"Is There Any Chance That He's Not Dead?" Asked Thatcher.

"I can't feel any pulse," Marten announced. "But half the time I can't feel my own. I—now what the hell?" He broke off to stare at his own hand, then peered more closely at Domínguez's closed fist.

"What is it?" Thatcher asked sharply.

"It's sand. Now will you tell me why Domínguez came here to the office with a handful of sand?"

"I have no idea," said Thatcher. "Who is Domínguez, anyway?"

"One of our foremen," Marten replied absently. "Benito Domínguez was the one who—" Then he stopped. "He was just one of our foremen, that's all."

Neither the broken sentence nor Marten's uneasy prowling up and down the side of the room was necessary to tell Thatcher there was more to it than that. If Benito Domínguez had been an ordinary foreman, presumably he would not now be lying here with his brains blown out. He had a strong suspicion he was going to learn more about Domínguez before many hours had passed.

Books by Emma Lathen

Ashes to Ashes
Death Shall Overcome
Double Double Oil and Trouble
The Longer the Thread
Murder Without Icing
Pick Up Sticks
A Place for Murder

Published by POCKET BOOKS

EMMA LATHEN

THE LONGER THE THREAD

PUBLISHED BY POCKET BOOKS NEW YORK

POCKET BOOKS, a Simon & Schuster division of
GULF & WESTERN CORPORATION
1230 Avenue of the Americas, New York, N.Y. 10020

ISBN: 0-671-83491-6

First Pocket Books printing November, 1973

10   9   8   7   6   5   4

POCKET and colophon are trademarks of Simon & Schuster.

Printed in the U.S.A.

Contents

THE LONGER
THE THREAD

1. Bias Binding

Wall Street is the greatest financial market in the world, and the function of a market is to provide an arena for smooth and orderly transactions. So the New York Stock Exchange regularly distributes millions of brochures describing how Mr. Jones in Dallas, wishing to sell one hundred shares of U.S. Steel, and Mr. Smith in Minneapolis, wishing to buy one hundred shares of U.S. Steel, are brought together (at very slight cost) through the good offices of Wall Street. The facts as described are accurate, although Mr. Jones, Mr. Smith, the New York Stock Exchange—and U.S. Steel, for that matter —emerge as curiously bloodless entities.

Reality from the Battery to Maiden Lane is less tidy. True, docile buyers and apathetic sellers do exist on Wall Street. But other actors also appear: plaintiffs and defendants, inside accountants and outside auditors, stockholders and company presidents, the Internal Revenue and capital-gains acrobats. Their encounters are rarely bloodless. It is only in theory that competition and profit-maximizing have a Doric serenity; in practice they entail one battle after another. All men may be brothers, but Wall Street knows that Cain and Abel were brothers, too.

John Putnam Thatcher was reflecting on aggression in this special sense one bitter January afternoon. As senior vice-president of the Sloan Guaranty Trust, the third largest bank in the world, he had witnessed more than his share of combat. He himself had a very creditable win–loss record. Nevertheless, for some reason, unnatural bellicosity was surfacing on all fronts today.

The morning had begun with Hugh Waymark, of Waymark-Sims, on the phone. Waymark wanted to lead a search-and-destroy mission against a well-known financial weekly.

"Yes, Hugh—"

Waymark was not listening this morning. "Slanderous! Publishing any gossip! That magazine is completely irresponsible! Now, I happen to know that they're short of cash . . ."

The article in question, Thatcher recalled, had been titled *"Waymark-Sims, Aging Titan?"* When he hung up, he had no doubt that Hugh Waymark was on the warpath.

But Hugh was pugnacious by nature. Tom Robichaux, one of the partners at Robichaux & Devane, investment bankers, as well as one of Thatcher's oldest friends, was not. During business hours at least, Tom usually tended toward philosophic mournfulness.

Lunch at Fraunces Tavern had found him breathing fire. More surprisingly, he was mapping long-term strategy designed to pulverize an enemy.

". . . short-term credit. We can lend Bravura Chemicals three or four million. That should tide them through the next six months *and* fix Joe Frisch's wagon!"

Thatcher broke into this recital. The object of Robichaux' wrath was an energetic hotel tycoon who had recently mounted a proxy fight against Waldoboro Computers. Proxy fights, as Thatcher knew, always make conservatives mutter about piracy and unprincipled looting. But this daring raid had failed.

"So why this ferocity now, Tom?" he inquired.

Robichaux downed his fork and leaned forward confidentially. "This Frisch fellow," he said darkly, "has a tremendous cash flow. No telling where he may strike next. The time to stop him is now!"

Thatcher could not accept this. "You're not gunning for everybody with liquid assets, are you, Tom? We've got a pretty good cash flow at the Sloan, too, you know."

Eyebrows quivering, Tom informed him it was no laughing matter. He then added cryptically, "Hotels."

Whatever the provocation, Robichaux was clearly readying an onslaught.

As he inched his way back to the Sloan through a near-blizzard, Thatcher was moved to congratulate himself for being a neutral in these various frays. But before he brushed the snow from his overcoat, he discovered he had a fighting war of his own.

Waiting in his office were two men who had not appeared on the schedule that his secretary, Miss Corsa, prepared each morning. Unfortunately, they were both valued members of the Sloan Guaranty Trust. Even more unfortunately, they were bristling at each other.

"I don't care how busy Thatcher is," said Innes, from International Division. "I have to see him this afternoon."

Before Miss Corsa could reply, the second man cut in. "Where do you get that 'I' business? Let's get one thing straight, Innes. If you see Thatcher, I'm going to be right there with you!" Pete Olmsted was one of the senior men in the Commercial Credit Department. A short, rosy-faced man built for good cheer, he was now stuttering with anger.

"And another thing, Innes," he went on inexorably, "I don't like this end play you're trying! If Milly hadn't found out you were sneaking up here—"

"Listen, Olmsted," Innes began ominously.

Just then the combatants sighted Thatcher poised in the doorway.

"John! Good! Now, it's important . . ."

"Thank God, you can put a stop to this . . ."

"Mr. Thatcher!" Without noticeable effort, Miss Corsa managed to penetrate the din. "Mr. Lancer is waiting for you. I am afraid you are already late."

George C. Lancer was certainly not waiting for him, as both Thatcher and Miss Corsa knew. But Lancer was chairman of the board of the Sloan Guaranty Trust. When Miss Corsa upstaged someone, she did it right. Innes and Olmsted were disciplined. They accepted, however grudgingly.

"But we've got to get this settled pretty soon," said Olmsted truculently.

"You're right about that at least," said Innes tightly.

An exchange of challenging looks.

Thatcher could play his part as well as Miss Corsa. Hurrying into his own office, he cast cold comfort over his shoulder. "Perhaps Miss Corsa can fit you in later this afternoon. If not, tomorrow . . ."

He closed the door behind him. His seething subordinates, he knew, could be left to his secretary. Miss Corsa's splendid indifference to human passion left her capable of suggesting to these two warriors that they prepare reports on the *casus belli*. Any woman who can tell a soul in torment to send a memorandum is worth her weight in gold. Thatcher only hoped that last Christmas' present, a marvel of leathercraft by Gucci, conveyed how much he valued Miss Corsa. He would never know. Miss Corsa was also splendidly uncommunicative.

"And what's all that about?" he asked when she arrived a few moments later to take dictation.

"Puerto Rico," she said simply. She then settled herself and waited for him to proceed. At hand was a strong letter to a Sloan customer who had developed an unhealthy interest in the commodity market. She realized that Mr. Thatcher was still waiting and amplified: "International and Commercial Credit have been fighting about Puerto Rico. I understand they've been talking to Mr. Withers." Her pause was an editorial comment.

"I see," said Thatcher. Any dispute within the bank that found its way to the desk of President Bradford Withers was bound to escalate. Brad routinely saw all points of view—in rapid succession. Nor was his executive function improved by his frequent departures. Yesterday morning, for instance, he had embarked upon what the Public Relations Department was euphemistically describing as a fact-finding mission to Fiji.

Anyone seriously interested in bird migration, Thatcher had often thought, could do worse than study Withers through the seasons.

"And he's dumped a mess of some sort in my lap," he said without undue resentment. Problems that Brad Withers touched usually did find their way to him, sooner or later. "Do we know exactly what there is about Puerto Rico that's set off Innes and Olmsted, Miss Corsa?"

She was evasive. "I've sent for the files. And both Mr. Innes and Mr. Olmsted are preparing memos for you."

Like Innes and Olmsted, Thatcher was disciplined. He realized that he was not going to hear any of the gossip and rumor that always swirled around these in-house feuds. Instead, Miss Corsa was going to present him with all the news that was fit to print, so to speak.

"Fine," he said, accepting the inevitable. He put Puerto Rico from his mind and concentrated on an ingenuous scheme to use Sloan money in the pork-belly market. "Dear Woolner . . . While we are interested in your model for estimating supply, we at the Sloan still feel that demand plays a part in price changes—even in pork-belly futures. Accordingly . . ."

But such peace was not destined to endure. Within two hours, Puerto Rico was monopolizing his attention. If nothing else, he reflected, he now knew why Brad Withers had fled to the Antipodes.

Innes and Olmsted had both sped back to their offices to dictate position papers at breakneck speed. Thatcher had just finished skimming through these documents, which were bulky, impassioned and mutually incompatible. He did not have every detail at his fingertips, but he could see, all too clearly, the shape of things to come. Puerto Rico did not represent a minor difference of opinion, it was a head-on collision.

He turned a page of Pete Olmsted's report. A month ago, Commercial Credit had lent three million dollars to Slax Unlimited, Inc., a manufacturer of ladies' slacks and sportswear.

"CC has been doing business with Slax for many years," said Olmsted's memo searingly. Not content to leave it at that, he appended statistics of every Sloan deal with Slax since 1952.

As he read about new plants in Georgia, about pension funds and short-term credits, Thatcher recalled a fact. Olmsted was the Sloan's expert on the garment trade. He was probably the only member of the bank who read *Women's Wear Daily* as religiously as he read the *Wall Street Journal*.

Slax, Thatcher read, was a family firm owned by Harry Zimmerman, son of the founder, and his sister. It had developed a well-known trade name, thanks to a product line aimed at the youthful, style-conscious, middle-income market. Zimmerman was pushing an aggressive expansion program that would, so Olmsted felt, very likely push Slax to the top of its field.

". . . new up-to-date production facilities," Olmsted wound up at white heat. "Naturally, Commercial Credit was happy to make a sound loan to an old and valued Sloan customer, who shows every sign of expanding significantly."

If Commercial Credit was happy, International was not. For while Slax Unlimited maintained sales, advertising and executive offices at 1407 Broadway, New York, production these days was farther afield—in Georgia and in Bayamón, Puerto Rico.

"I need not remind you," said Innes on page seven, "of the Sloan policy to funnel all relevant investments and credits through local Sloan branches. International Division, and in particular the Sloan Guaranty Trust (N.A.) in Hato Rey, Puerto Rico, is the appropriate coordinating authority for any credits extended to garment manufacturers when their facilities are located in Puerto Rico."

Neither Innes nor Olmsted was sticking to the high road.

"In case they haven't noticed in International," said Olmsted in a nasty parenthesis, "Puerto Rico is not a foreign country. It is part of the United States of America."

Innes, if anything, stooped lower. "We have developed in Puerto Rico a large expert staff, fully able to deal with usages, business practices and tax situations about which Commercial Credit knows little. It is our understanding that the only persons in CC who are fluent in Spanish, for example, are certain members of the typing pool."

All this unsuppressed emotion told Thatcher one thing at least. There was no use summoning the antagonists and ordering them to settle this squabble themselves. On the contrary, prudence suggested keeping Innes and Olmsted as far from each other as possible for the time being.

Thatcher swiveled around to watch the snow. This meant that he was going to have to make some decision about the Sloan in Puerto Rico. The one thing he could not do was let the situation fester. It was tempting to consider leaving it for Brad Withers, that eminent traveler. Or for George C. Lancer, who was the Sloan's real enthusiast for overseas branches. But God knew when Withers would reappear, and Lancer was currently trying to salvage something from unhappy developments at the London branch.

"Miss Corsa," he told his intercom resignedly. "Will you get Bowman to send up whatever he's got on Puerto Rico? I'm afraid this is going to be our baby."

Miss Corsa said she had spoken to the Research Department already.

"And you'd better schedule Innes and Olmsted for tomorrow morning," Thatcher went on.

"Separately," said Miss Corsa, anticipating him again.

Resolutely, Thatcher turned his attention to the problem.

It was indubitably true, as Innes maintained, that the Sloan's ever-increasing activities outside the continental United

States were coordinated through a whole phalanx of specialists in foreign parts. There were now massive edifices representing the bank from Rio de Janeiro to Paris.

Including one in Puerto Rico. It had been opened, with appropriate hoopla, some two years ago. Both Withers and Lancer had trekked south for the festivities. Thatcher, whose interest in the ribbon-cutting side of banking disappointed Miss Corsa, had not.

In theory, the Sloan Guaranty Trust, Hato Rey, San Juan, Puerto Rico, should be what the Sloan Guaranty Trust in Tokyo was. Commercial Credit was perfectly willing to leave Japan to International Division. Unfortunately, an American company on American soil was something else.

This was not a view that Innes could accept. For fully an hour the following morning he put his case to Thatcher. No one was claiming that Puerto Rico was a foreign country. Not at all. But it was not Long Island either. Doing business in Puerto Rico called for old Puerto Rican hands. Men who knew the language. Men who understood the peculiar economic situation. Men with contacts in the government . . .

Twenty minutes later found Thatcher's second visitor of the morning also pushing the old-hand line. Olmsted, however, was pushing the experience and knowledgeability needed to survive in the garment trade. He had even brought evidence with him.

"John," he said, his usual expansive self again, "I know how interested you are in our Slax loan. So when Harry here dropped by to pick up some papers, I told him I knew you'd want to meet him."

Thatcher found himself greeting Harry Zimmerman, president and owner of Slax. He was a solid middle-aged man with a vigorous handshake.

"I think we've hammered out a deal that's good for you and good for Slax," he said. "I don't know if Pete told you, but we've got big hopes for the new line we're introducing this spring. For pre-teeners. That's a big market, and I think Slax is going to be in a position to crack it."

"Are you producing it down in Puerto Rico?" Thatcher asked. "Or at your plant in Georgia?"

Olmsted, like a proud parent, could not restrain himself. "You should see the Slax layout in Bayamón, John. It's one of the most modern garment plants in the world, isn't it, Harry?"

Thatcher's attention was captured by Zimmerman. He had a ruddy, fleshy face, with shrewd eyes. A few moments earlier he had radiated confidence and ease. Suddenly he was completely expressionless.

"Yes," he said flatly. "And we're getting good cost results from Georgia too. We'll be producing in both plants. But the important thing is distribution these days. We've just made some new arrangements . . ." He went on to describe Slax's distribution system.

"Do you ship by sea from Puerto Rico?" Thatcher asked.

Again Zimmerman froze briefly. "Sometimes we air-freight runs up," he said. "If you miss the right season, you've lost most of your sales."

The conversation proceeded politely until Zimmerman rose to leave. It had a curiously lopsided quality. Olmsted's leading remarks about Slax's model plant in Puerto Rico, like Thatcher's few civil questions, simply prompted Harry Zimmerman to move the discussion into different channels.

"Makes you wonder, doesn't it?" said Thatcher, once Olmsted returned from escorting his client to the elevator. "He seems curiously reluctant to talk about Puerto Rico, doesn't he, Pete?"

Olmsted was obviously puzzled. "Harry didn't sound like himself. The other day—hell, you couldn't shut him up about what they're doing down there."

Thatcher saw with some amusement that Pete Olmsted had forgotten the contest about territorial imperatives. He was back in the garment trade with a vengeance. A good thing, too, Thatcher thought. Zimmerman was a hardheaded businessman. Any successful manufacturer of ladies' slacks had to be rooted in reality—in wages and output, in price lines and advertising budgets.

What would make that kind of man turn evasive about his modern facility in Puerto Rico?

"It might be worth the Sloan's time," Thatcher suggested, "to find out."

2. Following a Pattern

Ten miles outside San Juan, there were three men who could have explained Harry Zimmerman's reluctance to talk about Puerto Rico. They were sitting in the Bayamón office of Slax Unlimited staring gloomily at a table on which lay a rumpled pair of white slacks.

"Harry airmailed them down so we could see for ourselves," David Lippert explained unnecessarily. He sighed before adding, "I guess there isn't any doubt about it."

"None at all." With fastidious distaste Cesar Aguilera used a pencil to prod the exhibit away from his end of the table. "How many pairs did you say have been returned?"

"Four thousand, so far," Lippert muttered.

"Christ!" Eric Marten was a vociferous, exuberant man, in good times and in bad. "That's just in the last ten days, too. We may end up with the whole run back on our hands."

David Lippert was about to protest, but he was cut off by Aguilera.

"That, I should say, is inevitable. I still don't know what went wrong. But the entire run was handled the same way. So all the slacks must have been affected." As production manager for Slax he spoke with authority.

"Well, we'd better find out what the trouble was—and fast." Marten paused to scrape a kitchen match savagely and light a long black cigar. "I suppose that's what Harry's howling for."

Lippert shifted slightly as the other two men turned to him. "Yes. But Harry wants Norma sitting in on this. She should be here any minute."

"Of course," Aguilera murmured with instant courtesy.

"Fine, fine!" Marten said too heartily.

David Lippert silently cursed. He was younger than the other men and, in theory at least, their superior. Usually

17

the situation created no problems. Aguilera was busy with the production line. Eric Marten, Slax's commercial manager, was almost always in motion, overseeing the arrival of raw materials, conferring with government officials, expediting the flow of finished goods to New York. When they met in conference each had his own area of expertise, and Lippert could forget that he was general manager because he was the husband of Norma Zimmerman Lippert. That is, he could until Harry regarded affairs as critical enough to require the participation of Norma herself. These occasions were an agony to David. Over the past year, his malaise had infected the other two.

"I suppose she knows what's happened?" Aguilera prompted.

"Harry's explained it to her in general. God knows," Lippert burst out, "it's not all that complicated. We did a big run for the cruise season. White nautical bell bottoms, with navy-blue accent stitching. Harry gave it a big promotion, with spreads in all the Sunday supplements and the magazines. The ads pushed the easy care of these slacks. You know— machine-washable, tumble-dry, no-iron." He ended with a groan.

"And now," Aguilera concluded for him, "it has developed that the navy-blue thread was not dye-fast. The first time the slacks are washed, the color runs and they are ruined."

Eric Marten mashed his cigar out and flicked it into a wastebasket. "Great!" he summarized.

Just then they were interrupted. Norma Lippert arrived with a rush.

"I'm so sorry I'm late," she said breathlessly. "But traffic from Isla Verde is getting worse and worse."

As she spoke, she brushed a lock of sleek auburn hair from her face. Tall and slender, with elegant wrists and ankles, Norma looked more like a model for Slax than its part owner. Not that this status absorbed much of her attention. She was far more interested in raising her two young children and making a happy home.

For Norma was the optimist of the Lippert family. Unlike her husband, she had never doubted for a moment that he was ready to take charge of Slax's new plant here in Bayamón. She had known that she would enjoy living in Puerto Rico. She expected David Lippert to be a great success.

Nevertheless, she brought a certain forthrightness to everything she did. She wasted no time on preliminaries. Before the men reseated themselves she was saying, "Harry told me all about the returns. How big was our run?"

"Nine thousand," her husband replied tersely.

"My God! How did it happen?"

"That's what we're going to find out." Lippert turned to his production manager. "Cesar, this is your territory. I don't mean it's your fault, but you must have some idea how the bobbins could have been loaded with the wrong thread."

"They weren't."

"What?" Lippert stared.

Cesar Aguilera remained composed. It was very rare that he was anything else. An assured man with classic Latin features, he moved through the daily maelstrom of the production floor always calm, always correct, always slightly reserved.

"The only navy-blue thread we should have had in sufficient quantity was exactly the thread we ordered for this run. We can check the inventory records, if you wish. But you'll come to the same conclusion. There can't have been any mistake about loading the bobbins."

The frown cleared from Lippert's face as if by magic.

"But that's wonderful, Cesar!" he said enthusiastically. "That means it wasn't our fault. The supplier must have sent us the wrong thread. Don't you see? Harry can get our lawyers after Crockers. We can sue them if they sent us non-colorfast thread."

Aguilera was strangely unresponsive. It was left to Norma to sound a warning note.

"But that can't be right, David," she said in bewilderment. "Crockers doesn't make any thread that isn't dye-fast. They haven't for over twenty years."

Lippert subsided. For a moment he failed to see the alarming implications of her statement. He was trying to suppress his irritation. It was somehow unfair that Norma, with her very casual interest in Slax, should know more about the garment trade than he did. But Norma's father had talked about women's ready-to-wear at the dinner table. David's father was a dentist.

Eric Marten was not deflected by side issues. "I'd like to get this clear. Cesar says the junk thread can't have been

loaded by mistake at the plant. Now Norma says it can't
have been supplied by mistake because there isn't any at the
supplier's. Where in hell did it come from?"

"You mean there wasn't any mistake at all?" Lippert was
following the argument, almost reluctantly. "You mean it
was done deliberately?"

"Let us go a little more slowly," Aguilera suggested. "I said
there wasn't any other navy-blue thread in the shop. Is there
any possibility there is some at the warehouse, Eric? I don't
know what you've advance-ordered for the spring line. I
confess I don't see how they could get substituted, but it is
worth considering."

Eric Marten was apologetic as he shook his head. "No. I
don't blame you for wanting to cross out all possibilities,
Cesar. But it won't work. There isn't any navy thread at the
docks. This was no accident."

"All right, then let's face it." David Lippert sounded grim.
"You're saying this was a piece of spite work. It shouldn't
be hard to figure out who has a grudge against us. First we'll
get a list of everyone on the payroll who might have access
to the bobbins. Then we'll run through their records with the
foremen. Then, if necessary, we can have them on the carpet,
one by one. We'll get the guy who did this."

There was an awkward lull following David's forceful
statement. Norma looked impressed by his decisiveness, as
she always did. But, for Eric and Cesar, David's words
touched another sore point at Slax. David did not speak
Spanish. This meant that he was severely limited in his dealings with Slax personnel. Some of the staff spoke English, but
most did not. In order to communicate with the women who
worked the sewing machines or the men in the cutting room,
David Lippert had to rely on interpreters.

Cesar Aguilera did not point out that what David proposed, somebody else would have to implement. Instead he
said, "No, I am afraid we cannot do that."

"Why not?" David shot back.

"At the moment," said Aguilera, "we have to walk very
softly."

Eric Marten intervened. "Cesar's talking about the plebiscite," he said bluntly. "Until it's over, we all have to be very
careful about how we deal with the line. And the foremen."

Lippert was impatient. "What the hell does a lousy plebi-

scite have to do with somebody sneaking junk thread onto
our bobbins?"

There was another awkward silence. Most people who had
arrived in Puerto Rico a week ago, let alone two years ago,
knew the answer to that question.

"The plebiscite," Eric Marten said overpatiently, "has
something to do with everything that happens in Puerto Rico
these days."

His tone made Lippert flush, but Norma was eager to
understand.

"I'm not sure that I follow you, Eric," she said. "According
to the papers, there isn't much doubt that people are going
to vote overwhelmingly to keep commonwealth status for
Puerto Rico. They say the statehood party doesn't really have
much of a chance. And neither do the people who want independence."

"That is probably correct," Aguilera agreed.

But Marten was not inclined to gloss over the subject.
"Every day things get more complicated, Norma," he said.
"Both the independents and the statehood boys are putting on
a big campaign."

"Oh, I know, I know," she said quickly. "All that advertising—"

"They're crazy," said David Lippert sourly. "They don't
know when they've got a good thing."

Marten again took up the cudgels. "It really is complicated,
David. The independence and statehood parties don't expect
to win. They're building support for the next elections."

"Cheap politicians," David said resentfully. "Everybody
with any sense wants to keep Puerto Rico a commonwealth."

"The business community, yes," said Aguilera. "But there
are others. And not only cheap politicians."

"Well, we're not here to talk politics," said Eric Marten.
"But what Cesar is not saying is that feelings are running high.
Probably it will pass, but right now there is some anti-
Americanism. Of course, it's mostly radical students. You have
seen what people are scrawling on walls? *Yanquis go home!
Culebra for the Culebrans—not the U.S. Navy!* And the
paint thrown at all the street signs in English? Well, American
businesses could be a target, too. Now is no time for strong-
arm tactics with workers in an American-run factory."

Lippert was stung. "Strong-arm tactics!" he snarled. "We

have a model plant with model social benefits. We have full air conditioning! We have a cafeteria where we're serving three-course hot lunches for thirty cents a day—and you know how much that's costing us! What are you talking about?"

Cesar Aguilera smiled wryly. "Student radicals do not talk about such things, David. They talk about rich Americans coming down to Puerto Rico—because the labor is so cheap. It can be made to sound like exploitation."

Before her husband could reply, Norma intervened. "Anyway, Cesar and Eric have a point. Before we do anything, David, don't you think we should see how Harry feels? He's already steamed up. If we're running any risk of political trouble, he ought to know."

Both Aguilera and Marten were too wise to utter a word. They let the specter of Harry do its own work.

"Oh, all right," Lippert grumbled. "Though how you can expect Harry to have any ideas about the situation down here, I don't know. After all, we're the ones on the ground. But I suppose we ought to tell him about it."

Cautious as a cat, Aguilera rose. "You'll want to talk to him alone. And I want to check the daily total so far. I'll be back in half an hour."

He was ably seconded by Marten. "I'll come with you, Cesar. I want to show you some of those invoices."

They made it to the hall without being recalled.

"Don't worry, Cesar," Marten chuckled. "Norma will see that Harry gets the message. That girl has her head screwed on right."

"Thank God," Aguilera replied. "I realize that David has had a lot thrown at him this week. But I don't like to think of the turmoil we could create by not handling things delicately."

Eric Marten, in spite of his Danish forebears and his slight Scandinavian accent, was as much a permanent resident of Puerto Rico as Cesar Aguilera. He had married into a Puerto Rican family with commercial interests, and the coming plebiscite was important in his life.

"I agree with you, but I don't like it," he said, stiff-arming the heavy swing door that separated the offices from the production line. Automatically he raised his voice to adjust to the new noise level. "You can say what you like, but nobody switched threads on us because of politics. Basically David is right. This was a spite job. I don't go for being blackmailed into appeasement."

Aguilera was mentally conning the roster of employees. "Actually we don't have many troublemakers. Assuming, of course, that this wasn't some eighteen-year-old running wild and impressing the girls."

"When our eighteen-year-olds are on a Saturday-night spree, the last place they come is back to the plant," Marten rejoined. "And you don't have to have a lot of troublemakers. One will do. And he's coming right this way."

Aguilera duly noted the approach of his most troublesome foreman, Benito Domínguez. But he was far too experienced to frown. His face revealed nothing when the foreman hailed him.

"The morning totals are on your desk, Señor Aguilera."

"Thank you."

"I hear that something went wrong on that run of whites with the blue stitching."

"Yes." Aguilera knew it was impossible to keep this sort of news a secret. "The thread wasn't dye-fast."

Domínguez regarded him speculatively. "I suppose they'll try to blame the line," he suggested.

"I don't see how anyone could do that," Aguilera said mildly.

"Because they blame everything on us."

Domínguez was standing in the middle of the corridor, legs spread, in a posture of challenge.

"Then this is one time they haven't." Aguilera's voice was a masterpiece of indifference.

For a moment Domínguez debated tactics. "Times have changed," he finally announced. "Puerto Rican workers are not afraid any more. They will not pay the penalty when Americans make the mistake."

"But who has asked them to?" Aguilera asked smoothly.

Domínguez simply ignored the question. "You have to expect things to go wrong when outsiders give the orders. They don't know how we do things here, they don't know what we want."

But he had made an error. Aguilera would listen to him espousing the rights of the workers, but when Domínguez

strayed out of his jurisdiction Aguilera did not feel he had
to be patient.

"That's enough, Domínguez," he said crisply. "If management has made a mistake, they will pay for it. It isn't any of
your business if the line isn't being criticized."

"If Señor Lippert is taking any blame, it must be the first
time!" said Domínguez venomously.

"As you yourself pointed out, times have changed," Aguilera replied with unabated civility.

Domínguez glared. It was not the first time he had been
baffled by Aguilera's refusal to respond to his baiting. Finally,
with bad grace, he shrugged and stepped aside. As they passed
him, he was deep in laborious thought.

Eric Marten waited until they were in Aguilera's office
before commenting. "You handled him well, Cesar. I think he
was caught off base."

Now, Aguilera let himself frown. "Yes, he was surprised,
I think. I don't like it, Eric."

Marten understood. "So you got the same impression?"

"Domínguez was disappointed, I am positive of it. He was
hoping for just the kind of measures David was suggesting."

"I'd go further than that," Marten said. "I'd say he was
trying to egg you on to tackle the workers about sabotage."

Aguilera nodded somberly. "I thought this was simply a
piece of spite. I would not have been surprised to discover
that Domínguez did this himself to cause a financial loss—
and a loss of face, too—for Slax. I was wrong."

"You don't mean to say you've changed your mind about
Domínguez, do you?" Eric Marten was incredulous. "His attitude spoke for itself."

"His attitude wasn't what I expected. He should have had
that sly smile of his, he should have been openly jubilant
about the discomfort he caused. I think I'd be happier if he
had been like that."

Marten snorted. "What difference does that make? I still
think he did it."

"So do I. But for a different motive entirely. He wanted to
spark political trouble here at Slax."

"Selling nine thousand lemons is selling nine thousand
lemons, no matter what the motive. It makes me burn to see
Domínguez get away with it."

Aguilera lifted a worried face. "You don't understand,

Eric. It does make a difference. If he'd done it for spite, he
would have had the result he wanted. But if he did it to
start trouble with the workers, he hasn't succeeded. He's
failed."

"So?"

"So God knows what he'll try next."

3. Double Seams

It is possible to conceal bad news from creditors for long
periods, as headlines in the *Wall Street Journal* prove. It can
even be done when those creditors include such alert institutions as the Sloan Guaranty Trust. Wall Street's net is very
fine, but each year some fish slip through. It was a tribute
to the caliber of John Putnam Thatcher's staff that neither
the Pennsylvania Railroad nor IOS, not to mention scions of
the Du Pont family, had cost the bank one penny.

Duplicity, in the simple sense, was not the only peril.
George C. Lancer was currently enmired in London because
of other reasons. Rolls Royce had not misled its creditors; it
had misled itself.

Unfortunately for Slax, considerations above and beyond
the commercial had made the company of burning interest to
the Sloan.

It took Pete Olmsted less than forty-eight hours to learn
about the nine thousand ruined slacks. First, in a showroom
on Seventh Avenue, he heard somebody named Max gossip-
ing casually about production snafus at Slax's Bayamón plant.
Then, over a lunch complete with fashion show, he pumped
the buyer for a big Cleveland department store. Slax was
behind in some of its deliveries, said Miss Mellors. There had
already been one major snarl over an advertised special.

Miss Mellors wanted vengeance. "We took space in all the
Sunday papers. And where was our stock on Monday morning?"

After that, it took no time at all to find a buyer who *had* received delivery. "We had customers returning those slacks for weeks. And you should have heard what they called us!"

Olmsted pondered this information, then decided on Machiavellian cunning. Again he reached for the phone.

"Now, I don't want you to think that these Slax rumors are bothering me too much," he said in Thatcher's office, after reporting his haul.

John Putnam Thatcher maintained an unencouraging silence.

". . . still, I want to keep an eye on what's going on there. You know in the rag trade things happen overnight."

Thatcher was tart. "I thought Slax was supposed to be a solid well-established firm with a future," he observed.

Olmsted nodded vigorously. "Yes, but so was Allure Knits," he said. "Then within six weeks—down the drain! You have to keep on top of these boys. I'm not going to rely on Harry. I'd better go down and take a look at this Bayamón shop myself."

"Fine," said Thatcher.

"You know, John"—Olmsted was ostentatiously offhanded—"this underscores the point I was making the other day."

Thatcher had let his attention drift back to the papers on his desk. He looked up.

"It takes someone who knows the garment industry in and out to pick up these rumors in time," Olmsted went on modestly. "After all, we do have three million dollars tied up with Slax."

"Sometimes," Thatcher remarked, "I fear that I am the only one who finds that fact interesting."

Olmsted was not abashed. "Now, I don't deny that International can handle our business in Puerto Rico when it comes to sugar refineries or supermarket chains—"

"No doubt they will be happy to hear you say that," said Thatcher.

"*But,*" said Olmsted, approaching his punch line, "I doubt if anybody in Puerto Rico knows enough to ride herd on Slax. Now, take these nine thousand slacks . . ."

His voice trailed off as Thatcher held up a minatory hand.

"Olmsted," he said kindly, "if you are putting your money

on your special mastery of Slax, perhaps you would find this interesting reading."

It was the document he had been studying when Olmsted talked his way past Miss Corsa.

"It is a detailed report—on Slax Unlimited," Thatcher went on inexorably. "It was prepared by the staff in San Juan. Innes has just forwarded it to me. You will find a very full consideration of the nine thousand pairs of slacks."

He broke off to eye Olmsted.

"I wouldn't presume to instruct you about the garment trade," he said genially, "but let me give you a word of advice about infighting at the Sloan. It doesn't pay to underestimate the opposition."

Olmsted was torn between indignation and curiosity. "How the hell do you suppose they heard?" he demanded.

Thatcher smiled. "Down in San Juan they feel that only local experts could be expected to pick up something like this."

He could not know how true his words were.

The one-hundred-man staff of the Sloan Guaranty Trust in the Hato Rey section of San Juan had many things to keep it busy, from a new CATV television station outside Ponce to a housing development in Dos Pinos. But the telephone lines between New York and San Juan had been humming. The word had been passed. Any tidbit about Slax Unlimited was to be seized.

The Sloan in San Juan had two distinct advantages over Commercial Credit. First was *esprit de corps*. There were moments—familiar to all worldwide enterprises—when the home office seemed like the enemy. Then, too, Puerto Rico is a small island, and American bankers and businessmen there move in a small world.

Information about Slax flowed in from many sources. A member of the Real Estate Department attended the Lions Club luncheon at the Caribe Hilton. His table mate, one Wesley Fagan, operated the largest trucking firm on the island. Fagan, as usual, was filled with complaints about his customers. A major culprit was, it turned out, Slax Unlimited.

"They yell for the trucks to come at five," Fagan grumbled. "Then they don't have anything to load. God knows what they think they're doing."

Young Becker pricked up his ears and hastened to report to his superior.

"Hmm," said Ettore Ildebrando. He had already heard from another subordinate. Mr. and Mrs. John Harley, newly arrived from New York, were subletting an apartment in Rio Piedras. Their next-door neighbors, as it happened, included Mr. and Mrs. Eric Marten. The newlywed Mrs. Marten had artlessly confided that Eric was working late many nights because of difficulties at Slax.

"Hmm," said Ildebrando again. "I think Mr. Humble will be interested."

Dudley Humble, vice-president of the Sloan Guaranty Trust (Puerto Rico), *was* interested.

"Hmm," he said, rapidly reviewing several long conversations with his allies back in New York. "You know, Ettore, that Commercial Credit lent Slax three million dollars."

"Without clearing through us," said Ildebrando.

He knew it. Everybody in the bank knew it.

"They're talking about sabotage at Slax, you know," said Humble keenly. "I doubt if Commercial Credit has any idea of the problems Americans can have down here."

Ildebrando doubted it, too.

"Especially now with the plebiscite," said Humble. "In fact"—a skilled observer might even have said he was warming to his theme—"I expect that things may get worse at Slax before they get better."

"Hmm," said Ildebrando.

"Maybe it would be a good idea if I had a friendly talk with this young fellow—what's his name? Zimmerman's brother-in-law."

"David Lippert," said Ildebrando promptly.

Back in New York, Olmsted might be underestimating the opposition. Down in San Juan, the Sloan Guaranty Trust was carrying the fight into the enemy camp.

Harry Zimmerman was not worrying about the Sloan Guaranty Trust. He was too busy worrying about his customers. His days were spent in a weary round—pacifying buyers who had been burned with the white bell bottoms, ensuring that other deliveries gave no ground for complaint, agreeing to produce overnight a style that one discount house insisted would sell like hot cakes if only it were available.

Even his suppliers came in for extra consideration. It is always a bad sign in business when a salesman forgets which end of the selling transaction he is on.

"Sure, Sid," he said during a chance encounter, "take as much time as you need on the buttons. As long as they're in Georgia by the twenty-first, that'll be okay."

Sid, scarcely believing his ears, gave Zimmerman no chance for second thoughts.

"Fine! This is where I turn off. Give me a ring about lunch sometime," he said and plunged into the crowd slogging uptown.

Harry, waiting for the light to change on Seventh Avenue, threw away his cigarette and turned up his collar against the biting wind. As usual the avenue was a madhouse. Boys were shoving pushcarts along in the street, models equipped with boots and wig cases hurried to appointments, vociferous knots of men flipped out fingers that represented changing sums of cash, cars inched cautiously through the human ramparts overflowing each curb. Every movement sent up a spray of icy slush. Above it all was the noise of boys yelling, truck drivers cursing, brakes squealing, carts squeaking. Every level of affluence was represented, from the grandees of the cloak-and-suit empires to the hole-in-corner jobbers. There were experts in zippers and hooks, in braid and frogs. There were young and old, black and white, rich and poor. They were speaking English, Yiddish and Italian. Many of them were speaking Spanish.

Disenchanted, Harry surveyed the scene. Practically every week, *Women's Wear Daily* announced another departure to New Jersey or North Carolina. Yet the density around him remained exactly the same as twenty years ago. Then Harry remembered that Slax itself was three times as big as it once had been. Maybe the movement out of town just about offset the growth in the industry.

This philosophizing carried him all the way back to his crowded and shabby office. Outside, in the modern reception hall, there was wall-to-wall carpeting, indirect lighting and expensive furniture. Here there were piles of papers, boxes of swatches, old photographs and new sample books.

There was also a call from Puerto Rico.

"Yeah? Oh, hello, David."

As David spoke, Harry's saturnine expression darkened slightly.

Finally he said, "Keep your shirt on, Dave. I've had the Sloan on my neck, too. . . . What? . . . How the hell should I know? Probably everybody knows by now."

Again the phone spoke.

Zimmerman kept his patience with an effort. "Look, Dave, don't kid yourself. Some things you can't keep secret —believe me. The word gets around. . . . What? . . . I told Olmsted that we've had a few little problems, but that everything is okay now. And that's what you're going to tell them down there, too. A big show of confidence—that's the ticket." As he spoke, he worked a cigarette from a crumpled pack.

For once, David Lippert was as emphatic as he was. "Look, Harry," he said, "I don't think you know how bad this is. First there were those damned white bell bottoms—"

"I know all about that," said Harry. "So does Macy's and Field's. And a helluva lot of others."

"All right," Lippert snapped. "Since then we've had a batch of linings mislabeled. If somebody in shipping hadn't caught them this morning, they'd be on their way to New York."

Harry was silent. The last thing Slax needed right now was more delay.

". . . Yesterday the conveyer belt was out. That held up the whole pressing room hours. And somebody took the keys to the pattern room. We've had to have the locksmiths—"

"Okay, okay," said Harry gruffly. "I get the picture."

"No, you don't," said David. "Someone's doing all this deliberately. Somebody's shafting us!"

Harry felt a throb of nervous tension. Then: "Keep calm, Dave. So we've got a troublemaker. But don't make it any bigger than it is."

David burst into speech, excited, uncontrolled. "Bigger than it is? Now they're talking about agitators—and anti-American feeling because of the plebiscite! They say we can't do anything about this! So we've got to sit and take it while somebody works us over."

The younger man's near-hysteria steadied Harry. "Listen, is Cesar there? Let me talk to him."

It was a mistake he did not usually make. For a moment there was no reply, only a low hum on the line. Then, stiffly, Lippert replied, "I'll have him call you."

"Okay, Dave," said Harry hastily. "Well, don't let it get to you. This is probably just some nut. If it doesn't clear up, we'll go to the police. We're not going to let anybody's crazy politics close down Bayamón."

But his brother-in-law was still offended when the call ended.

For a minute Harry glowered at the phone. That's all we need now, he told himself. Hurt feelings. Then he picked up his order books again. A little calculation showed him what he already knew. More mix-ups in Puerto Rico and Slax could be in real danger.

David Lippert was not a man to sit alone with his worries. It was Norma's afternoon for Spanish lessons, so he could not call her. His secretary was more interested in her engagement than in her boss. That left only one other source of comfort.

Cesar Aguilera's office was a glass-enclosed cubicle on the balcony overlooking the one-story Slax plant. Aguilera looked up as David strode in.

"My God, Cesar," David began without preliminaries. "I don't know what Harry expects us to do!"

Aguilera was conscious of the irony of the situation. Every difficulty at Slax had landed on Aguilera's shoulders. He had been caught between the growing tension in the front office and widening anxiety on the line. He had personally dealt with every breakdown, every delay. Now he had to comfort David as well.

"I do not think we have to worry much about the Sloan," he said after hearing David's tale of woe. "They have heard about our troubles, so they wish to talk with us. If nothing else happens—"

Just then the door was flung open with explosive force.

Eric Marten, red in the face, closed it behind him. He was fighting for self-control.

"More trouble!" he said, his big voice shaking. "This one is a catastrophe." The Danish accent was more noticeable than usual.

He hurled his briefcase onto Aguilera's work table.

"Look inside," he commanded.

Lippert drew out a handful of gaily patterned cotton. With a curse, Marten snatched it from him and stretched the fabric taut.

The red and blue stripes were defaced by an ugly brown stain. It had rotted and scorched the material like fire.

"Acid!" spat Marten, crumpling the cotton into a ball and flinging it back onto the table. "Thousands of dollars' worth of material! And every bolt has been soaked with acid!"

"Oh, my God!" David Lippert cried. "Did you hear him, Cesar? Acid!"

Aguilera ignored him. "Eric, is it all lost—all the cloth?"

For a moment Marten looked dangerous. Then he breathed deeply and said, "No, Tomaso is still checking through the warehouse. Someone threw acid around. All the bolts have to be examined. We cannot take any chances. But it will all take time. And the losses—well, I can't tell how much material has been ruined."

He subsided into a chair staring bleakly at Aguilera.

The knock on the door startled all three men.

"Señor Aguilera," said Benito Domínguez. "I will need your permission to order a new gasket."

He proffered the order pad. But as he spoke his dark eyes were flickering over the room, from David Lippert to Marten. And finally to the cotton on Aguilera's table.

Possibly they did need a gasket, thought Aguilera, reaching for a pen. But possibly the sight of Eric Marten storming through the line had brought Domínguez up here. Whatever his reason for coming, the important thing to do was get him out.

"Here you are," Aguilera said, scrawling his signature.

But Domínguez was enjoying himself. Deliberately he stepped forward and reached for the fabric. He picked up a corner and played it out between thick stubby fingers.

"So," he said in a low voice. "It goes on at the warehouse too? And still there is nothing you can do, señores."

"Enough, Domínguez!" Aguilera ordered. "You have work to do. Here is your form."

Eric Marten was more direct. "Get out!" he said harshly.

Domínguez' eyes narrowed to a feral glitter. But he was attacked from an unexpected quarter.

"Tell him," said David Lippert, surging from his chair,

"the fun's over! He's not going to ruin Slax—not while I'm in charge. Tell him to get this and get it straight! He's through with these games—or else!"

Aguilera moved between the two men. "David," he said in an urgent undertone, "this is not the time . . ."

But the damage was done. Benito Domínguez had been given his opening.

"We are not afraid of angry North Americans any more," he said magniloquently. "Now they must be afraid of us. Things are changing in Puerto Rico. Señor Lippert will have to learn this."

He would have continued, but Marten was bellowing, "My God, what kind of fool are you, Domínguez? What good is this sabotage doing you or anybody else? Slax is good to you. You have steady work here. Good pay—"

Domínguez drew himself up. "We know these tactics. Accuse us of sabotage! Charge us with crimes!" The voice had fallen into a singsong rhythm. "But no, señores. We are not criminals. We are Puerto Ricans! Good work and good pay, Señor Marten? Little children go hungry here while rich North Americans drain the lifeblood of Puerto Rico. You live like kings—you and your wives and your children—"

David Lippert made a blind convulsive move toward Domínguez, but Eric Marten was before him. Unceremoniously he put a massive hand under Domínguez' elbow and propelled him out of the office.

"That bastard! Don't let me get my hands on him or I'll kill him! The goddam sonuvabitch! I don't give a damn what happens! That guy goes—do you hear me?" Lippert's storming had a strangely hollow ring. After a moment, he fell as silent as his companions. From the shop, the hum of machines continued.

"What will they do next?" Cesar Aguilera asked colorlessly.

Eric Marten was trying to find an answer when David Lippert broke in.

"It doesn't matter what they do," he said angrily. "What matters now is what we do. I've listened to you two because you both know a lot more about Puerto Rico than I do. But I'm through listening."

Both Eric Marten and Cesar Aguilera were expressionless.

Lippert looked at them. "Things are worse than we
thought," he said dully. "A lot worse."

No one contradicted him.

4. Sewing the Wind

At the Sloan Guaranty Trust the situation was deteriorating
as well. John Thatcher, unfortunately, found himself living
proof of this.

Thatcher was ensconced in a large, air-conditioned office
in a towering structure that evidenced modern architecture's
obsession with plate glass. In the outer office, currently typing, sat a sensible secretary working with dispatch and
competence.

But Thatcher was not in his sixth-floor office on Wall
Street. He was on a twelfth floor overlooking Avenida
Ponce de Leon. In Puerto Rico. The distant typewriter was
being addressed not by his own Miss Corsa but by a bor-
rowed Mrs. Schroeder.

Mrs. Schroeder herself appeared in the doorway. A solidly contoured middle-aged woman with a jaunty gray coif-
fure, she bore no outward resemblance to Miss Corsa.
Fundamentally, however, they were sisters under the skin,
as Thatcher had discovered within hours of his arrival the
day before.

"Mr. Thatcher," she said kindly, "Mr. Humble is on his
way up. And Mr. Olmsted will pick you up first thing
tomorrow morning. Now, this afternoon you are seeing the
Governor at La Fortaleza. Then you won't forget dinner this
evening with the deputy director of Fomento . . ."

"No," said Thatcher, "I won't."

"Of course," she said reflectively, "you do have a rather
full schedule. I could tell Mr. Olmsted that you are busy."

Thatcher appreciated this identification with his interests. "Thank you, Mrs. Schroeder, but I think perhaps I'd better face the music."

The firmness with which Mrs. Schroeder withdrew told Thatcher that once again he had gone too far.

It was, in short, all very homelike. Only a confirmed opponent of business trips, overseas jaunts and similar dislocations—like John Putnam Thatcher—could complain.

Except that his time was fully occupied with other concerns.

"Ah, Thatcher!" said Dudley Humble, striding in athletically.

In Manhattan, Thatcher recalled, Humble had been pallid and sedentary. Two years in San Juan had wrought a transformation which was a tribute to Puerto Rico's many and varied recreational facilities. There was no doubt which island suited him better.

Now his heavily tanned face was fixed in a broad smile. He was half the proud host entertaining an honored guest, and half the deferential subordinate.

"Here's that study of Fomento," he said. "You know, that's the Economic Development Agency here. It has statistics on how many mainland companies Fomento has attracted to the island. There are lists of all the Fomento plants, classified by industry. As for tourism, you may be interested to read about the seven million dollars Fomento put up for the Caribe Hilton . . ."

It was small comfort to Thatcher that none of this was his fault. His presence in Puerto Rico had become inevitable when the sleuths from International discovered that Pete Olmsted was not the only trespasser from Commercial Credit. No fewer than five other ventures on the island had been bankrolled by the Sloan without Dudley Humble's blessing—or knowledge. To a man, International had claimed that intercession by a higher authority was necessary. Thatcher's unregenerate hope that the peak of the winter season would make it impossible to find flight space had died aborning. It was Miss Corsa's duty and pleasure to circumvent just such difficulties.

Triumphantly she had reported her victory over Pan American.

"Yes, yes," Thatcher had said impatiently. "I gather that

many people wish to go to San Juan. Please bear in mind that I do not."

Dudley Humble was not only proud of the Sloan Guaranty Trust (Puerto Rico), he was proud of the whole island. Thatcher's descent had spurred him into providing a crash course on its economics. Since a large measure of the current prosperity was intertwined with Sloan programs, there was no decent way for Thatcher to escape.

"Now, some of the other things you will want to see today are written up here," continued Humble, brandishing an agenda.

Thatcher looked at it and raised no protest. He was here to learn, among other things, and learn he would. He only regretted that it required so many field trips. He had already inspected a new Levittown in Arecibo, grain elevators in Cataño and a furniture plant in Vega Baja. He had conferred with officials from the government and the business community. Now more of the same lay in store.

"Everybody is certainly interested in economic growth," he commented in a notable understatement.

"Yes indeed," said Humble enthusiastically. "Why, since Operation Bootstrap—"

Thatcher interrupted. "Including the Governor and everybody else we have met."

Humble began to look uneasy.

"Now I see that there is a plebiscite coming up," Thatcher continued. "Perhaps it would be helpful if I could discuss the political situation."

Humble was torn. "We are careful," he said in a stately voice, "not to become involved in local politics. As you know, Puerto Rico is completely self-governed, internally. We try to avoid any hint of involvement."

"Yes, yes," said Thatcher skeptically. Let the bank broadcast these fictions to the public, not to him. "Now, I have noticed a good deal of publicity about independence."

Humble admitted that he had seen it, too. He did not sound as if he approved.

"I would be interested in talking to some responsible supporter of independence for Puerto Rico," said Thatcher thoughtfully. "God knows I've met a lot of supporters of the status quo. I'd like to talk to someone who is willing to give up that big tax advantage."

Dudley Humble might disapprove, but the dark shadow of Commercial Credit put him on his mettle.

Lunch at the Bankers' Club that day, according to the invitation, featured a talk on the construction boom in the metropolitan area. More immediately germane, it also featured a small table for four.

"John Thatcher is our senior vice-president in New York, Dr. Ramírez. John, this is Dr. Francisco Ramírez Rivera, a distinguished representative in the Legislature."

This was the public introduction. Earlier briefing had informed Thatcher that Ramírez, after operating for years as a successful real-estate entrepreneur, was now shouldering his way to the top of the Independence Party. In appearance he was a commanding figure, with massive shoulders topped by a hawk-like Indian profile and a thick mane of white hair.

"My secretary," he said, indicating the gangling young man at his side. "Ernesto Méndez Diego."

Murmurs of acknowledgment accompanied the scraping of three chairs.

"You'll excuse me a moment, won't you," Humble said artlessly. "I see someone I should have a word with."

Dr. Ramírez had also been briefed.

"I understand you are interested in our political situation, Mr. Thatcher," he said suavely. "To meet a mainlander who admits there is such a situation is a pleasant surprise."

"I have been here for only two days," Thatcher replied, "but it is difficult to find anyone talking about anything but the economy."

Ramírez shook his head. "Exactly. You have put your finger on the problem."

As this seemed to be the extent of his contribution, Thatcher proceeded. "I am of course grateful for the opportunity to see so much of Puerto Rico's industrial growth."

"Yes," said Ramírez with a sad, lofty smile. "All of our petty officials are very proud of each new factory and each new hotel. There is no denying it—the prosperity built up during the long administration of Luis Muñoz Marin has come to be identified with our commonwealth status."

In the last plebiscite, Thatcher quoted Dudley Humble, an overwhelming majority of the electorate had voted to continue commonwealth status.

"We are changing all that," said Ramírez with magnificent assurance. He was too wily to introduce any facts. "Economic prosperity is important—but it is not everything."

"Naturally."

Ramírez suddenly smiled brilliantly. "No, I am not speaking like a foolish child. You bankers make the mistake of thinking money is everything. We *independistas* know Puerto Rico can maintain prosperity when it becomes independent. Why not? What is required, after all, but certain tariff concessions by the United States?"

Thatcher was always willing to admire a political stance that rested on having one's cake and eating it, too.

"Tariff questions," he pointed out, "can become intricate."

"Tariffs are being renegotiated the world over," Ramírez said sternly.

Thatcher did not think this was the time to observe that much of the renegotiation centered on raising, not lowering, trade barriers.

Ramírez swept on to higher considerations. "By tradition, by culture, by language, Puerto Rico is part of the Latin-American community. No doubt there is much to admire in the Anglo-Saxon tradition, but it is not ours."

The secretary spoke for the first time. "The young people of Puerto Rico are proud of their heritage and are prepared to defend it," he said ringingly, if not very relevantly.

Ramírez closed his eyes briefly, then roused himself to hiss a command. "Ernesto! Mr. Thatcher requires another drink. Attend to it!"

After Ernesto had shambled off, Dr. Ramírez expanded just enough to say, in bitter resignation, "My wife's nephew."

Thatcher required no further explanation. He had been in too many offices from Washington to Istanbul not to recognize nepotism when he saw it. The only question had been whether the boy was a wife's nephew or a mother's cousin. He had, however, done Thatcher's dirty work for him.

"Speaking of Puerto Rico's young people," he said, seizing the opening, "we have, of course, been following the stories about student radicals and their conflicts with the police."

Ramírez became sardonic. "So it bothers the American

bankers in New York, the growing awareness of our students to the exploitation of Puerto Rico? But their tactics should not come as a surprise to you."

Thatcher agreed amiably that student riots were no novelty to Americans.

"But they are new to Puerto Rico," Ramírez said instantly. "They are not compatible with our culture. *We* are not a violent people. While I sympathize with the dissatisfaction of our students, I deplore their methods."

"Splendid," said Thatcher cordially. He had yet to hear any politician in the world approve of violence. He was more interested in another question. Was Ramírez numbered among those who expected to reap its benefits?

Dr. Ramírez was beginning to hit his stride. "Nevertheless, I look to these young people as the hope of Puerto Rico. They see the injustice and the errors of American influence on the island. They are awakening the people to the real needs of our country. It is true that they are young and heedless, but they are headed in the right direction."

Thatcher eyed his companion. "There would seem to be several fundamental differences between your program and theirs," he ventured.

"Certainly not." Ramírez was not defensive. If anything, he was condescending. "Our students have no real program. They merely wish to end the dominance of the Puerto Rican economy by outsiders."

As Thatcher had feared, Dr. Ramírez, like many a standard-bearer before him, was too busy deceiving himself to have time to mislead others. Thatcher decided to steer the conversation into more specific channels.

"I have been reading some of their literature, and it has certain features in common with the pronouncements of our own protesters. There are references, for instance, to a social revolution which would eliminate the power of private industry, no matter who owned it. Not to mention basic changes in the class system—as they see it."

Ramírez waved away the tenets of the New Left. "Those are mere effusions produced by the exacerbations of the U.S. presence. They are parroting your students, I regret to say. With the removal of North American materialism, our young people will rediscover Hispanic values."

Thatcher murmured that Cuba's rediscovery of Hispanic

values had entailed a trifle more than the ejection of Americans.

"We have the inestimable advantage of Cuba's example," Ramírez said coldly. "Their sugar crop alone should be a lesson to all hotheads. No, I am afraid that you cannot be expected to weigh these considerations accurately. When Puerto Rican industry is controlled by Puerto Ricans, there will no longer be any need for reform. There will be a natural understanding on both sides that can never be achieved under present circumstances. You cannot appreciate the emotions roused by alien domination. It is more than a question of economic interests. It is a matter of social morality. The Latin American instinctively feels for the self-respect of others, he . . ."

As the lecture flowed on, Thatcher wondered why every politician in the world thought he could instruct American businessmen on the subject of anti-Americanism. After all, the people with real experience in this area were sitting in front offices in New York. They had been expropriated in Brazil, confiscated in Venezuela and squeezed out in Chile. They had negotiated in Japan, lobbied in India and made deals in the Common Market. They knew, better than most, the difference between home-grown capitalists wanting the gravy for themselves and dedicated revolutionaries marching to a different drummer.

"Our students are performing an important service," Ramírez continued in tones of measured approval. "By dramatizing our national plight, our younger generation has become a model for all concerned Puerto Ricans."

It was unfortunate that Ernesto should have chosen this moment to reappear. Placing a daiquiri in front of Thatcher, who was drinking Scotch, he slouched into his seat and peered around the table with innocent pride.

"*Some* of our younger generation," Ramírez corrected himself.

"Then you feel that the activities of this group at the university may result in swelling the ranks of your own party?"

"Undoubtedly," said Ramírez with supreme confidence.

"But, Uncle," Ernesto protested, "the students are demanding a boycott of the plebiscite. They claim all political parties are reactionary."

"Ernesto!"

It took a moment for Ernesto's uncle to recover. Then, turning to Thatcher with regal courtliness, he launched on his peroration.

"I do not have to explain to you at least"—here he glared at Ernesto—"that I do not expect the immediate support of the students. But the great mass of the electorate, made aware of the ground swell for independence, will obviously look to those with mature judgment for the implementation of that goal. We are not hotheads, you need have no fear of that. I personally foresee a considerable period of adjustment. My party looks forward to an orderly transition that preserves all economic gains. Naturally we expect the United States to recognize its moral obligation to ease that transition. Generous financial aid, a preferential tariff policy —that is the least we have the right to expect."

Ernesto thought he saw his cue. Fixing Thatcher with a basilisk stare, he intoned severely, "Love Puerto Rico—or leave it!"

Given the current emigration statistics for Puerto Rico, this struck Thatcher as a singularly ill-advised sentiment. He noted, with interest, that it was the first contribution by Ernesto which did not rouse his uncle's wrath.

Francisco Ramírez Rivera, apparently, was above statistics in more senses than one. He did, however, modify his nephew's stirring battle cry in one particular.

"Ernesto has, of course, phrased the matter too simply. But in essence he is correct. Puerto Rico must obtain sovereignty in its own right. But I assure you there will be no violence. We *independistas* shall achieve our goals through a mandate from the people."

After all this, Pete Olmsted's more modest goals came as a distinct relief to Thatcher the following morning.

"Hell, John, I just want to know what's going on out there —at Slax."

He had been in Puerto Rico one day longer than Thatcher. But while Thatcher had been meeting luminaries, Olmsted had been wined and dined by Slax's management in downtown San Juan. He was more suspicious than ever.

"I get the feeling they're giving me the runaround. Lippert swears everything's okay. They all swear everything's okay. But that's not the way it smells to me."

They were speeding out to Bayamón in the bank's vast Cadillac.

"So," Olmsted continued, "I thought I'd look the plant over myself. And I knew you'd want to come, too."

Who was Thatcher to disabuse him? In forty-eight hours he had inspected almost everything else in Puerto Rico. Why not Slax?

"Here we are," said the driver.

They had driven through the older section of Bayamón, circled around a new housing development, and come to rest before a long, low building directly opposite a shopping mall. In appearance, at least, Slax was a showplace. White concrete walls, gleaming beneath the tropical sun, were dappled with shadow cast by breeze-stirred palm trees. A neatly edged path led to the main entrance.

"It's a far cry from Seventh Avenue," said Olmsted leading the way.

He and Thatcher had barely entered the modest reception area when Eric Marten emerged from an inner office. After greetings and introductions, he suggested a slight delay.

"How about a cup of coffee? We have to wait a few minutes. Everybody wants to be in on this conference, and Cesar has to get the day's run started. He won't be ready for another ten minutes. Dolores, page Mr. Lippert and tell him we'll be in the cafeteria."

The decision to have the entire management on hand for this meeting sounded promising, Thatcher thought. Maybe the runaround was over. Maybe Slax was ready to talk turkey. Whatever the decision, clearly nothing would happen until the full roster assembled.

Accordingly Thatcher leaned back and listened to a casual exchange between Olmsted and Eric Marten. They were discussing the sales outlook for the coming season. What he heard he approved. In many firms, the commercial manager becomes a glorified public-relations man, full of enthusiasm but weak on detail about his industry. This was not true at Slax. Eric Marten certainly projected enthusiasm, but he did so with a wealth of information. He knew a great deal about the garment trade and about Puerto Rico.

After an exhaustive discussion of coastal shipping along both Americas, he answered a question. "I've spent my whole life in the islands," he explained. "I grew up hearing about shipping in these parts."

David Lippert, when he arrived, made a less favorable impression on Thatcher. But that may have been because he was so clearly nervous. He declined coffee on the grounds that there would be insufficient time.

"Cesar is already through," he explained. "And I'm expecting Norma any minute. You know my wife's a part owner, don't you?"

Thatcher simply nodded. Privately he wondered what sort of bankers Lippert thought they were if they did not know who owned the controlling stock in a family firm. But he had no time for further reflection. The intercom announced that Mrs. Lippert was at the front desk.

They picked her up there and proceeded into the executive suite. Cesar Aguilera appeared from an office to join them on their way to the conference room. It was he, indeed, who threw open the door and stood back to let Norma Lippert precede him.

Behind her, the men could see only part of the room. It was enough to tell Thatcher that something was terribly wrong.

The conference room was not empty. Instead, the chair at the head of the long table was occupied. A man in work clothes lay slumped forward, his head and one outflung arm resting on the polished teak.

Norma had moved into the room automatically. Now she was the only one near enough to see the shattered skull, the pool of blood, the ugly ooze of matter.

She froze.

Her rasping intake of breath was the one sound in the room. She was struggling not to scream.

As her husband pushed his way to her side, she gasped painfully, "Oh, God! It's Benito Domínguez! Oh, no!"

Then she pitched forward.

5. Pinking Shears

While David Lippert struggled to support his wife, the other men stood fixed. Finally, Eric Marten took three strides forward.

He bent over the body. One look was enough to make him retreat, his face drained of color.

"Christ!" Then, his voice louder than ever, he snapped out commands. "Cesar, find the nearest phone and get the plant doctor here. And you'd better call the police. Olmsted, can you help Dave get Norma out of here? She shouldn't see this." A tight turn of his head indicated the bloody mess on the table. "And, Thatcher, do you mind staying here with me so we can vouch for each other?"

His peremptory tactics worked. The others shook themselves free of paralysis. In minutes, Thatcher and Marten were standing guard alone.

"Is there any chance that he's not dead?" asked Thatcher.

"You should see the exit wound. He must have been shot in the back of the head. The bullet tore his face apart, coming out." Marten groaned. "My God, what a mess!"

Thatcher could not decide whether he was talking about the victim or something else. Marten himself seemed to feel there had been ambiguity in his words. Shrugging restlessly, he again approached the table. Cautiously he placed his fingers on Domínguez' wrist.

"I can't feel any pulse," he announced. "But half the time I can't find my own. I—now what the hell?" he broke off to stare at his own hand, then peered more closely at Domínguez' closed fist.

"What is it?" Thatcher asked sharply.

Marten was half murmuring to himself in bewilderment. "It's sand. Now will you tell me why Domínguez came here to the office with a handful of sand?"

"I have no idea," said Thatcher. "Who is Domínguez, anyway?"

"One of our foremen," Marten replied absently. He was still rubbing some sand between his fingers. "Benito Domínguez was the one who—" Then he stopped. "He was just one of our foremen, that's all."

Neither the broken sentence nor Marten's uneasy prowling up and down the side of the room was necessary to tell Thatcher there was more to it than that. If Benito Domínguez had been an ordinary foreman, presumably he would not now be lying here with his brains blown out. John Thatcher did not ask any more questions. Very soon other people with greater authority would be doing that. He had a strong suspicion that he was going to learn more about Domínguez before many hours had passed.

It did not take that long. The doctor and a patrol car arrived almost simultaneously. While the doctor assured himself that Domínguez was dead, the policeman made a call to headquarters. To no one's surprise, this call produced a very superior officer. Captain Vallejo's rank, his efficiency and his familiarity with manufacturing premises marked him as a specialist. He was the man who handled trouble at any of Fomento's cherished transplants.

He was also dauntingly well informed.

"It will save time, I think, if I tell you there are certain things I already know," he said when he joined them in the room where they had been waiting for him. "For instance, I know that there has been considerable industrial sabotage here at Slax Unlimited."

There was total silence. It was surprising, Thatcher thought, how guilty Slax's executives looked as they all avoided each other's eyes.

The lack of response exasperated Captain Vallejo. "You must understand that I know this without asking a single question, merely from the gossip that has been busy in the last few days. You are in the best position to know how much I will learn from interrogating the entire work force."

Cesar Aguilera stirred unhappily.

"Is that really necessary, Captain?" he asked.

"You do not think so?" Vallejo was gravely ironic. "I am

not, after all, receiving much assistance from the management of this company."

"What do you mean by that?" David Lippert burst out. He was sitting on a couch, holding his wife's hand. Norma, pale but composed, had refused the police offer to drive her home. "What can we tell you? We don't know anything. We marched into that room to have a conference, and Domínguez was there, dead! That's all we know!"

"You could tell me something about the background," Vallejo paused. "Instead of leaving me to find out for myself—possibly from more hostile sources."

"What does background have to do with it?" Lippert persisted. "Somebody shot Domínguez. It's your job to find out who."

"Exactly. Perhaps it would help if I tell you what I already know. First we have a dead foreman in your executive offices. That in itself is rather unusual. There are two entrances to the executive block. One is through the front door, past the receptionist. The other is through the door to the plant, past a number of people on the work floor. That door is used only by executives and foremen. Anyone else using it would cause comment. Finally, we have the hour of the day. Work begins on the line at seven-thirty o'clock. Normally the executive offices begin work at eight. But today Mr. Lippert, Mr. Aguilera and Mr. Marten were all here long before eight. In fact, you were all here at the time the murder must have been committed."

"You have not forgotten, Captain Vallejo, that today we had a conference with our bankers scheduled for eight o'clock?" Cesar Aguilera interposed quietly. "Our presence is readily explained."

"You may have an explanation for being here. Nevertheless, you *were* here. Now we come to the question of sabotage." Vallejo looked around the quiet circle as if waiting for a contribution. When none came, he went on. "There are certain similarities in all cases of industrial sabotage. In small plants, management always has suspicions as to who is responsible. This leads to certain bad feeling. The bad feeling usually erupts in some way."

"Horseshit!" Eric Marten snapped. "We don't know what you're talking about."

He looked at his colleagues for support. He did not get it.

"That won't work, Eric," David Lippert said bluntly.

Thatcher was interested to note that in this crisis, at least, the realist at Slax was not Marten but young Lippert.

Aguilera was shaking his head sadly. "You are forgetting my office has glass walls, Eric."

Captain Vallejo viewed this dissension with approval. "That is more sensible. In time, I will find out everything that has happened. But what went on behind glass walls I will know before the morning is out. My assistants are already questioning the men on the line."

Marten groaned.

David Lippert tried to counterattack. "Why don't they start a search for the gun instead? I'm not trying to tell you your business, but we've already had one murder here. I'd feel a lot happier if I didn't think some maniac is still running around the building, fully armed."

"We have found the gun—in your executive suite."

Someone in the room caught his breath sharply.

"It had been dropped into the wastebasket in the conference room," Vallejo continued smoothly. "Needless to say, it had been wiped of fingerprints. And now perhaps we could return to the subject of sabotage."

He received unexpected assistance.

"Yes, I think you should tell the captain everything that happened," Norma said with a troubled frown. "I'd like to know myself."

Lippert looked down at his wife in dismay. Both Eric Marten and Cesar Aguilera broke into speech.

"Very little happened . . ."

"You've got the whole thing wrong . . ."

Between the two of them, a simple story emerged. There had been no overt hostility, no serious threats, no real suspicion. There had only been natural irritation when several major losses prompted tactless remarks by Benito Domínguez.

"He did not have a sympathetic manner," Aguilera said.

"He was enjoying the whole damn thing," Eric Marten said more forthrightly.

But Slax had been too wily to be provoked into retaliation. Benito Domínguez had not been fired, he had not been threatened in any way.

"Why did you tolerate him?" Vallejo asked.

It was Cesar Aguilera, Thatcher observed, who presented the official position this time. "We considered firing him several days ago, Captain," he said frankly. "But only yesterday we came to the conclusion that it would not be wise, not before the plebiscite." He paused, then added persuasively, "You must understand that we did not suspect him of the sabotage. We were simply offended by his attitude. It is true we exchanged harsh words with him. Who would not? But that was all, absolutely all."

"You haven't forgotten those glass walls, have you?" Vallejo reminded them, almost jocularly.

Marten did the best he could. It might have looked worse than it was, he said. When Domínguez had interrupted a conference, David Lippert had been angry and shown it. But he had not laid a finger on the man.

"Actually I was the one who hustled him out of the office," Marten ended.

Captain Vallejo leaned back, nodding to himself. John Thatcher did not believe that the police captain was satisfied with this story. For that matter the Sloan Guaranty Trust, as represented by its senior vice-president, was not. Vallejo was simply satisfied that this was all he could get for the moment.

"That will do for now."

Marten and Aguilera heaved sighs of relief. David Lippert closed his eyes. Thatcher was sorry for them if they thought the worst was over. Then he met the eyes of Norma Lippert. She, at least, had no such illusions. She had gasped once during the recital—when Marten had glossed over David's anger. Clearly the scene with Domínguez was news to her. But she was not weeping over spilt milk, she was looking to her defenses against future attacks.

Thatcher's reverie was interrupted.

"Mr. Thatcher, if you and Mr. Olmsted will review the morning for me once again, I think we might be able to end this session."

Captain Vallejo was being conscientious. He had already mastered the morning timetable better than the two bankers. But dutifully they re-covered the ground. Eric Marten had come from the executive suite to greet them at the entrance.

"So you were already in the suite, Mr. Marten. Were you with anyone?"

"I've already told you. I was alone in my office, except when I looked for David on my way to the reception desk."

"And Mr. Lippert wasn't there?"

"No, he wasn't!"

Undiscouraged, Vallejo continued his questions. They had all adjourned to the cafeteria, Thatcher reported, until the intercom produced David Lippert.

"And where had you been, Mr. Lippert?"

"I went into the plant to Cesar's office. I intended to remind him to get through as quickly as possible so he could join us."

"But Mr. Aguilera wasn't there?"

"No, one of the foremen told me he had already gone through to the other side."

"So you went ahead to the cafeteria?"

"That's right."

There was very little else to tell. Thatcher repeated that they had waited until Mrs. Lippert's arrival, then proceeded to the executive suite, where they were joined by Mr. Aguilera.

"Is that correct, Mr. Aguilera?"

"It is. I finished getting the day's run started earlier than usual because of the meeting with Mr. Thatcher. Then I went over to the executive side, where I have another office. I waited in there with the door open until the others appeared, heading for the conference room."

"And none of the clerical help was around at that hour?"

"They just started coming in during the last five minutes."

Vallejo nodded to the patrolman who was acting as stenographer. "We'll have those statements typed up for signing," he directed before turning back. "You see what we have done? We have established that all three of you were alone for significant periods in the executive offices. We may be able to determine the times more accurately after we have questioned the receptionist, but the main issue cannot be avoided. All three of you were there. You do not admit seeing each other. You do not admit seeing Domínguez. You do not admit seeing anyone else. And it is extremely unlikely that anyone else was there."

He was not permitted to go to his next point.

"You've left something out, Captain." Norma Lippert was calm, almost apologetic. "Someone else was there. *I* was."

Vallejo was visibly annoyed. He knew very well that the fewer the suspects, the more pressure he could bring to bear.

"I hope that you are not being foolish, Mrs. Lippert?" he said curtly.

"You mean trying to share suspicion with the rest?" She was almost amused. "Oh, no. You'll find out when you talk to Dolores. After I got here I told her not to page the cafeteria until I was ready. Then I went into the executive offices and didn't come out for about ten minutes."

"And during those ten minutes?"

"I was in the ladies' room. And, before you ask, there wasn't anyone else there. The secretaries hadn't arrived yet."

Captain Vallejo compressed his lips. "It rounds out the picture," he admitted. "Everyone who had something to lose by Domínguez' activities was present."

Eric Marten snorted. "What makes you so sure about Domínguez' activities? There's no proof he was behind the sabotage. Maybe he was up to something else. We all had good reason to be in the offices, but what was Domínguez doing there? Did you notice that he was holding a lot of sand in his fist? Why don't you find out about that?"

"I noticed, but this is the first I have heard about your noticing, Mr. Marten." The black eyes narrowed. "You were busy while you waited for the doctor. What else did you discover in your search?"

Marten flushed. "There was no search. I was trying to see if there was a pulse. You can ask Thatcher. I wasn't alone with the body for one second."

It was Vallejo's turn to be amused. "A shame. If you had been free to go through Domínguez' pockets, you and Mr. Aguilera might have told a different story. You really didn't suspect Domínguez of sabotage, I believe you said. It was only his unsympathetic manner that irritated you. You never feared that he was an anti-American agitator."

Cesar Aguilera had a one-track mind. "We are not concerned with politics," he said urgently. "And even if Domínguez *was* behind the sabotage, anti-Americanism had nothing to do with it. He may have been neurotic, he may have believed he had a personal grievance."

Norma Lippert was quicker. "Never mind about that, Cesar. What did you find on Benito Domínguez' body, Captain?"

"Something his murderer never thought would be there."

Vallejo was enigmatic. "In his wallet is a membership card in the Student-Worker Radical Independence Party. In the pocket of his shop coat is the party's latest proclamation—exhorting workers to join the fight against American industry in Puerto Rico."

6. Tacking Together

Captain Vallejo's interrogation of the work force at Slax proved both more and less informative than he had hoped.

On the credit side was the volubility of his informants. Fifteen years ago, he knew, the same people would have instinctively retreated into sullen silence—they would have seen nothing, heard nothing, known nothing. But affluence had worked its usual miracle. The men and women on the line no longer thought of themselves as predestined victims. In addition, the grapevine had operated well in advance of Vallejo. Everyone knew that suspicion centered on management.

And with good reason.

Because, even under normal circumstances, workers and foremen chorused, it would have been impossible for anybody to go through the door from the plant to the executive corridor without arousing curiosity. Today, of all days, it would have been doubly impossible.

"What was so special about today?" Vallejo asked.

Benito himself had made it special, they replied. He had started the morning with the boast that the front office was on its knees. He was being invited to a special conference. The bosses, terrified by the damage they were sustaining, were about to plead with Domínguez, bargain with him, recognize him as the people's tribune.

Captain Vallejo pounced. "What do you mean by 'the bosses'? Which man was Domínguez going to meet?"

But the answer was a series of regretful shrugs.

Benito Domínguez had been more interested in striking

heroic poses than in revealing information, another foreman said acidly.

"We were used to him," he went on. "Benito was strutting around like a gamecock, talking about the conditions he would impose. Naturally I, a man of sense, did not take this seriously. If he had, in truth, been summoned, it was because they were going to throw him out! So we were all waiting with some eagerness. To see Benito deflated once and for all was worth a little wait. You understand, it did not occur to me at the time that instead of throwing him out they would murder him."

Captain Vallejo understood the human desire to saddle someone else with the crime. "It did not occur to you this morning, but now it seems reasonable to you?" he asked severely.

"Since this morning," the foreman said, "things have changed."

"You think Domínguez was killed because he was responsible for the industrial sabotage here. Then you yourself have no doubts that he was behind it?"

"Not now. Before, I did. It would have been like him to seize on the event, to produce mysterious half-smiles, to drop hints. Just to seem like a bigger man than he was." The foreman shrugged fatalistically. "Benito, you understand, was the kind of man who needs an audience. He did not brag, so I assumed he did not do it. But the Radical Independent card changes all that."

"You mean he must have been a different kind of man than you thought?"

The foreman made an impolite noise. "What kind of man chooses to associate with adolescents? No! I mean that he was doing his boasting elsewhere. Also, Benito was only taking orders. He was merely a tool. It is not surprising. That was the kind of man he was."

Captain Vallejo wanted character assessments of the suspects as well as the victim. But they were harder to come by. The foreman, when asked, appealed to others.

"Señor Marten laid hands on Benito," said an elderly cutter disapprovingly. "He forced him out of the office. We could see it all from the floor."

A younger man disagreed. "That was because Señor Lippert

was about to attack Benito. I was watching closely. Señor Marten intervened to prevent violence."

"It is possible. I can believe that you were watching closely." The voice was sarcastic. "It is rare indeed that you are watching your work."

A woman was impatient with these fine distinctions. "Señor Lippert and Señor Marten are always losing their tempers. They have not been well educated. It is only Señor Aguilera who is always polite."

"Ah!" breathed someone softly. "It is the quiet ones who are dangerous."

The foreman favored them all with a malevolent glance. "It is also well known that where you have women, there you have trouble."

Captain Vallejo was not certain whether this contribution was a broadside at women workers or a reminder that Norma Lippert was, at least theoretically, as suspect as her husband. He was not given the opportunity to probe further. His next question was interrupted by cries of alarm and sounds of tumult from the cutting room. It was here that the few superior male workers carried out their demanding craft.

"Jesus Christ! Jesus Christ! Jesus Christ!" someone was shouting with monotonous blasphemy.

"Get to the emergency switch!" someone else was yelling.

"Get the police!"

"Get Señor Aguilera!"

Vallejo shouldered his way through the rapidly growing mob to the scene of the disturbance. He was not much wiser once he got there. At the very core of the confusion several men were standing motionless, staring at a machine that was now lazily spinning to a halt. Several bolts of chewed-up fabric dragged lifelessly down to the floor. But a spectacle that merely bewildered Captain Vallejo was charged with sufficient drama to draw a bloodcurdling screech from the foreman, who had followed him.

"How did this happen?" he finally stuttered, shaking the fabric under the noses of the cutters.

This produced a group wail. "We don't know! It just started to go crazy!"

The foreman's voice deepened to a threatening hiss. "Fools! Blockheads! This means the bearings have gone. They must

have been going for days. Don't you even look at your own
work?"

Several backs stiffened alarmingly. The senior cutter fought
back. "Our work is inspected. Every day, every hour. There
was nothing wrong."

"How can you say there's nothing wrong?" Faced with the
unexplainable, the foreman was near apoplexy. "Do you call
this nothing wrong?" More shaking of fabric.

The charges and countercharges might have continued
apace for some time, but a calm voice sounded from behind
Vallejo.

"What is the meaning of this, please?"

As if by magic, the scene dissolved. Workers who did not
belong in the cutting room vanished. Junior cutters retired to
the rear. Cesar Aguilera was left confronting Captain Vallejo.

"There is something wrong, Captain?"

"Don't ask me," Vallejo barked, conscious of his ignorance.
"Everyone has gone insane simply because one of your machines isn't working properly."

"Simply!" raged the foreman. "Señor Aguilera, look!"

With a gesture worthy of the stage, he stepped aside and
revealed the machine. When the full enormity of the circumstances had been given time to penetrate, he went on bitterly.
"And these so-called cutters noticed nothing. Everything, they
say, was all right until now. Do bearings magically melt,
then?"

But he had not held his listener. Impatiently Aguilera
waved him into silence, then stood frowning massively.

Despite himself, Vallejo was caught by the tension. Like
everyone else, he waited silently.

Finally Aguilera looked up.

"I know you must be impatient, Captain, but if you will
give me a moment, I think I may be able to explain something that has been puzzling you."

Brusquely Vallejo nodded.

Aguilera advanced and scrutinized the cloth carefully. He
asked a few simple questions about the inspections. Then
suddenly he seemed to make up his mind.

"The lubricating oil, where is it?" he demanded.

A large nozzled can was produced.

Deliberately Aguilera squirted several gouts of the black
viscous mess onto his palm. Then he rubbed his fingers

together and nodded, as if his deepest fears had been confirmed.

"That's it, Captain," he said sharply. "That's what Domínguez wanted the sand for. He doctored the lubricating oil with it. Do you realize what this means? Already the bearings on one machine are ruined. But it's far, far worse than that. We will have to stop production completely and examine every machine on the premises. God knows how much damage he managed to do."

Now that he again knew where he stood, Vallejo was in full control. "Compose yourself, señor," he advised. "You seem to forget that somebody has already done substantial damage to Domínguez himself."

When he wrote his interim report that evening, Captain Vallejo contented himself with telling his superiors that there were four suspects, with no evidence favoring one more than another. He added that, in the interests of civic peace, he had made no reference to the Radical Independent connection in his remarks to the press.

The last sentence of Captain Vallejo's report was self-serving. He knew perfectly well that someone at Slax, probably before his own departure, would have called the newspapers. Two days later this suspicion was confirmed in banner headlines.

"INDEPENDENCE WORKER SLAIN AT AMERICAN FACTORY," proclaimed the pro-independence weekly.

"INDUSTRIAL SABOTAGE TIED TO RADICAL INDEPENDENTS," charged the pro-commonwealth daily.

Both papers were lying on David Lippert's desk.

"I don't see why you think it's so important, Cesar," he was saying impatiently. "We knew all about it before the papers printed this story. After all, the police showed us Domínguez' membership card."

Aguilera sounded discouraged. "It was of no consequence if *we* knew about it, so long as it wasn't made public. But now it will be a windfall for the Radical Independents. They will use it for propaganda."

"Aren't you forgetting the other side of the coin?" Lippert was growing angry.

"It doesn't make any difference what commonwealth supporters say," Aguilera continued doggedly. "They're in favor of American industry on the island no matter what happens."

David Lippert's voice rose with exasperation. "For Christ's sake! The Radical Independents are against American industry no matter what happens. I don't see where the big advantage in propaganda value is."

Aguilera's silence convinced Lippert he had scored a point. He turned to Eric Marten. "Do you go along with Cesar on this, Eric?" he demanded.

The Scandinavian spread his hands in a huge pantomime of helplessness before replying. "You're damned right I do! Look, Dave, I'll put it into words if Cesar won't. The only charge against the Radical Independents is that one of their people was responsible for some sabotage. They don't mind that. Hell, they're probably proud of it! But the propaganda against us is going to be dynamite. They're going to accuse us—I mean somebody in this room—of murdering Domín-guez!"

"You really mean that they're going to accuse *me*, don't you? I'm the general manager of Slax, I'm the one they'll go for."

"It does not really matter which one of us they single out." There was a hint of reproof in Cesar Aguilera's voice. "They'll do an enormous amount of damage."

David Lippert pushed aside the papers savagely. "We've got more important things to worry about. The police are working on the theory that we were the only ones in the front office with Domínguez. Vallejo is the one we should be worrying about!"

The hush that followed these words was broken by Norma Lippert. She was curled up in a corner of the small sofa against the wall, slightly removed from the three men.

"I think you're all getting much too excited," she offered now. "We should be looking on the bright side."

A harsh crack of laughter broke from Marten. "Which bright side, Norma? Point it out to us and we'll look at it."

"All three of you are being distracted by side issues." She put down her coffee cup with gentle finality. "Have you noticed that production is up again?"

Aguilera was taken aback. It was a moment before he replied. "Yes, of course we know that, Norma. But is that so important right now?"

"Harry thinks it is."

"Harry is safe in New York," David Lippert commented bitterly.

"There isn't anything for him to do here. We don't have a real problem," Norma continued serenely. "It was only a week ago that we were all desperate because of what was going on here at Slax. We'd lost thousands of dollars' worth of merchandise, and our good will was going down the drain. We didn't know what would happen next. Now that's all over. Harry's taking care of things in New York, production is running smoothly and, thank God, no real damage was done to the machines. And what you all seem to forget, we don't have to worry about where the next thunderbolt will hit."

"So everything's roses," Eric Marten growled derisively. "We shouldn't bother about little things like a murder investigation or a political mess."

"What does it all amount to? So Captain Vallejo doesn't think an outsider came into the executive suite the morning of the murder. That doesn't help him much," Norma pointed out. "He can't prove that no one else was here. And he certainly can't narrow down to a single suspect. Of course it's unpleasant. But it will blow over. You'll see."

"I don't think it will," her husband grated. "Domínguez made a lot of trouble for us when he was alive. He's going to make a lot more, dead."

Cesar Aguilera was looking curiously at Norma Lippert. "And even if he doesn't, it still means we have a murderer at large. Doesn't that worry you at all, Norma?"

"Not much." She remained unruffled. "It worries me a lot less than what was going on before."

7. An Elastic Band

If Cesar Aguilera and David Lippert really wanted to keep abreast of Puerto Rican flashpoints, they were reading the wrong newspapers. John Putnam Thatcher, settling down for a nightcap and an hour's desultory reading in his hotel room, could have told them as much. By some evil mischance, every section of the Sunday edition of the *New York Times* was a variation on the same theme.

The letters column of the travel section throbbed with anguished complaints about the low-fare night flights between San Juan and New York. "These cattle cars, unfit for human habitation," shrilled one correspondent, "are a brazen exploitation of new arrivals even before they set foot in New York." The magazine section had let itself go with an article of monstrous length and microscopic content about the Young Lords in Spanish Harlem and their painful search for Hispanic identity in the midst of an urban ghetto. The education column in the Review of the Week was less fiery in an analysis of demands by several community school boards for Spanish-speaking teachers. Even the television page, normally guaranteed to miss any sociological problem, had taken another look at the fare provided by commercial networks, dismissed it contemptuously, and turned to a discussion of the sunrise program providing instruction in the English language for Spanish speakers.

If all this was going on back in New York, thought Thatcher as he dumped the mountainous pile on the floor, almost anything could be brewing here in San Juan. His last thought, as he switched off the light, was for those bewildered children roused at dawn to watch television, then dispatched to classrooms from which English had been effectively banned.

The next morning, brilliantly sunlit with a balmy breeze,

encouraged a more optimistic outlook. Disembarking from his taxi and entering the Sloan building, Thatcher decided that the only person in the world likely to see a connection between yesterday's issue of the *Times* and the problems currently bedeviling Slax was the Sloan's chief of research. Walter Bowman no doubt was already busy photostating and circulating. But once the elevator had wafted Thatcher upstairs to the office and secretary that were now second home, he discovered that the far-flung Sloan family harbored yet another assiduous clipper. Every single article he had read the night before was waiting for him on his desk, in a neat file folder.

"I thought you might want to look at these Puerto Rican items, Mr. Thatcher," Mrs. Schroeder said briskly.

Each day he learned more about Mrs. Schroeder. For instance, he now knew she was originally from Indiana. After eight years in San Juan, she spoke Spanish with complete fluency and an unyielding Hoosier accent. Indeed, several times when she had been speaking to someone else in his presence Thatcher had caught himself straining to understand her, unwilling to believe that those familiar Midwestern intonations could actually be forming foreign sentences. In spirit, he had already decided, she resembled Miss Corsa. In form, however, she was her own woman.

"Call me Patsy," she had trumpeted cheerfully only yesterday.

But just as there was something familiar in her Spanish, so was there something all too familiar in her attitude toward her temporary superior. She was trying to organize him, trying to make decisions for him, trying to make him feel guilty about her wretched clippings.

"I have already given the *Times* a very thorough reading, Mrs. Schroeder," he said austerely. "And I believe I have an appointment with Mr. Humble."

"In fifteen minutes." She was wounded. "Can I get you anything in the meantime, Mr. Thatcher?"

"Yes, please. I'd like a cup of coffee, if you please—Patsy," he capitulated.

Oh, well, he thought philosophically. He knew by now that what a secretary wanted to be called reflected how she thought of herself. Miss Corsa was very definitely Miss Corsa during office hours, whatever she might be otherwise. Mrs. Schroeder at all times and under all circumstances thought of herself as Patsy. It was a different view of self that in no way precluded an identical view of function.

Fortified by his coffee and his insight into Mrs. Schroeder, Thatcher greeted Pete Olmsted and Humble a quarter of an hour later. He knew the session was not going to be easy, but he intended to bend it to his will.

"Now, Dudley," he began before the other two were fairly seated, "I came down here to settle our chain of command on Puerto Rican financing in general. I assure you, that question will be settled. But this murder at the Slax plant is going to force us to concentrate on Zimmerman's operation first."

Dudley Humble was too shrewd not to capitalize on this. "Yes indeed," he agreed readily. "Murder is something new as a client difficulty here. I can see how it changes the order of priorities."

Score one for Dudley, thought Thatcher. He had neatly conveyed the idea that Commercial Credit was responsible for insinuating this innovation into the Sloan's procedures.

"Just so," Thatcher went on. "Perhaps we'd better start by asking Pete how this murder has affected things out at Slax."

"All their lines are in full production," Olmsted announced defensively. Honesty then compelled him to add, "That is, they have been since they got this sand problem licked. You heard about that?"

Registering two blank looks, Olmsted explained about the sanded lubricating oil and the need for a new cutting machine. "But they got one air-freighted from Georgia. So that's fixed up now."

The news caused Humble to click his tongue disapprovingly and John Thatcher to muse.

"So that's the explanation for the sand."

"Yes. They figure it was Domínguez' last bit of sabotage."

"I'm glad, of course, that they have that cleared up. But it wasn't quite what I had in mind. Have they made any progress on the murder?"

"The police asked a lot of questions. I think they're pretty well satisfied that Domínguez was behind all the sabotage."

"But there's no talk of an arrest yet?" Thatcher persisted.

Olmsted was earnest. "Not yet. You know the police have a lot on their hands. On top of everything else, the students out at the university have called some kind of protest meeting. I guess the police are afraid it will turn into the kind of riots they had last year. You wouldn't believe . . ."

Thatcher forced himself to be patient. What he would not believe was that homicide investigations came to a halt whenever youthful protesters threatened to act up. After all, murderers had been arrested during the Battle of Britain and the Russian entry into Berlin. Still, it was clear that Pete Olmsted did not want to talk about murder. Like many another middle-aged man, he wanted to talk about student violence. And in this context, Thatcher knew, murder did not rank as violence.

It was left to Dudley Humble to bring the conversation back to earth with a thud.

"In the Bankers' Club," he murmured, "they're saying that the police have narrowed down the murderer to someone in the management."

Thatcher was pleased to see that, even in the face of deliberate provocation, Olmsted retained enough balance not to constitute himself the universal champion of Slax's front office. "I know that's what it looks like," he replied slowly. "But, for the life of me, I can't see it."

"But how well do you know them, Pete?" Thatcher asked reasonably. "Most business executives don't look like murderers at first blush."

"I know I've handled most of the financial details with Harry in New York. But I have met the others. And look what the police theory would have to be! Say Domínguez had a pocketful of sand from his last wrecking operation. Say he was insane enough to take a fistful of it and shake it in someone's face. Then he brags that he's been behind all the damage and has just caused more. Can you imagine Marten or Aguilera doing anything but reaching for the phone to call the police?" Olmsted gulped and continued resolutely. "Even Dave Lippert, and I grant you that he's the dark horse, even he would have howled for the cops. He might have gone slightly hysterical. But you're talking about someone going totally ape!"

Dudley Humble was prepared to see the thing through. "In the Bankers' Club," he said cautiously, "they're saying that Mrs. Lippert is without an alibi, too."

"Oh, for God's sake!" Olmsted turned to Thatcher in appeal. "John, you tell him. When we met her at the front office, did she look to you like a woman fresh from murder?"

Thatcher knew his duty. "No, she did not," he said firmly.

What he did not say was that, of all four suspects, Norma Lippert was the one most likely to have dropped the murder gun daintily into a wastebasket and wiped the whole distasteful episode from her mind. And the gun itself, come to think of it, was a powerful argument against the spontaneous-combustion theory of murder.

"I do not think, Dudley," he said instead, "we will get anywhere trying to solve the problems of the police. So why don't we address ourselves to the Sloan's problems?"

Humble and Olmsted instantly looked alert. Thatcher was not deceived into thinking either one had forgotten the fundamental contest.

"Regardless of the murder," he continued, "we have here a situation in which one of our clients has been the object of persistent sabotage and suffered considerable loss. Action against the sabotage has been hamstrung by the fear that it might boomerang in a delicate political climate. Now, first we should consider how delicate that climate really is. And second, how likely are other Sloan clients here to become similar targets? Dudley, you're the expert on local conditions."

Immediately Dudley Humble began to exhibit his more trying characteristics. "I am not sure that the real problem is political in a meaningful sense," he said magisterially.

No one outside the Sloan would have realized that Humble was, in his own way, as redoubtable a font of information as Walter Bowman back on Wall Street. Thatcher, however, was willing to grant that Dudley really did know more about Puerto Rico than most Puerto Ricans, possibly including Francisco Ramírez Rivera and certainly including most youthful radicals.

But here the similarity ended. Bowman was an enthusiastic disseminator of what he knew. Apart from protecting his sources, he was generous to a fault. Ask him about the eccentricities of the Federal Reserve or the drinking habits of an important fund manager, and the problem was to keep your footing as the tidal wave of facts broke over your head. By contrast Dudley Humble, and all of International for that matter, reminded Thatcher of witch doctors in some primitive African tribe. They acted as guardians and protectors of sacred mysteries, jealous of their arcane methods. Dudley and his colleagues doled out information, driblet by driblet.

". . . politically Puerto Rico is a commonwealth," he was unbending enough to say, "and it will continue to be so. It—"

"Why?" Thatcher interrupted baldly.

Humble was startled enough to give an equally bald answer.

"Costs," he said tersely. Recovering himself, he began to elaborate. "Statehood, by introducing federal corporate taxes, would end the island's special attraction to industry. Independence, in addition to introducing the costs of sovereignty such as defense, would raise a tariff barrier between the island and the mainland. Even the last plebiscite figures understated the strength of the commonwealth. Most commonwealth opponents are thinking in terms so distant as to be illusory. Asked what they want right now, most of them would probably settle for what they have. That, of course, is a gross simplification. The situation is far more complex."

He paused, his head bent in thought over his steepled fingers, a man overwhelmed at the task he had set himself.

Thatcher thought he saw a shortcut. With deliberate malice he said, "I was talking to Ramírez the other day. He says that there has been a dramatic growth in the independence movement."

"Ramírez!" There was a snort. "The man is as biased as they come."

"He admitted that."

As Thatcher had expected, what Dudley was unprepared to disgorge as simple information he was prepared to marshal as refutation.

It was fashionable in certain circles to be for independence these days, he conceded. There was the inevitable friction arising from the American presence on the island, ranging from sailors on leave to trouble with the Federal Maritime Board. There was, among the younger generation, a cultural renaissance emphasizing the Hispanic tradition. There was the ethnic and nationalistic fever gripping the whole Caribbean area. There was the stunning impact of Cuba, the usual fringe of Marxists . . .

"None of these factors is important by itself," Humble lectured. "They merely create a climate. In the absence of an incident giving them some cohesion, they will continue to be unimportant. But the right incident at the right time could give Ramírez and his friends enough votes to make them a power. I don't mean anything like victory. I mean the power of being the officially recognized opposition."

Dudley Humble, Thatcher decided, was finally beginning to talk horse sense. "And you think that is a delicate enough situation to have caused Slax's reluctance to follow up on the sabotage?"

Humble became judicious. "It was certainly reasonable for them to be cautious."

"You do realize that at first there was some doubt as to whether Domínguez was acting on behalf of the Radical Independents or simply working out some personal spite."

"Good heavens! The radicals aren't important." Humble was genuinely surprised. "It's the workers who are important. The Radical Independents are a pitifully small group. They got a bad name when so many people were injured in the ROTC riots last year. Now they just number a few hundred. Their new leader is much better at getting headlines than at getting adherents. Even the students are leery of him. If you walk through the University of Puerto Rico, you'll hear more evangelists preaching in the courtyard than Radical Independents. Unless they move out of the university and broaden their base, the party is of no importance. And that doesn't seem very likely."

Thatcher reviewed what he had heard before coming to a conclusion. "You seem to have answered my second question, Dudley. We don't have to anticipate a wave of terror and sabotage against all our other clients."

"I may be wrong, of course." Dudley Humble grinned boyishly at this absurdity. "But I think it most unlikely. It's an anomalous position, I grant you. A company hit by sabotage would have to be very careful. It could trigger a wave of anti-Americanism. On the other hand, the probability of sabotage is minute. I think there was trouble at Slax simply because the Radical Independents had a member working there. And that is a real rarity. I'm surprised they had even one member in Domínguez' kind of job. As I said before, there's been no attempt to broaden their base, and offhand I don't see what inducements they have to offer to labor."

Pete Olmsted smiled broadly. Even Thatcher was forced to

acknowledge the detachment of Humble's discourse. Because if sabotage and Puerto Rican politics were not going to play havoc with American industry, then there was substantially less need for the peculiar expertise of Humble and his colleagues in International.

"That's a damn fair statement, Dudley," said Olmsted in a wave of gratification. He would have continued in this vein if he had not been interrupted by the opening of the door. It was Mrs. Schroeder.

"Mr. Olmsted, I have a call for you out here. Do you want me to switch it?"

"Can't it wait?"

"They said it was urgent."

Olmsted sighed and indicated he would take the call on her desk.

As the door closed behind him, Thatcher felt honor bound to pay his own tribute to Humble's performance. "I'm relieved to learn that our problems seem to be localized in Slax. And I won't deny that the Sloan has always liked the idea of a man who knows steel in charge of making loans to steel mills. But there is more to doing business in Puerto Rico than I anticipated. And I expect the situation will get more complicated."

This seemed to be a day of unbroken selflessness for Dudley Humble. "No doubt we're all going to have to become broader in our interests. There is no reason Olmsted can't learn the ins and outs of the Puerto Rican situation. In the same way, I'm sorry you won't have a chance to meet Gregorio. But he's in the hospital having his slipped disk attended to."

"Who is Gregorio?" Thatcher asked, at a loss.

"Gregorio is our new garment-trade expert."

Humble's hearty chuckle was still resounding when Pete Olmsted burst into the room.

"That was Aguilera from the Slax plant," he said tightly.

"My God, what's happened there now?"

"They just got an anonymous call. You were dead right, Dudley, about the Radical Independents needing to broaden their base." His lips stretched in a parody of a smile. "They're planning to do it in a big way."

The new look in the Student-Worker Radical Independence Party had started the night before, when two hundred people had straggled into a building on Avenida José de Diego, near the University of Puerto Rico.

Outside, the signs read:

RADICAL INDEPENDENTS PROTEST MEETING!
PRUDENCIO NADAL SPEAKS TONIGHT!

Inside, the hall was much too large for the assemblage. Most of the audience had huddled together in the first bank of folding chairs. But throughout the auditorium there were scattered groups and individuals who seemed to prefer isolation from their fellows. Some of them were students, feet draped over one seat, head lolling back over a second, books and belongings piled on a third. Some were intense young women. Some were amorous couples. Some were clearly visitors from another world. On one side of the entrance was a table where a bored girl sat, soliciting contributions. On the other, an unshaven youth hopefully offered for sale a smudged news sheet. The bare walls and high ceiling of the near-empty room cast back cavernous echoes of each word from the speaker.

"Benito Domínguez Sánchez is a martyr to the cause—the cause of workers, the cause of students, the cause of humanity!"

Prudencio Nadal was a slight young man with dark eyes burning in a thin face.

"He died—unknown and unrecognized—for his comrades! While we were speaking and dreaming with each other, he was daring. Unsupported by us, even unrecognized by us, he took our words—and acted. While we hesitated, he marched forth alone—and was killed. Benito Domínguez died for us. Did Benito Domínguez die in vain?"

"No!" roared one hundred lusty young voices. Several people at the back of the room moved forward to be closer to Nadal.

"No, he did not die in vain," Nadal agreed. "He has shown us what we were forgetting. He has shown us who our brothers are. He, a simple man, had the courage to defy the exploiters of Puerto Rican workers and students. Now the time has come for all workers and all students to join fraternal hands in his battle—the battle for social revolution!"

There were ragged cheers.

Nadal shook his head slightly. "But it is not enough for us to know our friends. We must know our enemies too. Who is draining the lifeblood of Puerto Rico? What forces have brutalized and dehumanized our society? Why have we become the pawns of every power interest?"

Prudencio Nadal, for all his youth, was a practiced orator. He had spoken on the campus, on street corners, in many halls like this. Now that his audience was leaning forward expectantly, he broke off and laughed softly.

"We know who our enemies are by now. They run our government, they own our factories, they spread their lies in our newspapers. They do all this because the commonwealth makes Puerto Rico a colony for Yanqui exploitation! I spit on them! I spit on the millionaire Governor in La Fortaleza! I spit on capitalistic American imperialists!"

He took a deep breath. He still had one finger raised for his remaining target.

"And I spit on their hireling, the Independence Party that has sold us out to both of them! We know their version of independence—the same corrupt hierarchy entrenched forever, bigger and better hotels, freeborn Puerto Ricans turned into pimps for American tourists!"

During the blast of approval that followed, a man sitting inconspicuously in the rear said, "I don't like this."

His companion protested. "But you've always laughed at him before, Uncle. He's no wilder tonight than he usually is. You always say the Radical Independents are just a lunatic fringe."

Francisco Ramírez Rivera was grim. "Don't be an idiot," he snapped. "A handful of students may be a lunatic fringe. Nearly a million workers are not!"

"But I don't think there are any workers here," Ernesto pointed out.

"Nadal won't be talking here much longer," Ramírez said cuttingly. He looked back toward the speaker. "Why do you think he's suddenly emphasizing this anti-Americanism? He's never done that before."

Ernesto, who had been his uncle's proxy at other Nadal performances, had to agree.

"Now that he has a martyr for his cause," said Ramírez thoughtfully, "I think this young man may have big plans."

Up on the platform Prudencio Nadal was already outlining

the first of them. "The Radical Independent Party hereby calls for a massive strike and demonstration against Slax Unlimited! We will lead the workers to the picket line. We will provide them with instruction and support. We will make their cause our cause. Shoulder to shoulder, Puerto Rican workers and students will begin the revolution!"

"Viva!" yelled an excited member of the audience.

The party stalwarts recognized their cue. Their feet began to pound a remorseless tempo on the wooden floor.

"Viva!" they shouted. *"Viva la huelga!"*

The chant was taken up by everyone as feet drummed enthusiastically, and the scattered chorus became disciplined. The room rang with enthusiasm.

From the back row, Francisco Ramírez Rivera hastened to the door.

The news reached Harry Zimmerman in New York at the same time it reached the Sloan Guaranty Trust in Hato Rey. For the first time he was near despair. A strike would cripple Slax for good. But what could he do? If three hundred and fifty workers wanted to strike, there was nothing to be done. It was useless to argue with them, it was useless to appeal to the authorities. The weapons were all on the other side. He needed big guns and he didn't have any.

Suddenly the frown lifted and a gleam came into Harry's eye.

"Of course!" he exclaimed. "I'll get Annie!"

8. Union Maid

Anna Luisa Galiano was a woman who had become a legend in her own time.

There are, of course, different varieties of fame. One kind reduces its subject to living in the constant glare of publicity. If he enters a supper club once, he doubles its earnings for the

next six months. He cannot get on or off a plane without
flashbulbs popping. His marriages, his divorces, his children
and his pet beagle are fodder for in-depth reporting. Then
there is the other fame. The subject is virtually unknown to
the world at large. His private life can be conducted with
decent decorum. But within a restricted group he assumes the
dimensions of an epic figure. As the inner circle consists of
all the people whom he ever wants to influence, cajole, persuade or terrorize, this is a very satisfactory state of affairs.

Annie Galiano's fame was of the second sort—which was
not surprising. Most things did become satisfactory from her
point of view, sooner or later.

She had been a power in the International Ladies' Garment
Workers' Union for twenty-five years—yet she had never been
commemorated by a profile in *The New Yorker* or a column
in *Time*. She was a Puerto Rican—yet she had never served
on a commission about minority rights. She was a woman—
yet she had never been publicly asked for her views about
equal pay for equal work or about new life styles. The only
time her picture had ever appeared in the *New York Times,*
she was in the second row of a group of union notables eulo-
gizing David Dubinsky upon his retirement.

Annie was certainly no publicity hound. It helped that her
work did not include negotiating major contracts, presiding
over the opening of union health centers or announcing which
candidate had union endorsement. Annie was not attracted to
the making of general policy. She liked to sink her teeth into
hard facts—and hard opponents too.

As a young woman, she had been invaluable when Puerto
Rican workers first began trickling into Seventh Avenue.
Patiently she started educating employers. She insisted on
bilingual shop stewards. She set up Spanish lectures on work
practices, health standards, Social Security, and unemploy-
ment benefits. With the migration of textile and clothing
manufacturers to North Carolina, she turned her attention to
the South. Her bulldozing tactics taught more than one small
town about the existence of organized labor. But, as her
knowledge of the industry broadened—and as recessions took
their toll—Annie Galiano made an interesting discovery: there
is little point in wresting benefits from a company that then
goes bankrupt.

At this point, Annie really came into her own. The same

abundant energy that had leveled every obstacle to employee well-being was now applied to the problems of the employer. She became an expert in balance sheets. She hobnobbed with efficiency experts. She recommended cost-cutting programs. More to the point, she frequently provided union loans to help small companies switch over to modern methods. She knew exactly when a family firm should go public.

The years had left their mark. Her abundant black hair, swept back into a careless knot, was now liberally streaked with wiry gray strands. Her once-slim figure had thickened into rugged solidity, firmly planted on low-heeled oxfords. Her clothes now looked as if they came from the Salvation Army. And after decades of unlimited black coffee, cigarettes and whiskey, the high enthusiastic screech of her youth had deepened to a basso growl.

Nevertheless, she looked like a guardian angel to Harry Zimmerman.

"If these crazy kids really pull off a strike, Annie, we won't be able to ride it out. Slax will have to leave the island. We'll sell off the plant at distress prices." He paused to let it sink in. "And you know what that means. Three hundred and fifty of your people will be thrown out of work. For months at least. Maybe forever, if the plant is used for something else."

Annie grunted as she ground out a cigarette. "We'll see about that," she said martially.

The president of Slax Unlimited was satisfied by those simple words. True, Annie's career had never led to a bout with Che Guevara. If it had, Harry would have put his money on Annie any time.

"How soon can you leave?" he demanded.

When Harry Zimmerman gave the order to reserve two seats on the morning flight to San Juan, he was smiling for the first time in days.

His smile did not survive their arrival at the gates of the Bayamón plant. Instead of the sunlit languor that usually prevailed, there was milling confusion. Bearded students, waving placards, and uniformed police jostled for space. Standing aboard a pickup truck, a speaker with a hand microphone exhorted passing workers to lay down their tools. Somebody had been busy with a paint pot. The white wall of the office wing now proclaimed in blood-red letters, "DOWN

WITH AMERICAN IMPERIALISM!" At the corner, two young
men were thrusting mimeographed flyers at shoppers drawn
from across the street.

"This is your movement! This is your strike!" Prudencio
Nadal harangued. "Power to the people!"

"Power to the people!" the beards chorused.

Harry Zimmerman was frozen in his taxicab. "Christ!" he
moaned.

But Annie Galiano did not share his negative reaction.
Airports and highways, offices and hotels, were merely tiresome way stations for her. But a garment factory had the
same sweet beckoning smell that the boxing ring has for
a heavyweight, that Everest has for the mountaineer.

"Let me handle this," she said, brushing aside one hundred
and ninety pounds of sportswear manufacturer.

Her door was already open. She was plowing toward the
eye of the storm. Disdaining such effete supports as trucks or
microphones, she swept aside a pile of underground newspapers, picked up a box and planted it in a strategic spot
facing the crowd. She mounted with the magnificent confidence of a great Othello making his entrance and commanding
the entire stage. For all practical purposes, she was saying,
"Keep up your bright swords!"

What she actually said was, "Greetings, Local Six Hundred! Salutations from headquarters. I am Annie!"

As if on signal, the shop stewards emerged from Slax,
leading an enthusiastic snake line shouting, *"Viva Annie!"* The
ensuing celebration between Annie and the workers achieved
a fervor that left Prudencio Nadal stupefied.

It was a mystery to Harry Zimmerman too. How could
either of them guess that Annie had phoned ahead to the
shop stewards, relying on the magic of her name? And why
not? At Slax they heard about her constantly from sisters,
cousins and aunts in New York, they read about her in the
union newsletter, they knew about her activities in the same
way that the line at General Motors knows all the work rules
at Ford.

"I still don't see how you managed it," Harry was grum-
bling two hours later when Annie had at last been able to
tear herself away from her admirers.

"Never mind," Annie commanded briskly. "I think we can
kill this strike business."

Everyone at the table, except Harry, brightened.

"That would be wonderful," said Norma Lippert.

Cesar Aguilera almost shed his reserve. "I would be profoundly relieved."

"It sounds too good to be true." David Lippert was incredulous. "What do you have in mind?"

"It's not just the production," Eric Marten said buoyantly. "But I'd like to see that Nadal kid fall flat on his face."

Annie shook her head at him reprovingly. "Bah! They are simply children," she said with indulgence. "They want attention."

"Children!" Eric Marten almost choked. "Look, you're new down here. Maybe you don't know what these children have been up to. First they recruit one of our foremen. He sabotages us so that one run is completely ruined, thousands of dollars' worth of raw materials get the acid treatment, and a batch of sand goes into the lubricating oil. Then the foreman turns up murdered and, if you ask me, these particular children were behind that too!"

Annie was unmoved. She had already heard most of this from Zimmerman. "But this charge of murder is new." She became grave. "And serious. I didn't know the Radical Independents were suspected of killing Domínguez."

Cesar Aguilera cocked an eyebrow at his colleague. "For that matter, Eric, it is new to me too."

"All right! All right!" Marten was red-faced. "So I haven't said anything about it before. But I've been thinking, and it makes sense to me."

"I thought the police had decided it must be one of us," Norma Lippert said with a detachment that made her husband stir restively.

Eric Marten pounced. "And why did they decide that?" he demanded. "Because Domínguez told people he was going to meet one of the bosses. But what if he had one of his radical buddies stowed away here? He couldn't very well tell anybody that. So he made the obvious excuse for coming into the office wing."

"It would explain a lot. And nothing these radicals did would surprise me." David Lippert's eagerness faltered. "But the police have pretty well decided that an outsider couldn't have gotten in and hidden anywhere."

"Vallejo was thinking of an outsider getting in by himself."

Marten continued to hammer his point home. "But what if he had Domínguez to help him? It wouldn't have been very hard for Domínguez to sneak someone in before the receptionist arrived that morning."

Aguilera, as usual, was inclined to be cautious. "What you say is true, Eric. But you still haven't explained why the radicals should murder Domínguez. After all, they were on the same side, weren't they?"

"You could still explain it." Marten was uncharacteristically hesitant. "Now, don't say this is crazy until you've heard me out. What was the point of all this sabotage anyway? The radicals aren't interested in simply doing us some damage, you know."

"Oh, no?" Harry Zimmerman was sarcastic. "So what do you call what they've been doing? Helping Slax? You're talking through your hat, Eric. Of course they want to damage us. For God's sake, look at what the radicals back home are up to. Throwing bombs every time you look around. That's their specialty, causing damage."

Marten disagreed. "The radicals here are different, Harry. They've got a concrete goal, and that's to get the Yankees off the island. This Prudencio Nadal wants us out. He needed a big issue. And he didn't have one until Domínguez was murdered."

There was a long silence.

Then Aguilera, polite as ever, said, "It still sounds crazy to me, Eric. You mean the radicals murdered one of their own simply to drum up popular support? I don't believe it."

David Lippert was not so sure. "I don't say it sounds likely, Cesar. But it's not impossible. We don't know what went on between the radicals and Domínguez. For all we know, he may have been trying to blackmail them. 'Pay me or I know someone who will pay me.' "

"No." Aguilera shook his head with finality. "That, Domínguez would not have done. You do not understand his kind of man. He wanted the satisfaction of seeing us injured. He would have regarded money as beneath him in such a context."

Harry Zimmerman was scornful, but before he could speak Annie Galiano seized the floor.

"All of this makes no difference." With a brusque horizontal gesture she dismissed blackmail and murder. "The police will take care of the killing. That's their business. But your business is averting a strike. Let's talk about that."

Harry Zimmerman immediately lost interest in the theorizing of Aguilera and Marten.

"We're waiting for you to tell us what to do, Annie, and . . ."

"And?" she challenged.

Zimmerman's face twisted into a rueful smile.

"And how much it's going to cost us," he said.

Never, in all her beneficent dealings with manufacturers, did Annie forget that her primary aim was improved conditions for the labor force. And not a segment of that force, not any particular local, but garment workers in general. Harry had known all along that she would exact a price for her cooperation. He was anxious to see what it was.

"Well," Annie began, knitting her brows furiously, "you understand that you have to offer the line some kind of reward. Something emotionally satisfying, which is what the radicals are offering."

"You mean like finding themselves out of a job?" Zimmerman asked ironically.

"Don't laugh, Harry. In the short run, they'd have the excitement of demonstrations, protests, meetings. Besides, they probably don't believe Slax would actually shut down. Nobody ever does until it happens. So your best bet is to offer them a victory of some sort."

"Sure. And I suppose you have a particular victory in mind?"

Annie grinned. "I've been talking to some of the girls. That's what held me up for so long. Tell me, Harry, what do you think about a day-care center for children of women workers?"

Harry was thunderstruck.

"A day-care center?" he said blankly.

David Lippert gaped at her. "A day-care center?" he echoed. "Where did you get that idea? Most of our women live with their parents or their husbands' parents. The grandmother takes care of the children." In spite of her expression, he continued fluently, "So, you see, there really is no need for one. I don't know who you've been talking to, but—"

"Why don't you let Annie go on?" Zimmerman said hollowly.

Annie nodded regal thanks. "Our women live that way because they have to. A day-care center would let families live where they want. Why should you be surprised? All over the world people are trying to get away from their in-laws. Haven't you noticed?"

David was ready to continue the argument, but Harry was having none of that. He knew perfectly well that Annie had her guns trained on New York, not on Bayamón. If a leading garment manufacturer sponsored a day-care center that really worked, Annie would be supplied with ammunition for future bargaining sessions back home.

"I suppose," he said wearily, "that it would have to be something pretty special in the way of nurseries."

Annie bobbed her head pleasantly. "Not just special, Harry. Outstanding," she said firmly. "One that people all over would want to copy."

Norma Lippert felt that she was peculiarly qualified to take part in any discussion about child-raising. She failed to recognize that this was not a discussion, not even a negotiation. This was a bill for services rendered.

"I really don't see the necessity for too much expense," she said. "Of course, in principle I am in favor of day-care centers. There are too many children who don't receive adequate supervision if their mothers are working. And so often grandmothers don't enter into the interests of young children. But if we hired one qualified nursery teacher and made over the end of the packing wing, I don't see why that wouldn't do."

Annie eyed her coldly. "That was not what I had in mind, Mrs. Lippert. I was thinking of something much more ambitious—with preschool training, possibly Montessori teachers, all sorts of special programs. And I don't see any reason why it should be restricted to the children of Slax workers. It's a bad idea to start economic segregation at that age. If you make it the best nursery school in Puerto Rico, there's no reason why you shouldn't send your own children there."

Norma was startled. "My children!" she exclaimed in accents which told their own story.

"It would probably do them a lot of good," Annie assured her.

Harry Zimmerman leaped into the breach. "Well, well, there's no need to discuss that now. But I go along with the idea of the model day-care center, Annie. If we're going to do it, we might as well do it right."

Annie nodded solemnly. "Now, that," she said, "is a proposal I think I can take to the workers. And don't worry, Harry, it'll still be cheaper than a strike."

9. Buttonholing

With John Putnam Thatcher immersed in Puerto Rico and its problems, his post at the Sloan Guaranty Trust on Wall Street was occupied by Charlie Trinkam, his second in command. Charlie, although insouciant in private life, was an immensely capable banker. His personal style, however, was a far cry from Thatcher's. In some quarters this gave rise to friction.

"I don't blame John for hightailing it to the Caribbean," Charlie said breezily. Sleet was beating a rat-a-tat against Miss Corsa's window. "I wouldn't mind heading into the sunshine myself."

Miss Corsa did not welcome implications that Mr. Thatcher might be indulging himself, but she had learned not to join issue with Charlie Trinkam—at least not directly.

"Mr. Thatcher asked me to remind you about the meeting at Northern Lakes Shipping," she said.

"All taken care of," Charlie said, perching on her desk to riffle through the portfolio reports she had prepared. "Nicolls is going. And you can tell John we're keeping an eye on those clowns over at Boston Fund too."

Miss Corsa made a note and continued to treat Mr. Thatcher as spiritually present if absent in the flesh.

". . . and he wants to see a review of the short-term Treasuries that the Trust Department is holding."

"Fine, fine," said Charlie absently, initialing some carbons and tossing them into the basket. "Say, what's this Innes was telling me? He says someone got killed at that company Olmsted is mixed up with."

"Slax Unlimited," she said repressively.

Miss Corsa was always fully briefed. Thatcher's morning calls only supplemented her own conscientiousness. A duplicate folder of the clippings that Mrs. Schroeder had so thoughtfully provided in Hato Rey was currently on his desk here.

"I believe there has been some political unpleasantness," she added, skating over unsavory details.

"If I know John," Trinkam remarked tolerantly, "he'll find that a lot more interesting than Dud Humble. Well, thanks, Rose."

He pushed off from her desk and strode out. Long experience told Miss Corsa that, deplorable as it was, Trinkam was likely to be right.

Charlie, meantime, was heading back to his own quarters. En route, however he was interrupted.

"Ah, Charlie!" Innes beamed as if finding Charlie Trinkam at the Sloan was a happy surprise. "Tell me, what do you hear from John?"

"Not much," said Charlie cheerfully.

"We were wondering about his impressions of Puerto Rico," said Innes, falling into step beside him.

Like Miss Corsa, Charlie was loyal. But he was more direct.

"No use trying to pump me, Innes," he said. "I don't know anything about what's going on down there and, to tell the truth, I don't want to."

With some indignation, Innes refuted this reading of his motives. International, he wanted Charlie to know, would never stoop to anything underhanded in advancing its cause, no matter how righteous that cause was.

"Congratulations," said Charlie. "Why don't you stop by and try that line on Commercial Credit? I've already told them I don't know what John's doing. They were just making casual conversation, too."

On this thrust, he turned into his own office. There he found Everett Gabler.

"Hi, Everett," he said warily.

Gabler was the oldest, staidest and most single-minded of Thatcher's staff. During Thatcher's absences, when Charlie took the helm, Everett's normal foreboding intensified. There was only one way to deflect his disapproval. Trinkam, nobody's fool, was willing to give it a try.

"International and Commercial Credit sure take the cake! Both of them are digging for all they're worth to get John's thinking."

His bait was specifically designed to tempt Everett. Here was an opportunity to point out flaws in other divisions of the Sloan and to forget whatever imperfections existed in the Trust Department—or in Charlie.

Not for the first time, Gabler was too cunning for him.

"The Sloan's situation in Puerto Rico is inexcusable," he said severely, "and it is high time that it be rectified. My only complaint is that John should be the one required to do so. Particularly when we are so hard pressed. Now, Charlie, I am seriously concerned about our position in Stevenson Can. Especially with the market moving up . . ."

Charlie accepted defeat like the gentleman that he was. But when his secretary announced that George C. Lancer would like a few moments of his time, he rose perhaps more quickly than necessary.

"Sorry, Ev," he said. "Maybe we can get back to this later in the afternoon."

Everett rose, too. "As soon," he promised implacably, "as you are back in your office."

Charlie kept smiling. This was not complete hypocrisy. If George C. Lancer, chairman of the board, ran true to form, Charlie would not get back to his office till long after Everett had left for the day, taking Stevenson Can with him.

Lancer, just back from London, was a serious, hard-working executive. There was never any suggestion of carelessness or superficiality in anything Lancer said; there was never any suggestion of speed either.

"Charlie," he said, when Trinkam reached the magnificent tower suite. "Glad you were free." His meticulous courtesy was a byword.

"Good trip, George?" Charlie inquired.

"I suppose you could call it satisfactory," George said finally. "I think we're going to be able to recover everything from that secondary loan."

"That's better than I had hoped for," Charlie admitted.

George, although innately modest, was pleased. "It helps having someone from here drop in on the branches from

time to time. Otherwise—or so I find—they lose perspective.
That's why I am so glad that John is lending a hand with this
Puerto Rico tangle. I expect it won't take him long to
straighten things out."

"Sure," said Charlie. He was not the enthusiast for overseas branches that some of his colleagues were.

"You know," Lancer went on, "our liaison with Hato
Rey has not been as good as it might be. It may have been
a mistake to let our Puerto Rican branch report through
International. . . ."

In Hato Rey, John Putnam Thatcher was not straightening
out any tangles. He was talking to a policeman.

It was not the way he had expected to spend the afternoon.

Olmsted had been reporting. ". . . So Harry says that
Annie should be able to stop this thing in its tracks."

"She must be a redoubtable woman," Thatcher had remarked. "I look forward to meeting her sometime."

By now, Olmsted had no margin to spare for anything but
essentials. "That way, if Slax can keep the production lines
running, there's a good chance they'll meet their delivery
dates. Harry has wangled a couple of extensions without any
penalty. I don't say I'm optimistic, John . . ."

In view of what had been happening recently, Thatcher
was happy to hear that. Optimism about Slax at this juncture
would border on idiocy.

". . . a big run for Bloomingdale's for late spring. That
should help. With sportswear, some of this hard season
selling isn't realistic any more. Spreading out delivery dates
should help a lot."

Just then, Mrs. Schroeder put through a call. It was Captain Vallejo. He would very much like a word with Thatcher.

"At your convenience," said Thatcher cooperatively.

"I am in your lobby now."

"Then come right up."

Fluidly Vallejo made another suggestion. Perhaps a cup
of coffee across the street?

Thatcher appreciated the punctilio with which Vallejo was
treating all his North American witnesses. He was being
careful not to inflict the sensationalism of a murder investigation on the Sloan Guaranty Trust. Catch the New York City

Police Department doing as much! Even with this thought, another came. How long would this tact last?

Aloud, he replied he would be downstairs immediately.

"And I understand that Mr. Olmsted is with you? Perhaps he would be kind enough to join us?"

The three of them were soon in a small, bustling coffee shop half a block from the Sloan. It was located in the arcade of the Bank of Nova Scotia building. Down the street was the half-completed edifice that would be the new Bank of Ponce. Somewhere out of his line of vision, Thatcher knew, another skyscraper was going up—the new John Hancock building. He must remember this rash of construction the next time anybody lectured him about Puerto Rico's economic growth. When banks and insurance companies scurried to join other banks and insurance companies within the compass of six square blocks, Thatcher felt that the point had been abundantly made.

"I think it was you, Mr. Olmsted, who had met the people at Slax before Domínguez was killed? And Mr. Thatcher had not?"

"That's right," said Olmsted wearily. "But I don't know any of them well. I do most of the work with Harry Zimmerman—in New York."

Vallejo nodded, giving Thatcher the impression that he knew all about Harry Zimmerman.

Olmsted was painstakingly plodding on. "I've met David Lippert—oh, say four or five times. Norma maybe twice. Aguilera and Eric Marten I just met when I flew down this time."

"So they are casual acquaintances?"

"That's right," said Olmsted.

"That, perhaps, is why you noticed nothing unusual about any of them the morning of the murder."

"I don't think there was anything unusual!" said Olmsted, sounding tired.

Thatcher thought he could help. "You must remember, Captain, that we were there for a short time before Domínguez' body was discovered. Only something quite extraordinary would have registered in that time."

Vallejo persisted. "And nothing comes to mind?"

Silently Olmsted shook his head.

"I recall thinking that young Lippert might be nervous,"

said Thatcher, stirring his excellent coffee. "But since then I have discovered that he is a nervous type."

"So everyone tells us," Vallejo agreed. "Another question has occurred to us since we saw you last. Who arranged the timing of your tour of Slax?"

Olmsted was puzzled. "I don't see what you mean by that," he said.

Vallejo expanded. Perhaps he had put it badly. But who suggested the tour? When was it arranged? And, finally—Vallejo's voice was carefully neutral—how many people knew about it?

"Let's see." Olmsted was thinking aloud. "I got here the day before you did, didn't I, John? I got in touch with Lippert right away. We all had dinner that night. I don't remember who raised the subject, but we made arrangements for me to go through Slax. Then you got here. So I called back to say it might be a good idea—" He broke off. It did not seem like such a good idea now.

"Did Lippert take the lead in this talk?" Vallejo asked.

"No-o," said Olmsted, searching his memory. "You couldn't say that. It was a natural suggestion. They all took it for granted."

"And for what it's worth," Thatcher offered, "everybody at the Sloan knew about the tour. I assume all the secretaries at Slax did, as well. It was not a secret."

"You see our problem," said Vallejo. "So many people could have killed Domínguez. But why at that particular time? Was it perhaps because important bankers were arriving at Slax? Was Domínguez going to say something to them, show something to them?"

Olmsted was jolted by this thought. Even Thatcher was slightly startled.

Vallejo shrugged his shoulders. "It is only a theory, you understand. But we must not overlook it. Because it is still not clear why Domínguez was killed."

Indignation at being considered a catalyst for murder flavored Pete Olmsted's voice. "But he was some kind of political radical, wasn't he? Doesn't that give you a better lead?"

This time it was Thatcher who had to demur. After all, no other Sloan client in Puerto Rico had been troubled by anti-American outbursts. "These radicals seem to be highly selective," he objected.

Vallejo nodded. "That is true. It would, of course, be most convenient for the management of Slax if this were a falling-out of radicals. But it is hard to believe. These Radical Independents—they are good at riots. But a riot is a triumph of confusion. Everyone loses his identity. A rock flies out from the middle of a mob, and an ROTC cadet has a fractured skull. A shot is fired from a crowded student union, and a policeman lies dead. This does not simply mean harder work for the authorities. It means young people cease to be themselves and do things they would not otherwise do. All this is very different from a planned, cold-blooded murder."

"And certainly," Thatcher remarked, "whatever else you may say about Domínguez' murder, it was not inefficient."

"The real oddity," Vallejo went on, "is that Domínguez should have anything to do with these students."

Thatcher asked what kind of man Domínguez had been.

"He was not much respected," said Vallejo. "Not by the people who worked with him, not by his wife, not by his neighbors. They all say he talked too much—and sometimes foolishly. But still, he had learned his trade. He supported his family. He had risen to foreman."

There was silence at their table, if not around them. Dozens of office workers leaving for the day were crowding into the shop.

"If Domínguez was a foolish man," Thatcher suggested, "perhaps he didn't join the radicals on his own initiative. Perhaps they recruited him because they needed a Slax foreman."

Vallejo was interested, but dubious. "I don't see how we will find out. Nadal and his friends won't answer our questions, and Benito Domínguez never said a word to anyone else about the Radical Independents. If we hadn't found the card, we wouldn't even know he was a member."

This was too much for Pete Olmsted. "But there was all that sabotage at Slax!" he exploded. "Domínguez was running around throwing acid on material. And that sand—the sand he used to doctor the lubricating oil!"

Thatcher was willing to explore new ground. "I suppose," he said slowly, "it could be argued that Domínguez was killed because he caught someone else using that sand."

"My God!" said Olmsted.

Vallejo said only, "There are many possibilities. We are exploring them—all of them. So I am grateful for your co-operation today, as I shall be grateful for any other help you can give us."

He departed, after renewed thanks, leaving a worried Pete Olmsted.

"I hoped the worst was over at Slax," he said.

"The worst won't be over, Pete," said Thatcher bracingly, "until the police arrest Domínguez' murderer."

And even then, he thought, much would depend on just who that murderer was.

10. Cutting to Size

In spite of these forebodings in Hato Rey, morale at the Slax factory in Bayamón had never been higher. The management basked in the absence of sabotage and the production of a record output. The workers on the line were deriving a different enjoyment from bravura displays of combat every lunch hour.

For Prudencio Nadal did not simply fold his tents and depart. An issue such as the murder of Benito Domínguez was not likely to come his way again. Therefore every day he doggedly mounted his rostrum and loosed his eloquence.

At first the front office had been alarmed. But not for long.

"It gives everybody some excitement. Don't worry," Annie advised. "Leave this kid to me, and I'll smear him."

She punctuated this remark by mashing her broad spatulate thumb against the tabletop in a gesture which Norma Lippert, for one, thought the height of vulgarity.

The tone of the subsequent jousting sprang from the sense of moral superiority common to both contestants. To Nadal, Annie was a capitalist hireling, corrupted into opposing the revolution. To Annie, Prudencio was a rich boy, wantonly willing to close down a plant and throw poor people out of work in a show of self-aggrandizement. Given these views, neither was inclined to pull any punches.

Results, of course, were foreordained. On the practical level, Annie was speaking before people she knew, about problems they shared, in words they understood. Prudencio harangued his listeners as if they had just emerged from a course in sociology. It was the personal vilification to which both warriors rapidly descended that attracted large crowds.

The untroubled, tropical weather of Puerto Rico contributed to the entertainment. By the second day everyone in Bayamón seemed to be picnicking on Slax property. By the third day, people were arriving in buses from farther afield. Word spread rapidly that the opponents were reaching heights of abuse that were well worth hearing.

Here too Annie had the edge. She possessed a richly seasoned vocabulary, drawn from the storehouses of two languages and brought to a fine pitch by experience in the barrio and the ghetto, in the sweatshop and the union hiring hall. She was an instinctive debater, thriving on contention. Prudencio, instead, was an orator, limited to the epithets of the New Left and the few four-letter words popular in his circle. After all, as Annie said with jovial contempt, he was a middle-class boy, raised by middle-class parents, carefully shielded from the rougher elements of island life.

"Like you and me!" she said, underlining her point.

She was in high good humor. For Prudencio Nadal had mistakenly allowed himself to be lured into an exchange about the day-care center. It was a subject that merely bewildered him.

At first it had confused Slax employees as well. But many of them were mothers. They were fully alive to the advantages a day-care center would give their children. Now they were as enthusiastic as Annie had predicted they would be.

Prudencio, accustomed to the fads of his contemporaries, seized on the language issue. "A bilingual nursery!" he sneered. "So that your children can grow up enslaved by the speech of imperialism. In the university, you should know, we do not permit lectures in English."

Annie smiled broadly. "Naturally this boy doesn't care whether he learns English or not," she countered. "He has a rich father. He doesn't have to look for a job."

From there it was one pitfall after another for Prudencio. In vain he called Annie a union bitch, a cow milked by fat Americans, a whore sent out by establishment pimps. Annie had deadlier weapons. Prudencio's reputation for plain living and high thinking had gone before him. To the poor all over the world, it is inconceivable that anyone should voluntarily forgo pleasures of the flesh. Annie was swift to capitalize on this. When Prudencio, goaded by talk of sterilized bottles, disposable diapers and Montessori teachers, scoffed at the petty problems of domesticity, Annie did not make the mistake of treating him as just another man. She went straight for the vitals.

"What does he know of these problems? This *niño* who's never been on top of a woman, this choirboy whose voice hasn't changed, this beardless Che Guevara?" she asked.

By the fourth day, even Dudley Humble had been enticed from his aerie in Hato Rey so that the Sloan might have a Spanish-speaking expert on hand.

"That woman is a marvel," Dudley reported, bouncing with each word. "I haven't enjoyed anything so much in years. I don't know how she thinks up some of these things. Did I tell you she called him an avocado without a pit?"

But Dudley's enthusiasm was as nothing compared to that of Harry Zimmerman. All week long he sang her praises to anyone who would listen. And the praises became an anthem of joy when, on Friday, Prudencio Nadal finally announced that he was abandoning the field.

"The workers are not ready," he said severely. "They require further education."

His departure left Harry jubilant.

"We've licked it," Harry chortled. "Everybody have a good time over the weekend. You've earned it."

Socially speaking, Cesar Aguilera and his wife, Elena, led a double life. In their shuttered and tree-shaded home in the Miramar section of San Juan, they entertained their many family connections and the friends of their childhood. They both came from professional families rich in doctors, lawyers, architects and professors. The language of these gatherings was Spanish, the topics ranged from literature to politics. But though the community was close, it was not inward turning. Elena had been sent to Manhattanville College of the Sacred

Heart, in Westchester. She married shortly thereafter, and her first two babies were born in Cambridge, where Cesar was attending the Harvard Business School. As a result, the Aguileras had various ties with the American colony in Puerto Rico. When a management consulting firm in New York sent a man to study the sugar-cane industry, he was often a classmate of Cesar's. When a brokerage house opened a new office in the Condado, its manager was likely to be married to a classmate of Elena's. On the whole, the Aguileras preferred to entertain their American friends at their beach cottage out in Fajardo. There was swimming and fishing; barbecues and beach dinners were served; informality reigned.

The Lipperts always enjoyed themselves here. This Sunday, after the victory at Slax, they were enjoying themselves more than usual.

"Come and relax, Norma," Elena called from the patio. "It's much too hot to be energetic."

Norma, emerging from the house, obediently dropped into a chair. She had just changed from a bikini into slacks and a polo shirt. Close examination in the mirror had assured her that she was an attractive woman. But not, she ungrudgingly admitted, in the same class as Elena Aguilera. At thirty-seven, Elena effortlessly exuded ripe sexuality. And, from what Norma had seen of Puerto Rican women, Elena was going to be doing it for another twenty-five years. Happily, Norma had long ago come to the conclusion that anything so uncompromisingly feminine would have overwhelmed David.

Elena was thinking about her own husband.

"It's good to see them enjoying themselves, isn't it?" she asked lazily. "Cesar has been a mass of nerves ever since the trouble at Slax started. This is the first time in weeks I've seen him unwind."

The two women fell silent. They were idly watching a cluster of rocks a short distance from the shore. On these rocks their husbands, equipped with face masks and flippers, were superintending the skin-diving efforts of Cesar's two oldest sons.

"They've been out there a long time," Norma murmured. "I wonder if they're ever planning to come in."

Elena chuckled. "I've taken steps. María is bringing out the drinks in a minute. David and Cesar will be back as soon as they hear the gong."

"Meanwhile, tell me what you're going to wear to the fiesta tomorrow night."

Norma was looking forward to tomorrow's gala in historic Old San Juan. Its sponsors were predicting it would be the social event of the year. And many people seemed to agree with them. It was one of the few occasions at which the Aguileras' two worlds would meet. Elena was planning to do it full justice.

Five minutes later, when she was describing the black lace fan her grandmother had carried, the gong sounded. After a brief animated discussion, which even at that distance was clearly an exercise in paternal authority, all four swimmers headed ashore. The boys padded straight to the kitchen, while the men stripped themselves of their gear and fell on the tray.

David Lippert, stretched full length in the shade with a cold glass on his chest, sighed voluptuously.

"This is great, Elena, just great."

"I'm enjoying it, too," she replied, "but I'm still sorry that you couldn't get Annie Galiano out here. How I was looking forward to meeting that woman!"

"You may still meet her," Cesar said without much conviction. "But today she insisted on some meeting with the union local. And she swept Harry and Eric off to it, too."

"Well, I'm not sorry she isn't here," David announced. "I'm sick of the sound of her name. It's been Annie this and Annie that all week from Harry. I can do with a day off."

Norma looked down at him contentedly. David had been saying much the same thing for some time. But after a day at the office the words came out barbed and virulent. Now David sounded half amused.

"But all San Juan is talking about her," Elena protested. "Even my nephew at the university is quoting her. Is it true that she called Nadal a Samson that Delilah would have thrown back?"

David grinned. "That and a lot more. The trouble, of course, is that I can't really follow her Spanish when she gets going."

"You missed a lot," Cesar agreed. He lifted the pitcher of rum punch and carefully topped up glasses. "I admit that she's an unusual personality to have at Slax, but she is certainly giving us our money's worth. Apart from getting rid of Nadal, we've gotten more publicity on that day-care center than if we'd hired television."

"I'm not fighting you, Cesar," David said sleepily. "All I say is that I'll be glad when this is over. Then we can go back to running a factory instead of a three-ring circus."

Elena leaned forward to spear a savory little appetizer. "Men," she announced provocatively, "are all so conventional. Look at Cesar. He really wants each day to be a replica of the day before. He does not enjoy the unusual."

Thus attacked, her husband cocked an ironic eyebrow. "When the unusual takes the form of sabotage, murder and riot, you are right, Elena. I do not enjoy it."

"Annie Galiano isn't any of those," said Elena.

"Nevertheless, I shall be glad when she goes," Cesar said firmly. "I myself am looking forward passionately to the day when David and I can plan a run of three thousand pairs of white slacks and nothing more dramatic follows than the production of three thousand pairs of perfectly ordinary slacks."

"How dull!" cried Elena. "What I want is a husband looking forward passionately to tomorrow night—when he will be dancing with me under the stars."

But Norma was not thinking of the fiesta now. She was offering up silent thanksgiving. Only Cesar, she thought, would be tactful enough to paint David this picture of the promised land. He had referred only to Annie's going, without once mentioning that, when she went, she would take Harry Zimmerman with her.

"The way Annie's handling this, I'll be able to leave in two or three days," Harry Zimmerman was saying as Eric Marten drove him back to his hotel after their meeting at union headquarters.

"Handling it!" Marten snorted robustly. "You mean the way she's ramming it through."

"Annie," Harry said fondly, "doesn't take any guff, does she?"

They were leaving behind them the dazed representatives of Local 600, International Ladies' Garment Workers' Union. First Annie had read them a description of day-care centers that made the USSSR's program sound halfhearted. Then she had delivered a forceful lecture on keeping the peace at Slax. Finally she had ordered them to sign on the dotted line.

"She doesn't give a damn about winning friends, does she?" Eric remarked.

"You should see her in New York," Harry said, all admiration. "Why, I've seen her take on the CIO, the Black Panthers and the Mayor, all at the same time. And guess who came out on top?"

Eric Marten was an example of the conventionality of men that Elena Aguilera deplored. He thought that Annie might be too much of a tigress for such a small island. He was happy to work Sunday afternoon if that would speed her departure from their midst.

"It was a big help having you at the meeting, Harry," he said diplomatically. "It's too bad you didn't get to go out to the beach with the others."

"Oh, I don't know." Harry was clumsy about personal matters. "It's good for the youngsters to get away by themselves sometimes."

"Sure thing," Eric said stoutly. "David'll have a chance to relax. He'll be back in top form tomorrow, you'll see."

Eric Marten knew perfectly well that Harry Zimmerman was disappointed in the way his brother-in-law behaved under pressure. At the same time, Harry was trying not to add to that pressure. It would be interesting to see what he would do, Eric thought, if it ever got to a choice between watching Slax go under or popping up David's sagging morale.

"Anyway, I've got something else I want to talk about, Eric." Harry seized on a diversion. "Production has been great all this week, but what about shipments? We seem to have a lot of stuff stalled in the warehouse."

Eric turned his mind to his own special concerns. "The freight forwarders have been giving me double-talk," he admitted. "They won't say so, but it's easy enough to see what's happened. After all our troubles in the past month, they stopped holding space for us. Now we're at the peak shipping season, and they've got to scramble to find us enough cubic footage."

"Then make them scramble," Harry ordered. "Now's the time to use a little muscle. Tell them we can always find another freight forwarder if they don't cooperate. I'm going to be back in New York in a couple of days, and I want to be able to tell our customers that deliveries are coming through. I don't want any delays because our latest runs are backed up on the docks in Puerto Rico."

Eric Marten could be equally terse. "Right. I'll read them the riot act. Leave it to me, Harry."

"Good. I'm seeing the boys at the Sloan tomorrow, and I want to be able to tell them there isn't a cloud in the sky."

Eric Marten would have liked to study Harry's countenance at this statement, but no driver in San Juan takes his eyes off traffic for even a second.

"You don't count the police investigation into Domínguez' murder as a cloud, Harry?" he asked curiously.

"*I* count it," Harry answered, "but as long as we're making a profit I don't see why the Sloan should."

There was a short silence. Both men were considering the possibility that a police arrest might have a marked impact on profits at Slax. When Harry finally spoke again, it was with a diffidence alien to him.

"Look, Eric, just between the two of us, you wouldn't tell me who you think really shot Domínguez?" he suggested.

Eric Marten did not hesitate. "No, Harry," he said bluntly, "I would not."

"All right, all right," Harry growled. "Forget I asked. But look, there's one thing you could do for me."

"Yes?" Marten was very cautious.

"I know we've got a local lawyer down here. But I've had a lawyer in New York primed for the last two weeks. He can be down here on the first flight. What I'd like you to do, if things look bad, is give me the tip. In some ways, David and Norma are a pair of kids. They may not recognize trouble when it's coming. If anything threatens Slax, I'd like the best help we can get and I'd like it fast. Of course, I don't want to go off half-cocked. That kind of thing doesn't look very good."

Eric Marten was grimly amused. In spite of all the talk about threats to Slax, he knew what Harry was afraid of. Harry was afraid that David Lippert would be arrested. If worst came to worst, Harry might be able to voice that fear in awkward phrases about the miscarriage of justice and circumstantial evidence. The deepest fear of all Harry could never put into words.

"Yes, Harry. At the first sign of trouble, you'll hear from me."

After due expression of gratitude, Harry Zimmerman sat silently the rest of the way to the Americana. It was not a comfortable trip. Marten was glad that he had a legitimate excuse to refuse a drink.

"Sorry, Harry. But I have to pick up my wife. We're going to be late at her parents', as is." With a wave, he sped once again into the traffic.

Eric Marten's in-laws did not talk of literature at the dining-room table. They were all Puerto Rican businessmen. Unfortunately, they were hypnotized by events at Slax. They were eager for every bulletin, ready to speculate and prophesy endlessly. Marten could not leave Slax behind when he dined with his wife's family. Already he was busy editing the record of his day's work so that it could re-emerge as a suitable after-dinner story.

Stripped, of course, of certain details.

11. Pins and Needles

Old San Juan, the section of the city contained by the original masonry walls, was the background for the fiesta that Monday evening. Long since overwhelmed by the new city in extent and population, it retains its unparalleled site and its remarkable diversity. Lying at the very tip of a small peninsula, the land rises abruptly to a height from which Spanish fortifications command the most magnificent natural harbor in the Caribbean. Here there are breathtaking vistas along every inch of the historic walls. To the north, the long swells of the Atlantic end in breakers pounding endlessly against stone foundations many feet thick. To the south is the busy harbor and, beyond, the blue hills that form the spine of Puerto Rico.

Within the old city, open plazas alternate with rabbit warrens of sixteenth- and seventeenth-century Spanish architecture; precipitous cobblestone streets here and there yield to equally precipitous stone steps; majestic buildings which have housed the island's government since the Spanish occupation lie cheek by jowl with ferry slips for commuters. Both commerce and art have judged the location irresistible. Shopkeepers catering to the tourist trade were quickest. Now, in unbroken rows, they offer hand-screened fabrics, leatherwork, peasant blouses, basketry, jewelry and antiques. Painters and sculptors were next to move their studios here. The restorers came last, taking a single building and, with vast expenditure of time and money, turning it into a single perfect Hispanic gem. Between, around and above all these ventures, a resident population of twenty-five thousand people continues to thrive in unrestored bliss, serenely doing its laundry, buying its groceries and raising its children.

What had originally been planned as a modest social event, sponsored jointly by the restorers of Old San Juan and the promoters of native modern art, had mushroomed far beyond its initial dimensions. Every group with a vested interest in the old city had improvised its own addition to the entertainment. An outdoor art show had sparked a handicraft exhibit. A string quartet in the Plaza San José had brought guitarists, singers and rock groups to every street corner. Dancing in the Plaza de Armas was matched by a revival meeting in the Parque de las Palomas. The stores, bars and restaurants were all staying open. There was refreshment at every level, from stately dining rooms to taverns with fifty-cent rum drinks to stalls hawking mango and tamarind ice cream.

Everyone spent the first hour of the fiesta walking around. This exercise provided a bird's-eye view of the activities. It would also, John Thatcher profoundly trusted, provide him with an opportunity to shed his host and hostess, at least for a while. Norma and David Lippert were not successfully projecting their usual image of a harmonious couple. David's failure took the form of rather surly silence. Norma's, which was in many ways harder on the innocent bystander, took the form of brittle vivacity.

"You'll love the evening we have planned, I hope," she was saying, the words spilling out too quickly. "After the exhibition of native dancing, there will be some regular dancing. I promised the Aguileras we'd meet them there."

Thatcher and Pete Olmsted said they were looking forward to it.

"I thought we'd stay outside until after the fireworks. They're supposed to be marvelous. Then we'll be joining the sponsors' banquet at El Convento Hotel."

Manfully Pete Olmsted tried to keep up his end. "I suppose we'll be seeing Harry there. Is he coming with some other people?"

Norma hesitated one second too long. Then she flowed on. "Poor Harry found he couldn't make it at the last minute. It's such a shame. He's been looking forward to the fiesta all week."

"Sure," said David unpleasantly. "Harry's great on old Puerto Rican customs."

Fortunately a large family party on the narrow pavement forced them into single file at this point. When they coalesced again, Norma began to sing the praises of a local string quartet.

"I know it's quite a climb up to the plaza," she said, "but we really shouldn't miss them."

As they were currently plunging down a street that threatened to propel them into the harbor, Thatcher decided that Norma was beginning to panic. No rational response, however, was required. David Lippert was ready to denigrate any suggestion by his wife.

"Big deal!" he scoffed. "It's not as if they were the Casals Festival."

It was at this moment that Pete Olmsted proved worth his weight in gold.

"Well, now!" he marveled, ignoring the exchange. "What do you think of *that?*"

He was indicating a corner grocery that had been taken over temporarily by one of the many public groups active this evening. The sign read:

ILGWU
POINTING THE WAY!

But it was not the sign that was bringing people in off the street. It was the large photograph of a smiling woman and the invitation "Come and Meet Annie!"

"You said you wanted to meet her, John," Olmsted was continuing. "Here's your chance. Let's go in."

"Oh, for Christ's sake!" muttered Lippert.

Norma's voice rose a notch. "Yes, why don't you? But I do want to drop in at Cavanaugh's in the next block. David and I will wait there for you."

"We'll catch up with you," Thatcher agreed, promising himself that this reunion would not take place for at least an hour. He waited until the Lipperts were out of earshot before announcing this decision. "An hour should take us past the threat of this string quartet," he argued. "And, with luck, it will finish off this quarrel between the Lipperts, whatever it may be about."

"Trouble between David and Harry," Pete Olmsted diagnosed glumly.

"Is that just a guess, or did Zimmerman say so this morning? After all, he seems to be breaking appointments all over."

"No, Harry didn't say anything. He's not the kind who foists his family troubles onto business associates." Olmsted cast a look of deep disapproval down the street. "He just dropped by the bank for a few minutes. He said he was sorry to miss his appointment with us, but he had to get over to union headquarters. Even though he didn't say so, I could tell he was worked up about something. He was talking about clearing up a mess once and for all. Ten to one, he had a fight with Lippert about the way Slax ought to be run."

"And Mrs. Lippert has been sucked into the squabble," Thatcher concluded.

"Well, that's their problem," said Olmsted philosophically. "Would you like to take a look at this union storefront? It's not much compared to a Seventh Avenue rally, is it?"

Thatcher confessed, to his shame, that Seventh Avenue rallies did not come his way very often these days.

Olmsted shook his head sympathetically and shouldered the door open. Inside, thirty or forty people were crowded around the central figure. Annie was enthusiastically signing autographs and posing with people for snapshots. Several local union leaders looked on with pride. On the outskirts of the scene was a familiar face.

Eric Marten did not share whatever oppression had engulfed the Lipperts. "Hello!" he shouted cheerfully over the din. "I'm escaping from my wife. She's looking at a display of masks. And I can take just so much of that."

Stretching the truth somewhat, Thatcher remarked that they were fugitives from a string quartet. "And, of course, I've been hearing a good deal about Mrs. Galiano this past week. I thought I'd like to see her with my own eyes."

Marten immediately let loose a Scandinavian bellow. "Annie! Come meet Thatcher from the Sloan!"

Breaking out from her circle, Annie stumped across to join them. Olmsted was familiar to her from various loan negotiations. Thatcher she knew all about.

"I'm sorry I missed your bout with young Nadal," Thatcher said. "I've only heard the choice parts that everyone's quoting."

"That *chico!*" Annie chuckled. "You know, he's here tonight."

"Here?" Olmsted peered around the room.

Annie grinned broadly. "Not this close to me. He's got a pitch across from the revivalists."

"What the hell is he up to now?" Marten growled.

"Nothing much. He wants people to signal the uprising against American imperialism by charging the Convento during the banquet tonight. I hear he's in good form. You ought to take him in."

Marten stared down at her. "You call that nothing?"

"It's no threat to Slax," Annie replied single-mindedly. "And speaking of Slax, aren't you coming to my office to look over the agreement?"

"I'll try to drop by your place sometime tomorrow," Marten said impatiently. "Look, do you think there may be trouble at the Convento?"

Annie laughed. "Who's going to waste time tonight disrupting a banquet? There's too much else to do. Besides, everyone's having a good time. If you don't believe me, go and take a look at his audience. Prudencio's just part of the entertainment tonight."

Thatcher realized that Nadal's performance, whatever else might be said about it, would certainly be boycotted by the Lipperts.

"Why don't we take a look, Pete?" he suggested.

"You two go on by yourselves," Marten said. "I'm not as

broad-minded as you seem to be about that Nadal kid. I'd like to take a good swing at him."

When they left, Annie was chaffing Marten about his sensitivity to the New Left, and Marten was urging Annie to come discuss it over a drink.

Prudencio Nadal was, for once, having to compete for an audience. A small Hyde Park seemed to have sprung up on the green. A whole medley of impassioned orators was in full voice. Religion, politics, and aesthetic standards were being hotly debated in every corner. Thatcher and Olmsted had some difficulty locating their man. When they did, his discourse was, of course, unintelligible to them. But the tenor of his placards was not. More important, neither was the caliber of his listeners. Dedicated political shock troops are not recruited from people with small children, balloons, bottles of beer, ice cream cones and fancy hats.

"I suppose he might get twenty or thirty of the youngsters to try something," Pete Olmsted said skeptically.

"I think that's a handsome estimate," Thatcher rejoined. "And even if he did, he's been alerting the police to his target for some time. He'd need an army to accomplish anything."

His opinion seemed to be shared by Prudencio Nadal, who, having reached some kind of climax, now handed over his rostrum to a colleague and came down to be lost in the crowd.

"He's very young, isn't he?" Thatcher remarked.

"Well, that's no index of the damage he can cause, John. Just think of the ones back home."

"I wasn't thinking of the destructive trouble he can cause. I was thinking of the positive achievements he might be capable of. You know, Ramírez has high hopes that this kind of thing is going to swell his votes."

"Ramírez!" Pete Olmsted had always been a quick learner. "Dudley Humble thinks Ramírez is all wet."

"Dudley Humble thinks you shouldn't be handling the Slax loan," Thatcher observed dispassionately.

Olmsted was unabashed. "Dudley knows more about Puerto Rican politics than he does about a garment factory," he said cheerfully.

Thatcher should have known that was coming.

"So you've said before." He dismissed the subject. "Well, it's been over an hour. I suppose we should head for that plaza with the dancing. There's a limit to how long we can claim we were held up at the ILGWU."

Without pressing themselves unduly, the two bankers started to amble toward their objective. They stopped once, in mute wonder, to contemplate the spectacle of a band of teen-agers strumming guitars, with a large collection bowl bearing the legend "Please help us take our group around the world."

They stopped a second time for the drink they felt was necessary before re-exposure to the Lipperts.

"Honest to God, John," Olmsted complained, "I don't know what's come over these kids. What do you think would happen if you and I sat down on Wall Street with a sign asking people to send us around the world?"

"We'd probably be in Katmandu before we knew it," said Thatcher, firmly rising. "Come on, Pete, you can't stall forever."

But the Lipperts posed no immediate threat when the Plaza de Armas was reached. They were both dancing.

"But not with each other," Olmsted whispered portentously. Before he could enlarge on this theme, they were hailed.

"Mr. Thatcher. I would like to introduce you to my wife," said Cesar Aguilera. His wife, Elena, moved forward to his side.

It was several moments before Thatcher was conscious of anything else.

Elena Aguilera had combined the old with the new. She was wearing a contemporary white sheath and high-heeled white sandals. But her abundant dark hair had been piled in intricate coils atop her head, with high tortoise-shell combs supporting a black mantilla. Her plump hands, encased in black lace mitts, toyed with a fan embroidered with brilliants that reflected the sparkle of the single pendant hanging in the deep décolletage of her dress. Her eyes were enormous.

Once Thatcher recovered, he found himself in the middle of a conventional sentence about the success of the evening. Presumably he had negotiated the formal introduction. Olmsted, he was sorry to see, was still speechless.

Elena Aguilera clearly enjoyed the effect she produced. As the conversation proceeded, Thatcher decided that one element of her considerable charm was the unspoken invitation to share her own delight in her performance. Now she had lifted her fan and was peeping over it in open parody of the coquetry of a bygone age. But beneath the parody there was a playful confidence: *Anything my grandmother could do, I can do better.*

When she slipped a hand through his arm, Thatcher was delighted to fall in with her suggestion that they stroll up to a vantage point for viewing the fireworks.

"If we go now, we can get the best spot," she said.

Thatcher's only regret was that Cesar Aguilera found it necessary to wave at the dancers and indicate their destination. They could so easily have left the Lipperts to their own devices.

"You know, the fiesta is being sponsored by private groups, not the government," Elena explained. "But in honor of the evening, the Governor is permitting a firework display from the gardens of La Fortaleza."

"I imagine the effect, against the background of the harbor, will be spectacular." Thatcher was limiting himself to short contributions. Behind him he could hear Cesar Aguilera and Pete Olmsted making heavy weather of their climb. But Elena, he noticed, seemed to be gliding effortlessly upward, her hand light as a feather on his sleeve, her speech interspersed with light laughter. And all this in those sandals. Women, he reminded himself, are tougher than they look. Norma Lippert could probably do the whole hill without interrupting a marital diatribe.

"There!" Triumphantly, Elena led him to a spot by the city wall, from which they looked down on the water.

"And high time," said her husband, coming up to lean heavily on the rampart.

Elena ignored this display of masculine frailty. "I hope you had time for some of the sights in the old city, Mr. Thatcher."

Thatcher reviewed the evening thus far and said frankly, "I think the two most interesting things we saw we could have seen at Slax. We met Mrs. Galiano and heard young Nadal orating."

Neither of the Aguileras was surprised to hear of Nadal's presence, but Elena dismissed him.

"He can no longer be taken seriously," she said calmly. "Not after last week. I don't think there's anybody we know,

Cesar, who isn't repeating some of the names Annie Galiano called him."

Cesar, cautious as ever, observed that this did not nullify Nadal's nuisance potential. "Not until after the plebiscite, at least."

"Are you still going on about the plebiscite, Cesar?" a new voice called. David Lippert came laboring up out of the murky light. "I thought Annie was supposed to have solved all our problems." He nodded casually to the rest of the company.

"I was speaking about Nadal's over-all influence in Puerto Rico, David, not just about Slax," Cesar explained.

"You mean Annie didn't clean that up, too?" David asked.

Elena, without moving a finger, rippled smoothly into action. "There are limits, David," she said archly, "to what one woman can do."

David turned away from Cesar. "You can't really call Annie a woman, not that way," he protested.

Elena then made an error. Guided by the social instinct to turn conversation from a danger point, she said, "But where is Harry? I haven't seen him all evening." For once she was blind to a signal from her husband, even though it was clear to Thatcher. "He promised to come to our banquet."

She might as well have waved a red flag. Her good work was undone in one sentence.

"No, Harry isn't coming," David replied shortly. "He's left."

"Left?" Pete Olmsted was startled into repeating.

"He's left Puerto Rico. He went this afternoon," Lippert expanded.

"Are you sure?" Olmsted demanded. "He didn't say anything to me about leaving, and I saw him this morning."

David Lippert became defensive. "Harry made up his mind in a hurry. What's so surprising about that? He's been here long enough, hasn't he?"

"David." It was a lecture on prudence in one word from Cesar Aguilera.

Lippert jerked his head impatiently. "He's got an office in New York to run, hasn't he? He's got a plant in Georgia to bird-dog, doesn't he? He's—"

He would have gone on cataloguing Harry Zimmerman's duties, but suddenly there was a heavy thud far below, followed by a long-drawn hiss. Then a thousand pinpoints of color spangled the sky above them. As if by magic, the flag of Puerto Rico appeared emblazoned on the night, to hang lazily aloft for several seconds before expiring into the surrounding blackness.

"Oh-h-h!" gasped Elena Aguilera. "How beautiful!"

But Thatcher thought it sounded like a gasp of relief rather than of appreciation.

12. Separates

The steady explosion of fireworks, plus the arrival of Norma Lippert, effectively squelched David's snarled comments on Harry Zimmerman. After the display—which ended with a colossal set piece symbolizing art and industry in joyous union—it was time for the banquet.

El Convento, now a luxury hotel, had originally been built as a seventeenth-century nunnery. When they arrived, Thatcher examined its contours with interest. That windowless façade had been constructed to withstand far more ferocious attacks than anything the Radical Independents were likely to mount. Indeed, unless Prudencio Nadal was planning to parachute into the central courtyard, it was difficult to see what kind of onslaught he had in mind.

Thatcher found further cause for celebration in the seating plan for the banquet. He and Pete Olmsted had been separated. Thatcher himself had been removed from the orbit of the Lipperts. He was dining with the Martens. Mrs. Marten, a pretty young woman just celebrating her first anniversary, was ready to chatter happily about a variety of topics, ably supported by several other women in the vicinity. Thatcher had only one fault to find: Francisco Ramírez Rivera was sitting on the opposite side of the table and soon discovered from Mrs. Marten's prattle that an associate in one of his real-estate deals was a relative of hers.

"That would be Uncle Hector," she said, pleased with the connection.

After that, Ramírez was firmly welded into their group. Unfortunately, he overheard when Eric Marten dropped into his chair and apologized for being late, saying softly to Thatcher, "I was just having a look around outside. There's just a handful of kids there. I don't see how they can cause any trouble."

Ramírez seized the opening. "Ah, you have heard about Nadal's plans!" His teeth glinted briefly in a predatory smile. "It would be amusing, would it not, if he managed to disrupt this banquet. And the publicity would be prodigious."

"I don't see what would be amusing about it." Marten tried, not very successfully, to keep his tone light.

"That is because you do not see the irony so apparent to young Nadal. We have here a banquet heavily patronized by American industry"—a smooth gesture of Ramírez' hand encompassed the room—"theoretically in support of native Puerto Rican art, the very cultural form being stifled by the presence of American industry."

"I see the irony," Marten replied evenly. "It's the amusement I don't follow. What would Nadal accomplish by crashing El Convento tonight?"

"A display here by determined young Puerto Ricans would contribute far more to a resurgence of cultural energy," said Ramírez with a fluency suggesting previous use of the same phrases, "than any possible patronization by business interests."

Sometimes angels rush in, too.

"But, Dr. Ramírez," Mrs. Marten protested sweetly, "aren't you a businessman, too? You must be, if you work with Uncle Hector."

John Thatcher struggled to keep his face straight.

Dr. Ramírez cast a look of cold dislike across the table. "Indigenous enterprise is something quite different." The indulgence he extended to the youthful foibles of Prudencio Nadal clearly did not stretch to Margarita Marten. He shifted his ground to answer her husband. "You may be right, Mr. Marten. El Convento may not be a useful locale. After all, Nadal is not a beginner. Many people claim that he masterminded the demonstration at the university last winter. And that, you must admit, was very successfully planned."

This was too much for the matron sitting next to him.

"Successfully planned!" she shrilled. "With the riot squad called out, with three people dead and almost a hundred students hurt? It was a disgrace!"

Ramírez did not retreat. "Say rather a tragedy, señora. But my point is that Nadal is not an idiot. Last winter the riot squad was totally unprepared. The university police were helpless. The ROTC riot came as a complete surprise to the authorities."

"What does that have to do with tonight?" Margarita Marten was puzzled.

"It has everything to do with tonight," Ramírez replied. "Would Prudencio Nadal tip his hand so blatantly? Your husband said there were only a handful of students outside. Perhaps Nadal's speech in the Parque de las Palomas was a skillful feint."

Personally Thatcher believed it was folly to encourage Ramírez. But Eric Marten was still worried.

"What do you mean by a feint?" he demanded.

Ramírez shrugged his shoulders eloquently. "It is quite clear, is it not? He speaks violently about a charge at El Convento. The police are alerted. A few students are assigned to give substance to this threat. Then Nadal proceeds to a real coup elsewhere. Later he claims he was at El Convento all the time. Who is there to distinguish one student from another?"

Marten was frowning. "You mean he'll launch another one of his attacks against Slax?"

"You must not be so parochial, Mr. Marten," Ramírez chided. "There are many other American businesses in Puerto Rico."

"It's time they took some of the knocks," Marten said promptly.

Ramírez' response came smoothly. "But who else has had a foreman murdered in its executive offices?"

Bravely Mrs. Marten tried to hurdle the conversational paralysis following this remark. In so doing, she encountered the pitfall that gaped for all Slax wives this evening.

"You will have to entertain me alone, Mr. Thatcher." She pouted prettily. "These two wish to discuss serious problems. And otherwise, as you see, I am deserted." She indicated the empty place at her side and went on, "Mr. Zimmerman was placed here. But at the last minute he decided not to come."

Thatcher supported her efforts. "It's a shame," he agreed. "I understand that he has already left Puerto Rico."

"That's right." Marten steered a welcome course between Cesar Aguilera's overabundant caution and David Lippert's desire to tell the world his troubles. "Harry was out in Bayamón when we opened shop this morning. He said he was planning to catch a plane this afternoon."

"Curious," Thatcher commented. "He said nothing about leaving when he was at the Sloan today. Instead he was talking about clearing up some difficulties."

For a moment, Marten looked alarmed. Then he opted for frankness. "Oh, well, I suppose it's no secret he had a little dust-up with David this morning. He probably thinks David isn't handling things right. But that happens all the time. You don't want to take it too seriously. He probably has to rearrange some order shipments out of New York."

"That's Olmsted's version, not mine," Thatcher said readily. "I wasn't there."

"Harry can get pretty hot under the collar," Eric Marten conceded. "You get that all the time in these family companies. But it'll blow over, you'll see."

This time the entire group united in turning the conversation from the affairs of Slax. Dr. Ramírez and the ladies were conspicuously uninterested in family wrangles. Soon Eric Marten was enthusiastically discussing house hunting with one of the ladies; Dr. Ramírez, rather surprisingly, came forth in the guise of a baseball addict; and Margarita Marten told John Thatcher about the local business community's hopes for a free port.

"If Vieques does become a free port, it will be like St. Thomas as a shopping center. All the cruise ships will stop, and the money that goes to the Virgin Islands will be spent here," she said, one expert to another. It developed that several of her relatives were standing at the ready, waiting only for legislation to capitalize on this golden opportunity.

The end of the banquet, happily unmarred by lengthy speeches, released the celebrants to sample further amenities at El Convento. There was a floor show in the supper club, there was a gambling casino, there was an outdoor bar by the swimming pool in the courtyard. Olmsted and Thatcher joined forces to withstand certain blandishments by their hosts. It was not easy to explain tactfully to Norma Lippert that the one place a banker prefers not to be seen is at the roulette wheel.

"But don't let us stop you," Thatcher urged warmly. "I've been wanting to see the courtyard. I've heard a great deal about it. Perhaps you'll join us for a drink later in the evening."

Norma's resistance was drowned by the Aguileras, who swept her along with them.

"What's happened to Lippert?" Thatcher inquired.

"Heading for a bar, if you ask me," Olmsted said sourly. He had not had an enjoyable meal. "He was up and away with the last drop of coffee."

"Then let's choose a different bar. I've had enough of him for one evening."

Olmsted was too preoccupied to ask who had been the chief sufferer. "You know, Lippert was hitting that business about Harry's going back to New York again. Do you think he's just covering up because Harry was too sore to come to this shindig?"

"I wouldn't put it past him," Thatcher grunted. "But Marten says the same thing. And he's not making any bones about the fact that there's trouble brewing between Zimmerman and Lippert."

"I'd like to know what the hell's going on out there. They could pick a better time for their bickering."

"I expect the time picked them." Thatcher's spirits were rising with the absence of all Slax personnel. "After all, they had a major crisis in Bayamón. Zimmerman hears about it on the phone, plucks Annie Galiano out of thin air in New York, flies down and wraps the whole thing up. I assume that is Lippert's basic grievance, whether he knows it or not."

"That's no reason for Harry to flit without letting me know," Olmsted said hotly. "Ah, there's the woman who'll have the inside dirt."

He pointed to a table by the pool. Annie Galiano must have been the first person to reach the bar. Now she was leaning back, resting from her labors. She waved an expansive invitation.

"I didn't know you were coming to the banquet, Annie," Olmsted teased her. "It doesn't seem like your style."

"The union supports all sorts of activities," she said gravely. "You'd be surprised at some of the cultural events I've helped sponsor." She snorted richly. "Ballet, yet!"

Thatcher immediately suggested another drink to dispel the memory of *Swan Lake*. There was no nonsense about long rum drinks with spears of pineapple for Mrs. Galiano. She was drinking straight Scotch.

When he returned with the drinks, he found that Olmsted had wasted no time.

"Did Harry say anything to you about leaving today, Annie? That's the story Slax is handing out."

Annie's bushy eyebrows rose. "Leaving today? I don't believe it. He was on the phone to me last night, and he didn't mention it. Besides, we still have a few details to iron out."

"But what did he say today? He seems to have made some last-minute decision."

"I haven't heard from Harry today," said Annie.

Olmsted was persistent. "He said he was going up to union headquarters this morning."

"Maybe. I wasn't there this morning." Annie's interest was roused. "Was it about anything special?"

But here Pete Olmsted had to confess he did not know. Obviously he suspected fresh trouble at Slax which Harry was concealing from the Sloan.

"He might try to hide something from you. But not from me." Annie had no illusions about her role in Harry's life. "Hell, I'm the first one he'd come running to. And the one thing he wouldn't do is jet out of town. Take it from me, if there's trouble, it's family trouble." Internally Annie reviewed the situation. "And who wouldn't have trouble with that family?"

This rhetorical question led Annie and Olmsted, both specialists in their way, to a discussion of notable families in the garment trade.

"I ask you!" Annie was demanding within minutes. "Is a brassiere factory the place to bring your sex problems?"

Pete immediately countered with the tale of a married couple, joint owners of a small establishment specializing in ski wear, who had been divorced. Immediately following the court decree, came the ski boom with a fantastic rise in the firm's profits. "They were seeing more of each other after they both remarried than they'd ever seen before. Sixteen, eighteen hours they'd spend each day in the office together. And whenever the new husband or wife called up to complain, they'd get a blast, usually from the ex." —

"And did all these arrangements last?" Thatcher asked politely.

"Well, there was so much money flying around, nobody was willing to break anything up. But, of course, the original pair had a lot to sympathize with each other about. The new marriages may still hold, but the working arrangement isn't what anybody had in mind."

Reminiscences continued to flow. In Thatcher's opinion they made a pleasant contrast to the overriding concern with Slax and its problems which had been his lot so far this evening. Annie and Pete might have gone on indefinitely if they had not been interrupted by Cesar Aguilera.

"Have you seen David?" he asked quietly. "Norma is asking for him."

"He hasn't been in here." Pete Olmsted could not keep a note of self-congratulation from his voice. "He's probably in one of the other bars."

Ignoring this suggestion, Aguilera, after a punctilious request for permission from Annie, sank into a chair.

"No doubt you are right. Norma asked me to see if he was here in the patio." Aguilera was taking a very fine reading of his instructions. Probably he too had had enough of David Lippert.

Olmsted reluctantly abandoned anecdotes of Seventh Avenue and returned to business. "David and Eric are both saying that Harry's taken a plane out."

Aguilera nodded without any evidence of embarrassment, but he chose his words carefully. "Norma told me about it. I knew Harry was upset, but I didn't know he was leaving."

Olmsted was beginning to be exasperated at this further evidence that Harry Zimmerman had seen fit to take everybody into his confidence except his banker. "Oh, he talked to you too, did he?"

"Only on the phone." Aguilera sounded very tired. "He was irritated about something. Norma said that he and David had some kind of misunderstanding. She seemed surprised."

Aguilera, in his turn, could see no cause for surprise at a flare-up between David and Harry.

Thatcher, while admitting that he did not have Aguilera's experience with the principals, felt bound to object. "This is not the best time for the management of Slax to be diverted by personal quarrels."

"I don't believe you can call them personal." Aguilera smiled wearily. "Both Harry and David, in their own way, are thinking about Slax."

"And Norma?"

"In some ways she is the most single-minded of all. There was a problem at Slax. It has been successfully solved. She expects everyone to be happy."

Thatcher thought he detected an undertone he could not understand. Aguilera sounded almost too detached.

"You disapprove?"

Aguilera stared somberly into the depths of his glass before replying. Then he said: "In my opinion they are all overlooking a very important point. They seem to think that Slax's problems have been solved." His words were wry. "As for me, I cannot forget that we still have a murderer at large in Bayamón."

While Thatcher was coming to the conclusion that Cesar Aguilera was the only person at Slax capable of keeping an eye on essentials, David Lippert at last surfaced from his after-dinner retreat.

He came bursting onto the patio, his eyes glittering and his hands shaking.

"Been pouring it down like water," Olmsted whispered.

"Cesar!" David cried. "They just told me!"

Aguilera was startled. "I know Norma's been looking for you, but—"

"Never mind that!" David was shouting. "My God, why are you sitting there? We've got to get down there."

Cesar had half risen and grasped Lippert's arm. "Go where? David, get hold of yourself!"

David's eyes seemed to focus on Aguilera for the first time.

"They were paging me in the lobby when I came in." His shoulders slumped forward in defeat. "It was the police. Our warehouse down at the docks is on fire!"

13. Made to Order

For everyone connected with Slax, the fiesta was over.

Within minutes, Thatcher found himself leading Olmsted through the Convento lobby, outside to the car someone had summoned. David and Norma Lippert were just ahead, with Eric Marten and Cesar Aguilera a step behind.

"Okay, Cesar, let's go," said Marten, once they had all crowded into the car.

Aguilera, who had taken the wheel, threaded his way carefully through the thronged streets of the old city. But once on the expressway, he accelerated with a roar. Soon they were speeding past a city that seemed lifeless and somber after the dazzle of the fiesta. Finally, with a savage swerve, he turned the car eastward, heading toward the scruffy industrial no-man's-land that surrounded the docks of Cataño.

"For God's sake," Marten demanded from the back seat, "can't you go any faster?"

Thatcher glanced across Norma Lippert to study the driver by the dim light of the dashboard. Aguilera was concentrating with an intensity that created its own isolation. Thatcher doubted if he had heard Marten; he might have been alone in the car.

Marten was too keyed up for silence. "What did the police tell you, David? How bad is it?"

Lippert was slumped in the corner, next to Olmsted. "They just told me there was a fire," he repeated dully. "That's all. Just a fire. How long is it going to take us to get there, Cesar?"

There was no answer from Aguilera.

Norma, who was sitting forward tensely, did not turn her head. "It never takes more than twenty minutes, David," she said impatiently.

It was less than that when Thatcher felt Norma stir for the first time. He followed her gaze.

"Yes, there it is, I'm afraid," he said.

To their right, an angry red glow was silhouetting dark buildings.

"Oh, no," she said in a low, horrified voice. "It can't be."

No one replied. Aguilera turned off the highway and began weaving through a maze of cluttered streets, shadowed by gaunt wooden structures. Above them the pulsating glow in the sky was widening. After a third turn, Aguilera braked the car suddenly.

"I do not know how much closer we can get," he said.

Ahead of them was an inferno. Coils of smoke writhed upward in spirals shading from red to gray to black before disappearing into the inky tropical sky. Barely visible above the intervening buildings was a rim of white-hot light, from which geysers of flame spurted, probed the darkness, then flickered down out of sight.

Thatcher did not see any fire-fighting equipment or even the blazing warehouse itself, until Aguilera nosed the car around the final corner.

"We had better park here," he said. "They will not let us go any farther."

Eric Marten flung open his door and thrust himself out. Already he was loping ahead, toward the fire. More slowly, Pete Olmsted and David Lippert followed. In the front seat nobody moved for a moment.

The Slax warehouse was a large, ramshackle structure sharing the long block along the waterfront with other nondescript buildings. When Thatcher got out of the car, he could see that a cordon had been drawn around the area. Not thirty yards ahead he could see a barricade. Beyond, there was chaos— flashing red lights from the fire trucks, hip-booted men manhandling heavy hoses against the blinding glare, greasy pools of water reflecting the flames. The stench was overpowering.

By the time the others reached him, Eric Marten was shouting at one of the helmeted firemen.

"But, señor—"

Martin cut him short. "They're concentrating on the other buildings," he said viciously over his shoulder. "You can see what they're doing. They're letting our warehouse burn to the ground!"

"No," the fireman protested. "You do not understand. We hose the other buildings to keep the fire from spreading. But your buildings we must approach from the sea. There, look for yourselves!"

As he spoke, he dramatically swept his arm toward the pier. A fire ship was positioning itself. Spotlights clicked on, and a giant crane loomed over the whole scene. Jets of water began arching from the ship's tower directly onto the warehouse. They looked pitifully inadequate.

"We do what we can," the fireman said fatalistically. "But what can you expect?"

Aguilera asked a question that Thatcher knew was unnecessary. "What does that mean?"

The fireman became explicit. "This is no ordinary fire! You should have smelled the kerosene."

"Kerosene?" David Lippert echoed stupidly.

Marten turned on his heel and strode a few paces away, where he stood surveying the devastation with bleak eyes.

For once, Aguilera was blunt. "Arson, David! Somebody set this fire!" Then he too subsided, hands in pocket, watching the holocaust.

David Lippert must be the only one watching this spectacle, Thatcher thought, who had not immediately suspected sabotage.

A swirl of fire rose to meet the water pouring in from the fire ship.

"But they're not trying to save anything inside!" Norma cried with a half-sob. "Are they just going to let it burn?"

Without replying, the fireman went off to talk to the men who were bringing up another hose.

"What about all our material and supplies?" Norma asked distraughtly.

"Norma," Thatcher said to her firmly, "I don't think they can risk sending anybody into the building."

He paused to look at her. Norma's hair was disheveled. Her ivory satin pumps were sodden with the filthy scum being washed along the street. She seemed almost wild.

"I doubt if there's anything to be gained by watching this," Thatcher added. "Why don't you let us take you home?"

"No!" He barely caught her whisper before David Lippert spoke.

"God!" he said loudly. "Harry! I just remembered Harry! How am I ever going to tell him about this!"

Suddenly Norma's temper snapped.

"I'll call him if it bothers you so much," she said scathingly. "Or Eric or Cesar will. What difference does it make! Don't you understand, David? This is more of the same. We were all wrong about the sabotage. It wasn't Domínguez after all. We thought his murder solved everything and—"

She would have said more, but Cesar Aguilera seized her arm.

"Norma," he said urgently, "this is not the time."

He showed her the fire truck nearby—and the police car next to it. Standing there, seemingly intent upon the fire, was Captain Vallejo.

But Thatcher could see that the policeman was taking in every word.

"Did you notice Vallejo?" Eric Marten had rejoined them. "Now that it's too late the police are keeping an eye out!"

Aguilera was struck by a thought. "Eric!" he exclaimed. "The shipments! The shipments Harry was talking about—" He broke off with a quick glance toward Thatcher and Olmsted.

Olmsted was not reassuring. "It's no secret," he said. "Harry told us all about the trouble you've been having with freight forwarders."

"Maybe Harry told too many people," David Lippert said bitterly. "Don't look at me like that, Norma. It's true. They couldn't have picked a better time to hit us, could they?"

"David's right, Norma," said Marten. "There must be forty to fifty thousand dollars' worth of finished goods in there. They should have been shipped last week. Now"—he turned to look at the blaze—"they're going up in smoke, with the rest of the warehouse."

As if to punctuate his comment, there was an ominous rumble from the center of the fire. The roof was beginning to cave in.

The fireman came hurrying back. "We are moving the cordon back," he shouted. "You will have to leave."

Again Eric Marten had to speak. "Is anybody investigating this?" he demanded.

The fireman swore under his breath. "Can't you see we are busy? Is this the time for talk? Move back, move back."

They obeyed his orders, only to discover that, behind them, the street that had been almost deserted now held a substantial crowd. There were, at a guess, a hundred people, young and old alike, watching the cataclysm with rapt fascination.

"What's she doing here?" Norma's voice was a whiplash.

Thatcher peered into the gloom. Pushing her way toward them was the one person who had not joined them in the frantic drive to Cataño.

"She was going to fix everything just fine at Slax," said Norma savagely. "She knew how to handle Prudencio Nadal! Sure she did. She handled him, all right! Look what he's done to Slax now!"

Annie Galiano must have overheard Norma as she approached. But all she said was, "Harry sure picked a lousy time to leave, didn't he?"

It was a flat statement, addressed to the world at large. Thatcher recognized it as rough-and-ready sympathy. Nevertheless, he could have predicted that Norma would not.

"You keep your filthy tongue off Harry!" she spat.

"I was just—"

"Everything was supposed to be fine," Norma swept on. "You were going to take care of Prudencio Nadal, weren't you? Well, you did a great job! I hope you're satisfied now."

"Norma!"

"Norma!"

But Annie dismissed Norma as if she were a fractious child. She turned to look at the fire. "Looks like they're getting it under control," she said.

The unending streams of water, the plodding firemen, were gaining some sort of dominance. Flames still licked along the sills, but the inner cauldron had spent itself. There was little left to burn. The roof had collapsed, together with one of the walls. The interior had been gutted.

"I was just talking to one of the cops," Annie said. Her tone of level common sense came as a surprise. Everyone else, Thatcher realized, had been talking in voices transformed by emotion. Only Annie remained Annie.

"Someone got the watchman out of the way by cracking him over the head."

"Do we have a watchman down here?" Lippert muttered. "I didn't know that."

Eric Marten explained that a watchman for the whole

block made the rounds, including Slax as well as other warehouses. "My God," he said in dismay, "I forgot all about him. He wasn't in there, was he?"

Annie reassured him. "No, somebody clubbed him when he turned off the pier. He's not badly hurt."

A new voice corroborated her. "Yes, the watchman was lucky. They only wanted to get him out of the way for a few hours."

Captain Vallejo had strolled up and now surveyed them with his customary bland authority.

"When I heard of trouble at the Slax warehouse," he explained, "I decided to come down."

"Great!" Marten's explosion was a release of tension. "How much more of this do you expect us to take? When are you going to make some arrests?"

Vallejo did not reply directly. "To prove that anybody set a fire is not so easy, Mr. Marten," he said. "Unfortunately the courts demand evidence. So first the arson squad must work, when they can. No doubt they will find proof that this fire was set. But after that, things become more difficult."

David Lippert thrust his face at Vallejo. "What the hell do you want—a diagram? Jesus Christ, we need protection! Everybody knows it was Prudencio Nadal! Has he paid you off or something? Are you going to drag your feet—"

This incoherent spate froze everybody. It was hard to see Vallejo's expression in the flicker of light and shadow. He could have been smiling.

David slapped away Eric's minatory hand. "No, Eric, let me tell this guy. Who are you trying to kid, Vallejo? You don't need a complete court case before you make an arrest. Why don't you put Nadal where he can't do any more damage? Then get your proof!"

Vallejo was stiff. "You have a strange conception of our police procedure, Mr. Lippert. And there are other difficulties as well. You yourself know that Prudencio Nadal was busy in Old San Juan this evening."

It was Annie who made the obvious retort. "We were all in Old San Juan," she said. "And now we're all here in Cataño."

Vallejo was willing to make concessions to her. "We know that anybody could have taken the ferry from the old city to

Cataño," he agreed. "Crossing the harbor only takes fifteen minutes."

"What ferry is he talking about?" Norma demanded imperiously.

Annie was contemptuous. "The ferry I took when I came over. And the ferry most of these people took, too." She pointed to the crowd still growing behind the cordon. "That's how people who can't afford cars get to Cataño."

Cesar Aguilera hastily constituted himself Slax's spokesman. "So we are back where we started, Captain Vallejo?" he inquired. "We all know who set this fire, but you say there is no proof."

Vallejo enjoyed scoring points. "I said we needed proof. I did not say there was none. We have already made a beginning. *This* was pinned to the watchman's shirt."

He brandished a sheet of paper with crude lettering:

> FREEDOM FOR PUERTO RICO
> DOWN WITH IMPERIALISM
> VIVA NADAL!

14. A Dart Here, a Dart There

It was nearly dawn before Norma Lippert finally consented to leave Cataño. Now, some hours later, she was lying in her bedroom in Isla Verde, in a sleep so profound that it might have been drugged.

But downstairs, David was on the phone, as he had been for over an hour.

"Person to person, operator," he repeated. "That's Harry Zimmerman. Z—I—M . . ."

He mopped his brow. Still no word from Harry, and this was the fourth call. It was important . . . important . . .

Just then the front doorbell rang.

Hurrying to answer it, he almost tripped in his eagerness.

"Harry—" he exclaimed, flinging open the door.

But it was not Harry. It was two uniformed policemen.

Lippert was not the only one working early.

"I'm on my way back to the warehouse, John," Pete Olmsted reported by phone. There was the sound of a suppressed yawn. "I'll be talking with Marten about Slax's insurance."

"Fine," said Thatcher. At the same time he was shoveling papers into his briefcase. He had decided to return to New York on schedule, come hell or high water. Or, more accurately, sabotage and fire. "Let me know if anything interesting turns up, Pete."

Olmsted hesitated, then wished Thatcher a good trip before hanging up. He had been tempted, Thatcher guessed, to deliver a last-minute pitch on behalf of Commercial Credit. It would not have done him much good.

When the phone rang again, five minutes later, Dudley Humble proved to be less self-denying.

"So you're going back today after all," he announced, sounding too much like a man who has already played his eighteen holes. "Oh, by the way, John, have you heard about the fire at Slax—"

"*All* about it," said Thatcher emphatically.

Humble took the hint. "Well, everybody here in Hato Rey will be interested to know the Sloan's final decision about Puerto Rico."

Thatcher said that it would be forthcoming soon, then thanked Humble for courtesies rendered.

"And if there's any further information you want—about the situation down here?" Humble insinuated.

Thatcher was tempted to retort that he had too much information about Puerto Rico already. Instead he said, "No, I think I have everything I'll need, Dudley. I would be interested in anything new in the political situation."

"I doubt if we're in for any surprises," said Humble grandly.

"Don't tempt fate," said Thatcher, replacing the receiver firmly.

The taxi drive to the airport was, as usual, marked by enough near-misses to put from his mind any thoughts but survival. He arrived early.

There was an acquaintance sitting next to him at the coffee shop.

"I didn't know you were returning to New York so soon," he remarked.

Annie Galiano was frank. "Didn't know it myself," she admitted. "But I got thinking this might be a good time to talk with the boys at headquarters."

"About Slax?" Thatcher inquired. After all, sharing the small hours watching a fire made avoiding the subject absurd.

She replied obliquely, "That damned fire is the last thing they need. Especially right now."

Thatcher checked his watch. He had time to accept a refill from the cheerful counterman. "It didn't do Zimmerman much good to avoid that strike," he observed.

"Not Zimmerman," she corrected him firmly. "Annie."

Thatcher begged her pardon.

"Granted," she said graciously. "But to tell the truth, I think Harry could have handled it himself. The way I see it, anybody could handle that Nadal kid. He doesn't know which way is up."

This was a far cry from the Ramírez evaluation. Thatcher wondered if sex explained the difference.

"In fact," she went on reflectively, "they're all losing their heads out at Slax. Still, that's their problem. I've got a day-care center—that's the important thing."

Amused, Thatcher reached for the check and said, "You wouldn't use Nadal and the radicals for your own purposes, would you?"

"I'd use anything," she assured him. "Here, give me that."

Gravely Thatcher told her that it was the Sloan's privilege and pleasure to contribute to the American labor movement.

He rose and waited for her to gather her belongings, which included an amazing number of bags of one sort and another. Midway in the endless trek to the boarding gate, he missed one of her remarks.

"I said I wonder what they're doing here," she repeated.

Thatcher looked up.

A detachment of helmeted police was fanning through the airport.

At the same time that Thatcher and Annie were taking off, Pete Olmsted was clambering out of a taxi at the docks in

Cataño. By daylight, the scene was a tragic monument to loss. Under the brilliant blue sky the Slax warehouse was a charred ruin.

Eric Marten, moodily kicking a board out of his path, barely acknowledged Olmsted's greeting.

"A total loss," he said. For once, his burly figure looked defeated. He was drained of energy.

"Did you get any sleep last night, Eric?" Olmsted asked sympathetically.

"Hell, no!" said Marten. "After we packed David and Norma—" He broke off as if he regretted mentioning the Lipperts. "Cesar and I went back to Bayamón. We wanted to check our coverage."

"What's the bad news?" Olmsted asked. Insurance coverage is always adequate until after the fire.

"It could be worse. Harry kept us pretty well covered. It looks as if the insurance will meet most of the dollars-and-cents loss. But that's not the important thing right now."

"It helps," Olmsted commented, but he knew Eric Marten was right. Insurance could pay for the money Slax lost; it could not buy back infuriated customers.

"How's Harry taking it?" he asked. "He was pretty wild yesterday, even before all this happened."

Marten was terse. "David says he can't contact him."

The two men were trudging around the perimeter of the blackened shell. There was no possibility of salvage here. Slax was going to need a new warehouse. Olmsted said as much.

"That's one of the reasons we want to raise Harry," Marten said. "Cesar's back at the office trying now. We don't want to go ahead and rent a new one without his okay. And we've got stuff coming into port next week—hell, it's a mess. A goddam mess."

Olmsted knew that between the Lipperts, Aguilera and Marten, the Slax plant in Puerto Rico could operate almost independently. Still, everybody was hesitating, waiting on Harry. Olmsted did not blame them.

"What do you think Harry's going to say?" he asked.

"Who knows?" Marten was genuinely uncertain.

"You can't blame him for turning sour on Puerto Rico," Olmsted ruminated.

He had struck a spark. "God, Pete, do you think this is normal for Puerto Rico? Sabotage and arson? I've lived here for years. Cesar is a Puerto Rican! This doesn't make any sense to us either. You can't blame Puerto Rico for a bunch of crazy kids. I wish to God somebody would do something about them—something final!"

He subsided as swiftly as he had flared up.

"This doesn't help Slax much, does it?" he said with a bitter laugh. "I hope Harry is going to fight. But honest to God, if he decides to cut and run—well, I hate to say it, but I'd understand."

"How do David and Norma feel?" Olmsted asked.

There was a long silence. Then, in a voice that gave nothing away, Eric Marten said, "I don't know what they'll say, either."

Olmsted would have pressed harder, but they were interrupted.

"I thought you might be here," said Captain Vallejo. Behind him were two squad cars.

Francisco Ramírez Rivera was prepared to look beyond the fire in Cataño to broader possibilities. Although he had not abandoned the fiesta to watch the blaze, he knew all about it from many sources. Ernesto was not the only one of his supporters who had left El Convento to take the ferry and watch the Slax warehouse burn.

"Say what you will about Nadal, he is dramatizing the cry for independence," he said complacently.

Ernesto was too sleepy to follow this reasoning. "But, Uncle," he protested, "I thought we were committed to a peaceful transition to independence. Won't many voters be nervous about what Nadal is doing?"

When things were going his way, Ramírez enjoyed guiding his followers. "No one has tears for the property of Americans," he said expansively. "Bloodshed, personal violence— that is what frightens people. Who cares how much money Slax loses, except the people at Slax?"

Ernesto digested this, then raised a point that effectively dissipated Ramírez' good humor. "Well, then," he said, painfully working out his thoughts, "if the *independistas* like what Nadal is doing, won't they support him instead of you?"

Ramírez glared at him. "There is always that danger. A statesman learns to provide for the future. You will see,

Ernesto, that the voters will not approve of Prudencio Nadal for long."

Ernesto would have asked for more detail, but the telephone buzzed imperatively. Automatically, he answered it. "Yes, sir. . . . Yes, of course. . . . I will inform him immediately . . . as speedily as possible."

When he cradled the receiver, he was wide-eyed.

"Uncle," he stammered excitedly, "the Governor has summoned an emergency session of the Legislature."

For once, Ramírez stared back at him in wild surmise.

At the Capitol, later that morning, the Governor was eloquent, somber and decisive.

"Today, Puerto Rico faces a crisis which threatens the very foundations of our democratic way of life. An attempt to undermine the right of the people to determine their own destiny . . ."

Radio, newspapers and television summed up his long message tersely:

The Radical Independents had kidnapped Harry Zimmerman.

15. Out of Whole Cloth

The Governor's message signaled the onset of a state of emergency that swiftly pervaded all Puerto Rico. Everywhere, from the airport in San Juan to the waterfront at Mayagüez, police and security forces were already swinging into action—rounding up terrorists, confiscating firearms, hunting door to door. Even the isolation of the resort hotels was breached; police combed pool clubs, casinos, marinas. The crisis preempted newspapers and television. In place of disk jockeys, social notes and commercials, there were photographs and descriptions of the victim.

Over and over, announcers repeated the meager facts. "The

ransom note, delivered to the editor of *El Mundo* this morning, read as follows: *'We have Zimmerman. He will be released only when U.S. gangsters promise to free Puerto Rico! Radicals for Independence!'* "

Radios in homes, in bars, in automobiles, in stores blared another message:

". . . Anyone who can assist is urged to contact the police. Also desired is information about the whereabouts of Prudencio Nadal, aged twenty-two, formerly a student at the University of Puerto Rico. Also sought is a female companion, Antonia Viera, aged eighteen. Both are wanted for questioning. . . ."

Emergency measures were already disrupting the fabric of life. The university was closed; the National Guard was activated; military and naval installations all over Puerto Rico were put on the alert. Buses, cars, boats, trucks—everything that moved was halted, searched.

Some emergency measures were as visible as the Coast Guard helicopters scanning every inch of coastline. Others were not. Behind closed doors at La Fortaleza, a hastily appointed committee was in session. Their subject was the proposed suspension of the constitution.

"Unless, of course, Zimmerman is released safely in the immediate future," said the Governor's aide. "But we must be prepared for a longer ordeal. The experience of Canada, as well as Uruguay . . ."

Francisco Ramírez Rivera knew the line he had to take.

"The Independence Party protests," he said perfunctorily. "There is no need for precipitate action. It is a grave matter to suspend the constitution, especially in view of the plebiscite. We will have to take under advisement any measure—"

"Exactly!" a voice seconded him.

"To suspend the constitution," Ramírez went on, "is an extreme measure—"

"For extreme times!" the Governor's aide cut him off. "Puerto Rico demands unanimity, gentlemen."

This was not a threat; it was realism. The ground swell of popular support for vigorous action was growing by the hour.

He swept on. "The people of Puerto Rico will not condone this outrage—no matter what their political persuasion. They support every effort the Governor has proposed. The whole machinery of government is working . . ."

But hours of work by the whole machinery of government produced nothing. That day ended almost as it had begun—with one notable change. By evening, Harry Zimmerman had become part of Puerto Rico. He had been seared into the consciousness of people who had never met him or heard of him before. Total strangers worried about him, talked endlessly of his plight, prayed for his well-being and safe deliverance. In a way, kidnapping had made Zimmerman larger than life; he had become part of modern history.

But the people for whom Harry was real suffered a more wrenching anxiety.

"Why don't they call up, or send another note or something? Why did they kidnap Harry, if they don't want us to do something? My God, we could give them money if they want it. . . ." Norma had been talking feverishly all day.

"Norma, you have to control yourself. You are making things harder for yourself—" Elena Aguilera hesitated only a shade before going on—"and for everybody else."

Mechanically, Norma twisted and untwisted her handkerchief. "I'm all right," she said. "But Harry—oh, God, I know they're searching all over Puerto Rico. But maybe they've taken him out of the country. St. Thomas. Cuba. Have the police thought of that? Anyway, what if they frighten the kidnappers? Maybe we should wait . . ."

By now, Norma was unable to focus on anything but Harry. As for how her behavior was affecting others—including David—she was virtually unconscious. Since the news had first broken, she had been in the grip of uncontrollable tension. In those hours, the contours of her face had grown sharper; her eyes had become too bright. Her fingers, convulsively twitching, had turned into talons. If Harry's ordeal were prolonged, Elena knew, Norma would collapse.

"Why don't you try to get some sleep?" Elena murmured, although it was only nine o'clock.

"How can I sleep without knowing what's happening to Harry?" Norma asked, running a hand through her hair. "How do you think they're treating him?"

Just then the telephone shrilled. Norma wheeled toward the table, but David Lippert came hurrying into the room. He snatched up the receiver.

"Let me take it, Norma," he said. "Hello? . . ."

"Who is it? Is it Harry?"

". . . Yes. . . . Yes. . . . That's something. . . . Yes, yes. . . . No, there's nothing else. . . . Yeah, they say they'll call. . . . Okay. . . . Thanks."

"Who is it?" Norma screamed at him. "Is it about Harry?"

Lippert mopped his brow. "No, it wasn't about Harry, Norma. I would have told you," he said wearily. "It was Eric."

She stared at him.

"He says he got a call from the freight forwarders. They did manage to get one shipment moved yesterday. Before the fire, that is."

With an affronted silence, she tore open a pack of cigarettes.

David was almost dogged. "At least it's some good news."

"Good news!" Norma said, fumbling with the matches. "What do you mean, good news? With Harry in the hands of some crazy killers? My God, David!"

David frowned and flicked a beseeching look toward Elena Aguilera. "Norma . . ." he began.

"Oh, leave me alone!" she said pettishly. "Go tell Cesar all about this great good news!"

Moodily she stalked over to the window and started to pull back a curtain. Elena called out a warning. Outside the house, reporters and cameras were ringed like vultures, waiting to swoop. Any sign of life sparked them into action. All this intensified the garrison atmosphere inside the Lippert house.

With an angular motion, Norma threw herself into a chair, deliberately looking past David. Only the ticking of the wall clock broke the silence.

"We'll be through in a few minutes," David muttered, heading back to the study.

An unpleasant twist of the lips was Norma's only response.

Amidst the other emotions of an emotion-filled day, Elena Aguilera felt sympathy for David Lippert. For once, he was meeting crisis like a man. Since the first shock, he had behaved well, keeping a firm grip on himself. It was David who decided that the children should go to the Aguilera home. It was David who dealt with the police, the Governor's office, the FBI. It was David who composed and read a brief state-

ment to the press. It was David who was doing what had to
be done.

"How can he?" Norma burst out. "How can he? He doesn't
care what's happening to Harry!"

"Of course he cares." Elena was sharper than she meant to
be. "We all care!"

Norma dismissed this. "For all we know, he may be dead!"
she wailed.

"Norma, don't torture yourself," Elena said again. For how
long had she been conducting this one-sided dialogue with
Norma, going over the same ground again and again? "They
won't hurt Harry. This is just a move to get publicity."

She went on speaking, although she knew it was quite
useless. Since this morning, Norma had retreated into a shell,
inaccessible, beyond the reach of comfort or reassurance.
Elena thought she understood why. Harry was more than
Norma's brother. He was the rock, representing stability and
strength, on which his sister depended, perhaps more than
she had ever realized. Fears for him—painfully real, painfully
shattering—were only part of Norma's distress. There was
another element. With Harry in danger, Norma herself was
threatened, her own life was turned upside down.

She was retaliating in a frenzy, by lashing back—against
her husband, against her friends, against anybody whose concern for Harry did not match her own. In this state, she did
not approve David's self-command, nor was she grateful for
it. She resented it as indifference.

David returned, with Cesar behind him. Cesar went directly
to Norma's side, reached down and, without a word, pressed
her hand.

Her eyes brimmed. "Oh, God, Cesar, I'm so frightened."

"I know," he said softly. "But you must have courage.
These students are not so dangerous, Norma. They have made
a bold move—in order to get attention. But they will not
harm Harry. You will see."

While he spoke, David was busying himself at the bar,
reluctant to face Norma.

"Brandy, Cesar?" he asked, from across the room. "Elena?"

There was an uneasy pause while David provided drinks for
the Aguileras. Then, at last, he turned to the chair by the
window. "Norma?" he asked. He did not sound like a hus-

band to a stricken wife, but more like a wary trainer with a dangerous animal.

But Norma was not clawing. "Maybe a little Scotch," she said lifelessly. "Thanks, David."

She leaned back, closing her eyes. Nobody spoke. In part it was because everything had been said, and said again—what the Governor promised, what the police were doing, what the radicals wanted. But also, Elena realized, it was because they were all afraid of Norma.

Moodily, David rose and went to the corner to switch on the television. Involuntarily Elena moved to stop him, but she was too late.

". . . no news of the missing Harry Zimmerman," the newscaster was saying. "Searches of the dormitories at the university continue, and inquiries have been instigated in the Virgin Islands as well as the Dominican Republic. Elsewhere . . ."

Abruptly Norma set down her glass, not noticing the liquid splashing over the rim.

"You know what makes it worse," she said drearily. "I can't stop thinking that the last time I saw Harry, we had a fight. That's terrible, isn't it? After all Harry has done for us. To fight with him."

Cesar had not coped with Norma today as Elena had. He did not realize that consolation could not reach her. After a glance at David's rigid face, he said, "You and Harry will laugh about it."

"Laugh?" she repeated blankly.

Once again Cesar looked to David before he spoke. "It will all be something to laugh about, once Harry is back."

Stubbornly she did not hear him. "It's a terrible thing. To fight with your own brother. And then to have this happen. My God, I'll never forgive myself if . . . if . . ."

Suddenly her husband's silence infuriated her. "Don't you care, David?" she raged. "Don't you care that the last thing we did was fight with Harry? Doesn't that bother you at all? Don't you have any feelings at all?"

He sounded defeated. "All I care about is getting Harry back. That's what I feel right now, Norma."

She was poised on hysteria.

"Nadal will release him," Cesar said forcefully. "He is no

fool. All he wants is publicity. He has it. He will release Harry."

"I'm sure you're right," David replied quickly. "That's what the Governor said when he called."

"It is only common sense."

Their byplay was lost on Norma. She sank back into her own thoughts. Then, as David was describing the official promises to relay information at any time of the day or night, she suddenly stiffened. Her face had gone white.

"What if they don't release Harry?" she asked in a terrified voice.

"They will."

"But we were wrong about everything else!" she cried. "What if they don't? What if they don't?" Sinking her head into her arms, she broke into a paroxysm of sobbing.

With a muttered oath, David rose and went to her side.

"Leave me alone," she cried, rocking back and forth. "Leave me alone!"

David retreated a step and stood baffled. But the searing anguish in Norma's voice drew him forward again. He slipped an arm around her shoulders.

"No!" she screamed, trying to thrust him away. "Don't touch me!"

Instinctively he drew her into his embrace to soothe her wracked body. But Norma had abandoned every pretense of self-control. She pummeled his shoulders with clenched fists.

"Oh, my God, what have we done to Harry? None of this was his fault. Why should he pay?" she gasped hoarsely.

David's hands had slipped down Norma's arms to imprison her wrists. But she continued to struggle, writhing against him and throwing her head back to shriek:

"Let me go! I'm going to find Harry, I'll make them listen to me—I'll tell everyone!"

Across the room, Aguilera broke from his paralysis.

"Elena," he ordered brusquely, "get Dr. Salas—before anyone else hears her."

16. Blind Stitching

When John Thatcher arrived on Wall Street to be greeted by the news of the kidnapping, his first thoughts naturally were for the fate of Harry Zimmerman, the anguish of his family and the bewilderment of his colleagues at Slax. These concerns were shared by the callers who monopolized Thatcher's telephone for the rest of the day.

Pete Olmsted, on the long-distance line, spoke for the shocked American community in San Juan.

"My God, it's so senseless," he said over and over again.

When Thatcher asked about official action, Olmsted said that the Governor seemed to be determined and efficient. Police were combing known hideouts of the Radical Independents. Several students were already in custody. But Harry Zimmerman and Prudencio Nadal might have disappeared from the face of the earth.

Annie Galiano rang through later in the afternoon. Her normal liveliness had been muted by distress.

"Poor, poor Harry," she said sadly.

As she went on, Thatcher recalled that she and Harry Zimmerman had known each other, worked together and lived through the ups and downs of the garment trade for almost twenty years. She was not responding to a social outrage; she was worrying about the danger threatening a particular individual. Furthermore, her instinct for vigorous action was frustrated. What could she do? What could anyone do? On hearing the news, she had ordered the ILGWU in San Juan to denounce the kidnapping.

"And a fat lot of good that will do," she commented. "Every organization in Puerto Rico is issuing some kind of statement. I never would have believed that Nadal kid would pull anything like this. It'll boomerang so hard it will finish him."

"I thought you didn't have a high opinion of Nadal," Thatcher reminded her.

"I said he was wet behind the ears," she said grumpily. "Not that he was crazy."

Thatcher believed in facing facts, however unpalatable. "Ramírez claims Prudencio Nadal was the one behind the trouble at the university last year. If he started his career by gunning down the police, he doesn't have such a long way to go before he reaches kidnapping."

"That's different. Riots are so confusing that you get a confused public reaction. This is cut and dried." She was silent for a moment, before continuing thoughtfully. "Even so, I never heard that Nadal organized the riot. I thought he was just one of the kids who joined in. I'd better look into that."

Thatcher did not see what good this would do, other than provide distracting occupation. He avoided any remark, instead promising to pass on any information from Hato Rey as soon as it came in. With renewed expressions of sympathy, he hung up.

Dudley Humble called just before Thatcher left for the day. He had nothing further to report other than that Olmsted was presently closeted with the police, answering questions about Zimmerman's last known movements.

It was just as well that John Thatcher's Tuesday had been dominated by people genuinely concerned with the fate of Harry Zimmerman. On Wednesday, it was brought home to him that certain interests at the Sloan viewed the outrage in terms of their own parochial interests. This was not surprising. No one in International had met Zimmerman, and San Juan was a long way away.

Thatcher, when he emplaned for New York, had not expected to escape the problem which had been responsible for his journey. The dispute between Commercial Credit and International was still unresolved. He had avoided making a hard and fast decision. And what had happened in the interim? Murder, arson and kidnapping—that's what. It was too much to hope that Innes, and his cohorts in International, would not see a powerful object lesson in this sequence. They would strike while the iron was hot. There would be conferences and memoranda and research reports. There would be preternaturally intelligent displays of hindsight. There would be reproaches made more in sorrow than in anger.

So much for anticipation. The conferences, memoranda and reports all duly materialized. But so did something else. Innes, flailing his subordinates into prodigies of effort, had achieved a result he was the first to regret. The tidal wave fomented by his tactics had flowed past the sixth, seventh and eighth floors of the Sloan—which was all he had in mind—to wash over the executive tower. There a returned traveler was just checking in. So the tide, receding from its high-water mark, had casually dumped Bradford Withers, president of the Sloan, at the head of the conference table. He was prepared to bring to bear on the problem at hand all the resources of his intellect.

Withers' two outstanding characteristics were a commitment to perpetual globe-trotting and a massive indifference to financial matters. Normally the first defect canceled the second. When affairs at the Sloan became sufficiently critical to require front-office intervention, Brad was usually in some far-flung corner of the world. Today, alas, he was not. In addition, he felt he had special expertise to contribute to the proceedings.

"Now, John," he said chattily, "I've been reading this report about Puerto Rico and you'd be surprised at what's going on there. Why, they've kidnapped one of our customers! I don't think we should encourage that sort of thing."

To a man, his subordinates agreed.

"I can't imagine what's gotten into them," Brad continued. "Now, I haven't been there for a year or two, but I remember everybody was very pleasant. No one tried to kidnap *me*."

John Thatcher normally did not speak at meetings unless he had something to say. But the yearning silence which engulfed the table—as of men who look on the promised land—propelled him into action.

"I think, Brad, it's generally agreed that only a minority of the independence supporters are involved in these crimes. None of our other customers have had any trouble. Or anybody else's customers, for that matter. For some reason, the *radicalistas* have been concentrating on Slax."

"The *radicalistas?*" Then Withers' expression of chronic bewilderment cleared. He beamed with innocent pleasure. "So that's what they call their radicals, is it? Have I ever told you that I've picked up quite a bit of Spanish here and there, John? I expect Innes has, too. It'll be a big help to him, running things down there."

John Thatcher was too experienced in handling his superior to be surprised that Withers should toss off the very decision they were supposed to be deliberating.

"I'm glad you brought that up, Brad," he said firmly. "As a matter of fact, Pete Olmsted's operation has been making investments on the island." To guard against any request for further identification, he hurried on. "Commercial Credit and International have both been active in Puerto Rico. It's been suggested we consolidate our business there in one division. Innes takes the view that International should be in charge."

He was reaching for Walter Bowman's report to find a simple synopsis of the opposition viewpoint when Withers broke in.

"And I suppose Commercial Credit wants to stay down on those beaches," he chuckled genially. "But seriously, now, you can't deny that the only way to understand a country is to spend a lot of time there. And Innes has spent more time in Latin America than anyone else we have."

Innes was anything but gratified by this tribute. He knew what everyone at the table was thinking. Bradford Withers was walking proof, if any were needed, that it takes more than extended sojourns in foreign parts to perceive foreign problems. Withers, after all, had managed to spend considerable time on Wall Street while remaining splendidly immune from the slightest interest in American business. The delegation from International hastened to put its case on steadier foundations.

"Of course, our men are familiar with the languages and social customs prevailing in the Latin-American area. In addition to that, however, they are kept abreast of the current political and economic conditions. Stuart, here, will bear me out."

A small sandy-haired man snatched up a list and began to intone. If he were to be believed, International had predicted every turn of events that had surprised our neighbors south of the border in the last decade. They knew about that sugar-crop failure before Fidel Castro; they had given the Chilean election to Allende before the networks in Santiago had begun totting up; they had plotted Che Guevara's course before the Bolivian Army ever heard his name. No nationalization, no coup d'état, no devaluation had caught them unaware.

Stuart's audience was not markedly impressed by his recitation. John Thatcher, for one, knew too much about International's habit of hedging its bets. They could just as easily have produced confirmation of their omniscience if Guevara were President of Bolivia and Cuba glutted with sugar. Brad Withers was frankly restive. When he was lured down from the tower to attend a meeting, he did not care for tiresome historical detail. He wanted a nice, cozy talk about where the best scuba diving was and which yacht broker was reliable. As for the alert, terrierlike man from Commercial Credit, he was straining at the leash. Barely had the last encomium to International's foresight been presented when he seized the floor.

"That is certainly interesting, Stuart," he said insincerely, "and a remarkable testimony to International's efficiency. But I think we may be losing sight of essentials. The reason you have to know about conditions in Argentina before you do business in Argentina is because they affect your market—export restrictions, credit policies, socialization, all the rest. But the garment industry in Puerto Rico is part of the American market and—"

"So that's what they're doing down there." Brad Withers was pleased to know.

Quite rightly, the terrier ignored this interruption and forged ahead. "And the American garment industry is in the throes of upheaval. The introduction of the new double-knitting machines and the development of the polyester synthetics has revolutionized . . ."

Another spate ensued. Not unexpectedly, its message was that special knowledge of the garment industry was essential for Slax's banker in San Juan. By the time it ended, Innes was shedding his lofty detachment and becoming downright partisan.

"Now, look here, Finch," he said in the tones which had taken him through so many customs barriers, "that's all very well and good. But aren't you overlooking something? This isn't just a question of perma-press fabrics. So far we've had sabotage and kidnapping. Are you still claiming that Slax might just as well be somewhere on Seventh Avenue?"

Stoutly Finch maintained that sabotage and kidnapping

were not unknown in America. He even implied that they were merely two more of the day-to-day hazards of doing business in New York.

"Good heavens!" exclaimed Withers. "I didn't know that things were that bad."

"He's exaggerating a little, Brad," Thatcher said.

"American industry," Finch continued tenaciously, "deals with unions, race relations and corrupt officials. Before ever setting foot in Bayamón, Slax integrated a production line in Georgia and hammered out a contract with the teamsters. What more do you want?"

Thatcher disapproved of strong-arm tactics at in-house conferences. "Unfortunately," he said dryly, "the man who accomplished these miracles is Harry Zimmerman."

Innes picked up the cue promptly. "Yes, and Slax may have to do without him permanently. What about the management that's left in Puerto Rico?"

"We're talking about our investments in Puerto Rico generally, not just Slax," Finch replied warily.

"Ah ha! Then things don't look so rosy if Slax has to handle its problems in San Juan without Zimmerman."

Finch capitulated. "Pete tells me they might have to abandon the Puerto Rico operation. Slax will retreat to its plants in New Jersey and Georgia."

"And what about their plant in Bayamón?"

"They'll sell it off at distress prices."

"A plant that Commercial Credit helped finance," Innes said pointedly.

The terrier turned into a bulldog before their eyes. Forgotten were momentary dissensions. "Commercial Credit," said Finch in a voice of steel, "intends to get its money back. No matter what happens to Harry Zimmerman."

Thatcher had to approve of this goal. It was in the best tradition of the Sloan Guaranty Trust. Nevertheless, like Annie Galiano, he wished there were something somebody could do for Harry Zimmerman.

"It's a shame," he mused aloud, "that the radicals aren't a bigger political party. Then, with the plebiscite coming up, they might be willing to bargain for Zimmerman's freedom. As it is, they have nothing to gain and nothing to lose by negotiating about Zimmerman. They're a splinter group without any real power, except to create incidents. Nothing will change that."

Brad Withers waxed indignant. "Do you mean, John, that all this is for nothing? A bunch of guerillas blows things up just before an election, the government rushes around with all sorts of emergency decrees—I understand they're even searching people at the airport—there are meetings in Washington, the Coast Guard is patrolling the Caribbean, and nothing important is involved, except the safety of this poor man? Otherwise the only change is that they'll force a factory to be sold off? I would simply refuse to deal with these people."

Given the source, it was a reasonable attitude. Brad Withers, protected by money, position and privilege, often resorted to the stance he was advocating.

It was not easy to change his mind. Brad admitted that Harry Zimmerman should not simply be abandoned to his fate. He was the first to deplore insensate destruction of property.

"Fires do a lot of damage," he said almost intelligently. "Have I told you, John, about the trouble Thornet had when his place in Connecticut burned down? But what does all this have to do with the political situation? Why don't the police just round up whoever's responsible? They've got laws against this sort of thing, don't they?"

"The police are trying." Thatcher was not going to make a fool of himself explaining that airport searches and Coast Guard patrols were merely an attempt to achieve this end. "After all, Brad, it isn't easy to capture criminals like this, even in New York."

"It's not the same." Withers had a clear view of the difference between Puerto Rico and Manhattan, and he struggled to put it into words. "You expect trouble here. But there— well, you don't. Not with those beautiful white sands and the water, that crystal-clear water . . ."

But reality on the beaches of the Caribbean was a far cry from Brad Withers' dream world.

When Thatcher entered his office next morning, it was to find Miss Corsa, phone in hand, saying, "Yes, yes, I realize it's an emergency, operator. I'll have Mr. Thatcher return the call as soon as he comes in. If you'll just leave your— Oh, here he is now. Just a moment, please."

Muffling the receiver, she hissed, "A long-distance call from San Juan, Mr. Thatcher. The operator says it's an emergency."

A chill sense of foreboding descended on Thatcher as he strode into his own office and snatched up the receiver.

"John? Thank God I got you."

It was Pete Olmsted and he sounded drunk. Automatically Thatcher checked his watch. Nine-thirty in Manhattan and hence ten-thirty in Puerto Rico. It did not seem likely.

"Yes, Pete?" He tried to keep impatience out of his voice.

"It was Humble's idea. He talked me into taking a dip before breakfast."

So far, it did not sound ominous.

"But the beach in front of the hotel isn't good enough for Humble. No, he has to have some special beach, miles from anywhere, a beach no one else has discovered." Olmsted choked. "Well, never mind that, so we went there together this morning."

"And?"

"It was quiet, all right, quiet as a tomb." Olmsted caught what sounded like the beginning of a high-pitched giggle and steadied his voice. "I went right into the water. I didn't realize Humble wasn't behind me. He thought there was someone lying over by some rocks. He went to take a look. I was diving through the breakers. At first I didn't even hear him yelling."

Thatcher attempted the impossible feat of breathing reassurance over a long-distance line as if he were giving artificial respiration.

"Take it easy, Pete," he said very slowly.

"Oh, God, it was Harry Zimmerman, John!" The announcement turned into a howl as recollection broke over Olmsted. "It was what was left of him. And, John, they cut his throat first!"

17. Fly Front

The nightmare of that early-morning discovery sent Dudley Humble into shock and ravaged Pete Olmsted's sleeping hours for weeks to come. It also reshaped the form of government action against the radicals.

For public opinion in Puerto Rico had not firmed; it had set like concrete. The initial outrage at the kidnapping trebled with the final atrocity. Every newspaper on the island carried two pictures on its front page. One was a publicity still of Harry Zimmerman taken for the opening of the Bayamón plant. The other was a stark photograph of the shrouded stretcher being loaded into an ambulance for the grim journey to a police laboratory. The publicity shot was appallingly good. It hinted at shortcomings as well as virtues. It showed a man, happy at a moment of achievement, who was probably blunt and insensitive, who was probably kind, responsible and hard-working. Far too many people could identify with that man, could recognize a husband or a son, could visualize the moments when he had been kidnapped, when he had been murdered.

The Administration was not slow to get the message. When there was still hope of recovering the victim alive, the proper tactics included sudden descents, swift arrests, comprehensive searches. But now the government would have to prove its efficiency in a different way. There would have to be an arrest; there would have to be evidence; there would have to be a trial. Insensibly, the burden of crisis shifted from armed soldiers to trained policemen.

Relations between the police and students at the university had been tense all year. Only last winter a pitched battle between students had cost the life of the head of the riot squad. Before the violence was over, hundreds had been wounded. But, as Annie Galiano had foreseen, things were different now. Many voices had been stilled. There was no youthful professor saying, "The riot was caused by police brutality." There was no trooper saying, "If they shoot at us, we're going to shoot back." The closing of the university was accepted without protest.

Even the residents of the commune that was Prudencio Nadal's formal address were finding it difficult to rationalize Harry Zimmerman's murder.

"The American industrialist was not a victim of the Radical Independents," a girl with long dark hair stammered to the two policemen standing in the living room. "He was a victim of the repressive forces operating in our country and—"

"Who cut his throat?" demanded the sergeant.

The girl subsided unhappily.

"A warrant has been issued for the arrest of Prudencio Nadal," the officer continued. "It is your duty to assist us in finding him."

This sparked an automatic response from a young man currently attending the law school. "A fair trial is impossible in the courts of the commonwealth. They are institutions imposed on the people of Puerto Rico by an imperialistic occupying power. As such, they have no legitimate authority. The only tribunal before which Prudencio Nadal is accountable is the hearts of his countrymen!"

"If his countrymen get their hands on him before we do, Nadal will be lynched!"

This was so true that it caused a blanket of silence to descend. Finally the girl took up the cudgels again.

"This is what happens when the establishment learns to fear a radical. First they try to muzzle him. When he refuses to be silenced, they seek to discredit him. These charges are false. The evidence has been manufactured." She was growing more vehement with each phrase. "Have you not heard that the editor of *El Mundo* received a letter from Prudencio disclaiming any responsibility for this American's death?"

"When it was clear that the people of Puerto Rico were revolted by his tactics. What about the first letter, in which he was proud of everything he was doing?"

The girl was beginning to find her stride. "Lies! All lies!" she said immediately.

"I suppose he wasn't even responsible for the fire?" The sergeant was sarcastic.

"No, he wasn't. We have told you that before. We were all in front of El Convento until news of the fire came to us. Then we all went across on the ferry to watch. Prudencio himself saw what you would try to do. He said it would all be blamed on him. That was when he and Antonia left. He knew you would seize on anything, an accidental fire even, to throw him into prison!"

The sergeant's gaze was thoughtful, and his voice was soft. "So, you are going to provide Nadal with an alibi. How considerate. And, of course, you alibi yourself at the same time. And the fire was just an accident, in spite of gallons of kerosene. What about Zimmerman? Another unfortunate accident?"

"I know nothing of Zimmerman. I have never seen him!"

"How do you know? Perhaps he was at one of your meetings. Perhaps you should come to the mortuary to make sure?"

The girl went white and took an involuntary step backward. "No, I won't!" she cried.

"Ah, you do not wish to look upon your victims?"

"It was an accident," she gasped.

"Tell me about that accident," the sergeant purred.

"I know nothing about it," she said wildly, before she could control herself. She was sullen when she continued. "I meant that it must have been an accident. That is the only explanation. But I know nothing that would help you."

"You don't know much, do you?" The sergeant's contempt flayed her. "I waste my time asking you where Nadal is. You don't know that either."

This was too close to the bone. The three young people all looked affronted. They were the residue of the radical group that had inhabited the commune. After the warehouse fire half the members had fled. A sweeping raid by the police, hard on the heels of the Governor's speech, had removed many of the rest. Those left were the clerical force. They typed the letters which others dictated. They hired lecture halls. They distributed posters. The police regarded them as too insignificant to be worthy of notice.

The law student tried to bluster. "It is unnecessary that we know where Prudencio is. You will never find him. You fool yourselves if you think we are his only comrades. He is the voice of the common man, he is the common man!" he

declaimed. "Prudencio Nadal has only to seek sanctuary with
the workers of Puerto Rico!"

The sergeant's eyes were flat and hard as he rose.

"Even a student," he said, "should know better than that."

No one approved the new look in government countermeas-
ures more than Captain Vallejo. Armed soldiers were all very
well for putting down riots, for aborting revolutions, even
for mass roundups of terrorists. They were still proving their
usefulness. At this very moment, they were making exit from
Puerto Rico a cumbersome, lengthy process. Passengers for
airplanes and ships were scrutinized. Freighters were searched
from stem to stern before weighing anchor. The coastline was
being patrolled. Cruise ships had been advised to forgo their
stop in San Juan. But, in the last analysis, murder was the
business of trained policemen. And the murder of Harry
Zimmerman was peculiarly the business of Captain Vallejo.

Gone was any temptation to sneer at the troubles of Slax.
In the privacy of his own soul, Captain Vallejo had offered up
a little apology to Harry Zimmerman, then determined to
make amends in his own way. Without undue pride, he had
scrapped every preconception he had ever had about what
was going on in Bayamón. He was starting from the beginning.

"You're asking me about Domínguez again?" Cesar Aguilera stared at him.

"This whole situation has centered around Slax from the
beginning. Domínguez was murdered not two doors from
where we're sitting. Before that, there was sabotage. After
that, there was arson and murder. There must be some
connection."

Aguilera was very tired. But he forced himself to think. "I
thought you were convinced that Domínguez was murdered
by someone in our management, Captain."

"I tended to that conclusion, I admit." Vallejo frowned.
"But now I am not convinced of anything."

"Probably that should be a relief. But I am merely confused these days."

Captain Vallejo became more conciliatory as he tried to
enlist some assistance. "You understand, we have been active ever since Domínguez was killed. We have questioned his
family, his friends, his associates. Never was there the slight-

est suggestion of any political interests. It stands to reason that he must have been paid for what he did."

"I could have told you that Benito Domínguez was not the dedicated type."

"I am in accord. And that brings me to an inescapable conclusion. He would be a great help to me if he were still alive. A man like that would have told all he knew, at once. The name of his employer would already be part of our evidence."

Aguilera failed to see that this was important. "Surely there are other sources of information. What about the students in Nadal's organization? They are not all missing, are they?"

"They say they never heard of Domínguez." Vallejo raised a hand at Aguilera's sound of disbelief. "No, I am inclined to believe them. You understand, many of them are shocked by this atrocity. I think whoever hired Domínguez was very secretive about it."

Through his weariness, Cesar Aguilera began to sense a certain reticence in the Captain's phrasing. "The problem is evidence, is it not? Surely you don't doubt that Nadal hired him."

"You cannot deny someone has been active at Slax in behalf of the Radical Independents—since Domínguez' death. Someone knew that the warehouse was supposed to contain an unusual amount of finished goods. Someone must have located Mr. Zimmerman. I think there may be a missing link."

"You have been investigating our workers very thoroughly, Captain," Aguilera said cautiously. "Is that what you mean?"

Vallejo shot down this conjecture instantly. "Your people have been investigated back to the day they were born. I would go on oath that not one of them has the slightest sympathy with the Radical Independents."

Cesar Aguilera could not pretend to be surprised. It was axiomatic that Prudencio Nadal had been unable to attract the workers. Cesar knew that Vallejo wanted him to pursue the point to its logical conclusion, but today he was not prepared to indulge anyone. He shifted to an earlier remark.

"What did you mean about someone locating Harry, Captain?"

Vallejo was too experienced to show his chagrin. Now his

mission was to make an ally of Aguilera. With good grace, he
answered, "If you are going to kidnap a man, you must first
know where he is. We have very little information about Mr.
Zimmerman's movements on the day of the fire. But our radio
appeal has produced several taxi drivers. We know that he
was at the plant in Bayamón, at the docks in Cataño, at the
offices of the Sloan. And what is very interesting is something
he said to Mr. Olmsted. At that time he was going to clear
up some mess once and for all. That is why he canceled his
appointment with Mr. Thatcher. Now, tell me, what problem
was so big, so pressing, that Mr. Zimmerman would put off
his bankers to deal with it?"

Cesar Aguilera disliked being jockeyed into rote answers.
"I suppose there could have been a good many problems," he
said stiffly.

"Come, come. You don't mean that. Oh, granted, there
might be more than one problem. But do you not think it
conceivable that Mr. Zimmerman thought he could settle his
troubles with the radical students by a face-to-face confron-
tation with Prudencio Nadal?"

Aguilera examined the idea. He would have liked to find
a flaw. But finally, reluctantly, he nodded. "It is possible,"
he agreed. "Harry liked to deal with difficulties personally. I
doubt if he would have thought of such an idea by himself.
But if it were suggested to him . . ."

Vallejo leaned forward intently. "If, perhaps, it were put to
him in the guise of an invitation from Nadal? What would
his reaction have been?"

"I suppose he would have agreed." Aguilera fingered his
chin, frowning. "But I would have expected him to tell
someone. Is your theory that the invitation came in such a
way that Harry had no time?"

"Not exactly. The last thing Mr. Zimmerman told Mr.
Olmsted was that he must rush to the union headquarters.
Unfortunately Señora Galiano was not at headquarters that
morning. But you see my line of thought. Who had already
gotten the better of young Nadal? Wasn't she the logical person for him to tell?"

"Yes, that is sensible. But what does it have to do with
your idea of a missing link at Slax?"

Vallejo leaned back, watching Aguilera carefully. "Where
could Mr. Zimmerman have received such an invitation that

morning? He was not sitting in a hotel room, where anyone could have telephoned him. He was constantly on the move. He was not following any schedule. The message must have been delivered personally. And where? He was at the Lippert home, he was at the plant in Bayamón, he was at the dock in Cataño. And who were the people who had access to him? The people of Slax! Is that not true?"

"You make it very convincing, Captain." Aguilera suddenly surrendered to a jaw-breaking yawn. "I am sure there is something wrong with your reasoning, but I cannot find it."

"It is because you are tired that you think there is something wrong. You will see. When you are rested, you will agree with me."

"Then you may have to wait a long time."

Cesar Aguilera had not had a night's sleep since Harry Zimmerman's disappearance. His hours at the Slax plant had alternated with hours at the Lippert home. Now his fine-boned face had become cavernous, with sharp ridges defining his nose and cheekbones. He was hollow-eyed with fatigue.

"It is too much," Vallejo said sympathetically. "Trying to salvage Slax and help the Lipperts."

Aguilera set his chin firmly. "I am only doing what has to be done. Even if Slax closes down tomorrow, it must be kept going today."

Captain Vallejo in fact was putting in as many hours as Cesar Aguilera. After a full day in Bayamón, he returned to his own office and the inevitable accumulation on his desk. One report bore the legend *"Urgent"* in his superior's handwriting. He read it at once.

Five minutes later he was in his chief's office.

"I have just read the post-mortem findings. They must be wrong," he exclaimed.

"That is what we all thought. I assure you, Vallejo, there is no possibility of error. The stomach and its contents were in good condition. And there is ample testimony at the hotel about Zimmerman's breakfast."

Once again Vallejo stared at the document in wonder. "But the doctor says that, at the very latest, Zimmerman was killed late Monday afternoon. That was before the fiesta, before Nadal's speech in the Parque de las Palomas, before the fire."

With the satisfying savor that comes from passing on

one's troubles, his superior said, "The doctor put that in for a safety margin. He inclines to the view that Zimmerman was killed nearer to noon."

The full implication of the autopsy was sinking home, bit by bit.

"But that means," said Vallejo, at last realizing the magnitude of the readjustment required, "that Harry Zimmerman was never kidnapped at all!"

18. Women's Wear

John Putnam Thatcher had long since concluded that the only thing to expect from Puerto Rico was the unexpected. First a routine investment in the garment trade had plunged the Sloan, and incidentally its senior vice-president, into a kaleidoscope of crime and violence. Now CBS was telling him that desperate and lawless political extremists had not kidnapped Harry Zimmerman. Zimmerman had not been kidnapped at all.

He had, however, been murdered.

Thatcher was not sure whether this confirmed Commercial Credit's contention that Puerto Rico was as American as apple pie or International's view that its flora, fauna and dramatics were ineradicably exotic. He was confident, however, that fallout from this latest development would somehow or other drift back to his desk. After all, Harry Zimmerman—however his death came about—had been a Sloan client.

So, as Thatcher informed Miss Corsa, he was braced.

Miss Corsa, who had taken an inexplicable dislike to everything about Puerto Rico—from papaya trees to Mrs. Schroeder in Hato Rey—no doubt could have told him he was braced for the wrong thing. Certainly she was disapproving when she put through another call from San Juan.

Without regret, Thatcher set aside a report illustrating the power of heart over head. Some trust officers in the Sloan still yearned to buy Penn Central stock.

"What was that, Pete?" he asked. "I didn't quite catch what you said."

Olmsted was so indignant he was gabbling. Thatcher could not sympathize. The Sloan's three-million-dollar loan to Slax Unlimited depended on Pete Olmsted's keeping his head. So Thatcher was astringent.

"Did you say something about Mrs. Lippert?" he interrupted. "Please convey my condolences. But what . . . ?"

Olmsted was not wasting time on bereavement.

"Norma owns Slax now," he said. "Harry left her everything."

The police might find this interesting; Thatcher did not. In the first place, Olmsted had already given him a very complete review of Slax's ownership. In the second place, Sloan investments in family firms were protected, to the nth degree, against mishaps to principals.

"She's out to make trouble," Olmsted went on with distinct sourness. "She's lashing in all directions."

Thatcher valued precision. "Exactly what kind of trouble is Mrs. Lippert causing?" he asked. "And for whom?"

Olmsted started at the top of his list.

It was the first formal meeting of the Slax management since Harry's death. Pete Olmsted had arrived expecting general accord. Things did not work out that way.

David Lippert sat at the head of the table. "I've asked Pete to sit in with us so you'll all know the situation," he began. "He and I have gone over the figures, and unfortunately we don't see any other way out. We're going to have to close down the Bayamón operation gradually over the next month. It's going to mean extra work for all of us. And not work we enjoy. But I know I can count on you."

Eric Marten and Cesar Aguilera knew the financial realities even better than David Lippert.

"I wish I could give you an argument," Marten said sadly, "but I can't."

Aguilera nodded in resignation.

There was a short silence. Olmsted assumed that the last word had been spoken. He was wrong.

Norma Lippert had not been agreeing. She had been thinking.

"David, you haven't really given this enough time," she said. "Harry thought Slax could do well in Bayamón—and it has. It's been our most profitable operation for the last two years. We can go on with Slax in Puerto Rico. I know we can."

In the last three days Norma had lost weight. There was a new maturity about her. But the horror of Harry's death had not crushed her. She had been distraught when his fate was still uncertain. Afterward, she had wept uncontrollably. But there, almost abruptly, Norma's mourning ended. Grief she might feel; outwardly she was herself again.

"Honey, I haven't wanted to bother you," David said. "But if we don't sell off Bayamón, we may be in real hot water. It isn't just the Sloan that we have to pay off."

She smiled lovingly at him but addressed Cesar, sitting on her right.

"Do you really agree, Cesar? Do you think we have to sell the Bayamón plant?"

Aguilera chewed a lip. "Nobody here wants Slax to sell off Bayamón. But look at the damage that's been done. We have lost customers and we will lose more. We do not have a warehouse. Finally—" He broke off apologetically.

"Go on," Norma said steadily. Of all the people in the office, she was easily the most composed. In their various ways, David, Eric and Cesar, even Olmsted, were still caught up in the past. Norma was the only one who had put what had happened behind her and was looking to the future.

Cesar was not happy. "Harry," he said. The single word cast a pall. Harry Zimmerman had been washed ashore with his throat cut. The search for Prudencio Nadal might still be proceeding. But Captain Vallejo had returned to Slax with questions, questions, questions.

Nobody really wanted to face what that suggested.

With an effort, Cesar forced himself on. "When Harry was alive—I'm sorry, Norma—he ran sales from New York. Bayamón could concentrate on production. Now the situation is totally different. Perhaps without Harry you will find that Slax is too large."

Norma's reply was not what he had bargained for. "I agree with you—about Harry," she said. "That's why David has to go up to New York right away."

She startled everybody, including her husband.

David stopped studying his pencil. "But, Norma, I can't go to New York. I have to wind up things down here."

She reached over to clasp his arm warmly. "But now that we're not closing Bayamón, the important place for the man in charge is New York. Our whole future depends on sales and advertising. Now that Harry's gone, you're the logical person to take his place."

She left everybody speechless, except Eric Marten.

"For Christ's sake, Norma!" he exploded. "What do you mean, we're not closing down Bayamón? We can't afford to keep it open."

"We can't afford to keep it open if David doesn't take charge in New York," she retorted.

Marten's face darkened. He was on the brink of losing his temper completely.

Without waiting for others, Olmsted leaped into the breach. "The Sloan has gone over the capital budget and the income accounts, Mrs. Lippert, as I'm sure your husband told you. Before you lose more money, it would be a good idea to retrench. That means selling Bayamón. The sale will give you cash to meet your other obligations. It will also—"

As Olmsted subsequently reported to Thatcher, Norma was not giving an inch.

"I don't care what the Sloan advises," she said roundly. "We are going to keep Slax open in Puerto Rico as long as I—we —can!"

And I own Slax now! Although unspoken, the sentiment rang clear as a bell.

Norma shed imperiousness for cajolery. "I think you've all let yourselves get too pessimistic. Things aren't as bad as they could be. Remember when we were watching the fire in Cataño? We thought we had lost a warehouse almost filled with finished goods. But now we know the freight forwarder managed to ship everything out before the fire. So we're not any worse off than we were before. Isn't that so, Eric?"

"Sure," he said lifelessly.

"That means Slax *is* meeting its delivery dates," Norma said triumphantly.

"For how long?" Cesar intervened, but she ignored him.

"We can keep Slax going," she said. "You'll see, Mr. Olmsted."

It was almost physically impossible, Olmsted found, to remind Norma Lippert of the problems she had conveniently forgotten. Such as the murder of Harry Zimmerman -and those questions Captain Vallejo was asking.

But they were what he was thinking about in the taxi ride back to Hato Rey.

Marten and Aguilera, meanwhile, were heading for Cesar's office.

"I don't know, I don't know," Marten rumbled, once they were clear of the Lipperts. He led the way through the work floor. The familiar clatter of sewing machines, of voices calling for more material, of dollies wheeling past with heaps of finished goods, assailed their ears. Despite everything that had happened, Slax was working at top capacity. It was almost unreal.

They halted while Aguilera signed an order for a foreman, then continued upstairs.

"Even if nothing else occurs," Cesar began once they had reached his quarters, "do you think she can keep Slax running in Puerto Rico?"

"Without Harry?" Marten snorted. "David couldn't run a sewing machine, and you know it as well as I do, Cesar."

There was a pregnant pause, then he said, "And why the hell is Norma so hot to get him up to New York right now? He'll just ball things up there, too."

Cesar smiled enigmatically. "Norma says that New York is the place for the man in charge."

"Man in charge!" Eric scoffed. "David was born to take orders. I wonder what she really has in mind."

"I am afraid," Cesar said, "that Norma wants to get David out of Puerto Rico. At least to another jurisdiction."

Marten's jaw dropped.

"After all, Eric, it is clear where suspicion turns if Nadal did not kill Harry. To someone who benefits from Harry's death. And who benefits more than the Lipperts? You underestimate Norma. She is not Harry's sister for nothing."

He might have been amused to realize that Norma was returning the compliment in kind.

"Cesar's no fool," Norma was saying, more to herself than to David. "You know, when I went to pick up the kids I was talking to Elena. From something she said, I got the impression that Cesar is looking for a new job."

David rose and took a quick turn around the office. "Of course he is," he said gruffly. "Can you blame him? Listen, Norma, I know how you feel about keeping Slax going down here, but it just won't work. You heard what Olmsted said. Well, he's right. And unless you want to lose every penny you've got in Slax, the sensible thing to do is to sell. . . ."

She listened with flattering deference as he spoke. Since Harry's death, Norma's behavior to David had been, if anything, more affectionate than ever before.

". . . and besides, this idea of my going to New York isn't any good," he wound up. He was trying to sound masterful.

"It's a very good idea, David," she said emphatically.

"Why?"

She rose and searched vaguely for her purse. "Oh, you know we have to have somebody up there," she said.

He barred her way to the door.

"Why, Norma?" he repeated insistently.

"Because," she said, raising her chin, "they've killed my brother! They're not going to do anything to my husband! David, I have to get back to the children!"

With a swift kiss, she was gone. Slowly David closed the door behind her, then went to his desk and sat down. When his secretary came in for dictation, she found him with his head buried in his hands.

Norma, meanwhile, was driving herself back to Isla Verde. She was troubled by no second thoughts. Slax in Bayamón was going to stay open. David was going to New York as soon as possible. That was that—no matter what anybody said.

She cut in front of a taxi without seeing it. It was too much to say that Norma Lippert was contented with her work. But she had seen a problem and had solved it. In the last terrible days, she had found new resources in herself, new ways of thinking and acting. They surprised her, but they also strengthened her.

Although she did not realize it, Norma Lippert had stopped being a girl and become a woman.

She was not discomposed to discover a visitor waiting for her.

"Well, Captain Vallejo?" She was cool, supercilious.

"I am sorry to trouble you again," Vallejo murmured. He was deeply interested in this new Mrs. Lippert, so different from the woman he had encountered earlier.

This new Mrs. Lippert whose brother's death left her sole owner of Slax.

"I want to help in any way I can," she said distantly.

There was nothing new in their exchange. Yes, the last time she had seen her brother had been here at the house, the morning of his murder. Yes, there had been a quarrel.

"Your husband does not inherit any Slax stock?" Vallejo asked.

He touched a nerve. "What I have is my husband's," she blazed with a passion that mocked her earlier composure. "Everything I have is David's and the children's. And if you think either of us would harm Harry—" She broke off, but she did not weep. Instead, in a deadly voice, she said, "*We* weren't the last ones to see Harry. What about Mr. Olmsted? Harry went to see him, didn't he? Why don't you talk to him, not me?"

Vallejo's silence spurred her on.

"One of them is lying," she said. "Either him or that Galiano woman. Why don't you talk to them, Captain Vallejo? Not to us. We loved Harry! They didn't. And I'll tell you something else. Harry didn't trust either of them. So why don't you find out why they're lying?"

Vallejo wondered at the venom in her voice. All he said was, "We are exploring it, Mrs. Lippert, just as we are exploring everything else. Now if you'll excuse me . . ."

Norma had herself in hand once again. She nodded, in effect dismissing him.

"I may find it necessary to return to you," he said.

She looked unwaveringly at him. "I intend to stay in Puerto Rico," she said defiantly. "You can talk to me any time you wish, Captain Vallejo."

"A lot of goddam foolishness," Olmsted was saying irately. "Poor Harry. I've been doing business with him for years. If he didn't trust me, he didn't trust anybody!"

From what little he recalled of the dead man, Thatcher was inclined to doubt this. Harry Zimmerman was one of the breed who never trusted anybody implicitly, not excluding representatives of the Sloan Guaranty Trust. It would do Pete Olmsted no harm to realize that bankers are not always regarded as universal uncles.

"And as for Annie," Olmsted went on, "that's just Norma's

spite. Harry relied on Annie, which is more than you can say for that sister of his. And after this morning I can see why. Did I tell you—"

"Yes, you did," said Thatcher. "Well, Olmsted, I regret that you are entangled with the police."

Olmsted denied that he was entangled with the police. He had simply been asked to repeat his account of Harry Zimmerman's last day.

"When he broke his appointment," Thatcher remembered aloud. Why was Olmsted so testy? Was he coming clean? "Tell me, has Mrs. Lippert made trouble on this too?"

"She claims one of us, Annie or me, is lying." There was a buzz on the line. "Unfortunately, there seems to be some misunderstanding. I thought that Harry was going over to see Annie . . ." His voice trailed away.

"Olmsted, I can sense trouble as quickly as the next man, but I still don't see . . ."

Olmsted took a deep breath.

"Harry never turned up at ILGWU headquarters. Or, if he did, no one really remembers. Annie said she wasn't there that morning. Anyway, when the police asked Annie about it, naturally she said Harry hadn't been at union headquarters."

"If that's the most serious discrepancy the police have found, I congratulate them," Thatcher said dryly.

"Yes," said Olmsted again. "But somebody gave Annie the idea that I was trying to involve the ILGWU in Harry's murder."

"Oh," said Thatcher.

"Annie is on her way back right now," said Olmsted hollowly. "She just called me. She told me I've got an appointment with her tomorrow morning. She wants Dudley Humble to be there, too. She says she knows how Dubinsky would have organized this."

Unbidden there came to Thatcher's mind a vivid picture of Annie Galiano leading the ILGWU against the Sloan Guaranty Trust.

"Dudley," said Olmsted, "is a little worried."

Thatcher did not reply. He was busy consulting his calendar.

19. Without Embroidery

John Putnam Thatcher had no previous experience with Annie Galiano on the warpath. But his respect for the lady was such that he was not surprised, when he entered ILGWU headquarters in San Juan, to find her solidly planted behind a desk and laying down the law.

Olmsted, Aguilera and Marten hailed his arrival as if he were the cavalry relieving a siege. Annie simply glared.

"We've been trying to explain to Annie how the police got the wrong idea," Eric Marten said with less than his usual ebullience. Then he sat back and signaled that the ball was in Thatcher's court.

Thatcher was annoyed. "I am still not clear on what troubles the police."

Annie had several pungent suggestions about the basic trouble with the Puerto Rican police.

"Yes, yes!" Looking punch-drunk, Pete Olmsted tried to report to his superior. "Look, John, I suppose you could say this is all my fault. When Harry dropped by on the morning of the fire, he told me he had to rush off to union headquarters. When the news of the kidnapping broke, the police and everybody else assumed Harry had been snatched later in the day. I admit I should have been more careful, but it just didn't seem very important. I told them Harry said he was going to see Annie. Then there was a certain confusion about the story they got here at ILGWU headquarters."

Annie had begun to rumble ominously as Pete picked his way carefully through the mine field. Thatcher paid no attention, but barked, "What confusion?"

"At first they said Harry wasn't here. Then, when they saw some pictures, they said he was."

Thatcher turned expectantly to Annie. Open battle hung in

149

the balance for a moment. But, as Thatcher had hoped,
Annie's initial wrath had been dissipated.

"There's no mystery about it," she growled. "The receptionist doesn't speak English. Harry didn't speak Spanish. He
came up here looking for me, saw my office was empty and
left. The receptionist never did get his name."

Thatcher had already achieved a victory. By getting first
Olmsted's story, then Annie's, he had imperceptibly become
a mediator. To punch this home, he cocked his head thoughtfully and nodded to himself before he spoke.

"That could all happen very easily," he said at length. "I
cannot attach any blame to the receptionist or to Pete here. I
fail to see why such a natural misunderstanding should ab-
sorb the police."

Annie's eyes narrowed. She jerked her head at the Slax
contingent. "Ask them," she advised.

Cesar Aguilera hesitated. Not so Eric Marten.

"The time for a lot of pussyfooting is over," he rasped.
"You may as well know that Norma is doing her best to throw
dirt on everyone, and that includes the Sloan. She's been having a field day."

Thatcher did not have to explore the motives behind Norma
Lippert's behavior. "Have the police given up all idea that
Prudencio Nadal was behind Zimmerman's murder?"

"No, you cannot say that." Aguilera was scrupulously exact.
"They now have proof that Harry was killed early that Monday. There never was a kidnapping, and the kidnapping letter
was an additional piece of cruelty. I think you can only say
that the police have broadened the scope of their inquiries.
They're considering Nadal—and others."

"You mean Lippert." Thatcher did not have to be as
tactful as an employee of Slax. "What does Lippert say?"

Annie gave an unpleasant laugh. "He's in New York. His
wife got him out of town fast."

"And now she's trying to rope the rest of us into this,"
Eric Marten said with his old vigor. "No, Cesar, stop shaking your head at me. Besides all this bilge about Annie and
Pete, she's been busy with us too. She's been onto Vallejo
because she found out Cesar was looking for another job.
My God, anybody in his right mind would be looking for
another job!"

"Very well. I suppose that it must come out. But I want you

to understand," Aguilera said persuasively, "that Norma can scarcely be regarded as responsible. Not only is she making an enormous cry since she discovered that Eric went to the Water Board Monday morning—because the Water Board is several blocks from here—but she is also trying to involve Ramírez."

"Ramírez?"

"Norma thinks she understands Puerto Rican politics." Cesar Aguilera was at last showing signs of hostility. "She is explaining to Captain Vallejo in great detail that the murder of Harry has ended Nadal's potential as a competitor to Dr. Ramírez."

Annie looked up. "That's interesting. Vallejo must have enjoyed the lecture. I'll see how Ramírez is taking it tonight."

"Tonight?" Olmsted was puzzled.

"The election rally," Annie expanded, growing more human by the minute. "Life goes on, you know."

Annie, of course, was right. The search for Prudencio Nadal continued with unabated vigor. Captain Vallejo's daily routine intensified. But otherwise Puerto Rico was going back to business as usual.

And for every politician on the island, that business meant one thing—the plebiscite next week. The Commonwealth Party flexed its mighty muscles, the statehood advocates tried to convince themselves of new opportunities, and Dr. Francisco Ramírez Rivera dusted off old notes. There was only one howl of outrage, and that emanated from a commune near the University of Puerto Rico. The elections would be a fraud, shrilled the mimeographed newspaper. How could the Radical Independents campaign? Their leader was the object of a relentless manhunt, their executive committee was in jail, the university itself was in the hands of the forces of oppression. They would not lend their countenance to this farce. They would boycott the candidates' night sponsored by the AFL-CIO!

"You can't blame them," Annie Galiano commented. She was sitting in the front row of the speaker's platform, examining the packed audience. "If they showed up here tonight, they'd be lucky to get out in one piece."

Her neighbor did not take this offering in good part. "I am sure," said Dr. Ramírez, at his stateliest, "that the labor force

of Puerto Rico would give the Radical Independents a fair
and courteous hearing."

Annie was blunt. "The labor force of Puerto Rico doesn't
like murder."

"Certainly not." Dr. Ramírez frowned. "Mr. Zimmerman's
death was very unfortunate. But we cannot allow that tragedy
to color our thinking about the Radical Independents."

"You sound like that student editorial," Annie said unflat-
teringly.

"What editorial?"

"The one the radicals are complaining about. That's why
they're yelling about the forces of oppression."

"But that is their standard complaint."

Neither Dr. Ramírez nor Annie was struck by the fact
that she, a union official from New York, was explaining the
local currents to him.

"Oh, no. The students who run the college newspaper had
a big crisis of conscience. They decided they couldn't approve
the murder. So their editorial the other day said that, while
they sympathized with the arson, they were forced to deplore
Harry Zimmerman's death."

Ramírez' voice sharpened. "That," he snapped, "is simply
ridiculous."

"Well, don't blame me. I didn't say it."

A surge of music forced them to their feet. After the
audience had paid homage to their beautiful island, the band
swung into the tune which tells the initiated that the Governor
of Puerto Rico is about to make his entrance. On cue, he
appeared at a side door and mounted the podium amidst wild
enthusiasm.

He was not the man to waste such an opportunity. His brisk
speech was designed to flatten opponents on all sides and
bring home to his audience their good fortune in having him
and his party at the helm of state during these trying times.
There had been those, he marveled, who questioned the
viability of the commonwealth form of government. Let them
question no longer. Events had taken Puerto Rico from the
realm of theory into the realm of fact. The commonwealth
had proved it could do everything it claimed and more. It had
protected its sovereignty and repelled its enemies. Delicately
he hinted that excellence was to be found not only in the form

of government but in the person of the Governor. He sat down to tumultuous applause.

The statehood advocate who came next on the agenda was not under any illusions. He knew that the Governor's hand was stronger than ever. His goal, therefore, was to annex votes from erstwhile independence supporters. No one, he claimed, could be more grateful than he that the fabric of their present government had withstood the dark strains to which it had been subject. No one was more relieved at the strong stand taken by the executive. He ended by reminding his audience that any approach to statehood would necessarily be a protracted process, allowing ample time for necessary adjustments. The readiness was all.

It was Dr. Ramírez' unenviable task to follow these speakers and to support the theoretical goal of independence while anathematizing every single action taken by its advocates in the past two weeks. He did not do a bad job.

"Ah! I understand!" he cried, when the stewards failed to quell the wave of catcalls at the first mention of independence. "You and I are both revolted by these insensate acts of violence. The radicals call for a social revolution, and what do they give us as a first step in that revolution? The hand of brother turned against brother."

By the sheer drama of his oratory, Dr. Ramírez stilled his hecklers. He was an impressive sight, his noble face impassive while his hands sketched movements of majestic sweep. The organ notes of his deep voice supported his theme. He was a father addressing his children, pointing a moral for their edification. But oratory can do just so much. The only theme available was that the Radical Independents were abhorrent to all men of good will. And Dr. Ramírez knew better than anyone that the Radical Independents were not going to get any votes anyway. So, with a natural instinct for good theater, he allowed his speech to trail away into a grave and sober view of the immediate future. Independence remained the only desirable end. It was worth striving for, but it was a long way off.

The gentle clap-clap of applause was a tribute to the perfection of the performance, but it represented a low point in the evening's emotional temperature. Happily there was a stimulant at hand. For this was primarily a gathering of labor. They had come to hear the chief delegates of the parties, but they had also come to hear Annie Galiano.

As she advanced on the microphone, the gentle cloud of melancholy that had been generated by Dr. Ramírez disappeared. There is no official signature tune for the appearance of an ILGWU official, but the band improvised splendidly. It says much for the impact of the American labor movement on Puerto Rico that a Spanish version of "There Once Was a Union Maid" sprang readily to the lips of the audience. Like a prize fighter acknowledging victory, Annie clasped both hands together and waved them dementedly over her head. The eager response deferred the start of her speech for over five minutes.

She spoke without notes and, at first, seemed to be rambling her way toward a formless expression of camaraderie. Puerto Rico, she began, would always be home to her. It was the scene of her early childhood. And the Spanish Harlem of her later youth had simply been Puerto Rico in another guise. True, there had been no sunny skies and mild blue waters, but it was the sunniness that Puerto Ricans carried within themselves that made a home. All these vague statements were received with uncritical acclaim by the audience. But the very critical ears on the platform were not unduly surprised to find these opening chords modulating into a very definite theme. Within minutes, Annie was scattering statistics around like grapeshot. Economic problems could also be carried from one place to another—problems and solutions. Labor's needs were simple. Labor would not forget its friends. It was to be hoped that, after the election, the friends would not forget labor.

The continuing excitement which greeted Annie's appearance, accompanied her speech and wafted her back to her seat was not lost on Dr. Ramírez. Here was something he had been looking for a long time. Something that was, even under present conditions, a bigger draw than the Governor and the Commonwealth Party. Thoughtfully he pondered this phenomenon as the public presentations of the evening drew to a close and the notables retired to refresh themselves at a small reception. He acknowledged to himself that he was surprised. He had known, of course, that Annie's influence at the Slax plant was enormous. Without thinking about it much, he had been ready to assume that she would be equally powerful in other labor disputes, that her counsel on whether or not to strike, whether or not to ask for a new wage package, would be persuasive. He had not realized the scale on which she might sway a substantial body of voters. Señora Galiano, he decided, was worth cultivating.

When he finally arranged things so that he and Annie were alone together, slightly removed from the eddying throng, he thought he had struck out on a novel and unanticipated course. Annie, sipping her whiskey, looked at him enigmatically. She was waiting to hear what this latest in a long line of men wanting political favors was going to say. He did not realize it, but she was already comparing him with New York City borough presidents, candidates seeking the endorsement of the Liberal Party and people running for district judge in Georgia.

It had been, she agreed, a very stimulating evening.

Emboldened, Ramírez remarked that there was naturally no doubt about the forthcoming plebiscite. The Commonwealth Party would be upheld by a landslide. The very understandable outrage of the electorate with the atrocities of the Radical Independents had ensured that.

"It won't make that much difference," Annie said flatly. "There would have been a landslide anyway. It will just be a little bigger, that's all."

Ramírez hastened to agree. Sad to say, the magical influence of Muñoz Marin still prevailed. There could be no rational examination of the defects of the commonwealth system until political life ceased to be overshadowed by the memory of the father of modern Puerto Rico. He himself was working toward that day.

Annie cocked her head and listened in unreceptive silence.

"You may be in for a surprise," she announced when he came to a halt. "Has it ever occurred to you that the people of Puerto Rico support the commonwealth, not because it was spawned by Muñoz, but because it works?"

Ramírez stiffened. Like most great men, he was used to having his remarks accepted reverently in his presence. Opposition was something that appeared in the newspapers— and, unfortunately, at the election polls.

"In a narrow sense, you could say it works," he said, activating his rusty debating techniques. "There have been temporary economic benefits from American investment. But at what price? We are, after all, a people of Spanish culture. We are not Anglo-Saxons. We speak a different language, honor different values, move to a different daily rhythm. Is it right that we should be required to give this up? That we should cease respecting individuality, abandon our literary heritage and stop playing the guitar—because these are not the habits of North Americans?"

This impassioned plea left Annie cold.

"I don't know whether you've noticed, but there are a lot more transistor radios and pop records in Puerto Rico than there are guitars," she said.

Ramírez pounced. "Exactly what I mean. Our young people are being corrupted before our eyes."

"Why shouldn't they have the music they want?" Annie demanded. "Just because somebody has a romantic notion of what village life was like in the good old days? How many guitars were being played in starving families, do you think? For that matter, how much time do you spend twanging a guitar?"

Ramírez flushed. "That surely is beside the point."

"Oh no it isn't. Not by a long shot. When North Americans want to hear a steel band, they fly to Trinidad and ask where the natives are. That's pretty patronizing. But, my God, you want to be a tourist in your own country!"

"You speak for special interests yourself," Ramírez accused her. "Basically, you're simply interested in an environment which will produce a strong labor movement. That's why you favor American investment."

"Look!" Annie pointed a finger like a spear. "What do you think Spanish culture has ever given most Puerto Ricans? Nothing. What do you think American culture will give them? Nothing. And you know why? Because culture doesn't give things like a lady bountiful. Culture is something that's created. And Puerto Ricans can create their own as well as anybody else if they don't have to spend all their time struggling to survive. I don't say a transistor radio is great. But the villagers are competent enough to decide whether it's right for them, so long as they get a choice. You don't want to give them choices. You want to make the decisions yourself."

Ramírez reminded himself that here was something he hoped to use. He became more placatory. "I think you misunderstand me. I have never conceived of an independent state that would discourage American investment. I look forward to full sovereignty—but in the context of a special relationship with the United States which would secure and, indeed, increase the economic benefits you are so attached to. I have never advocated the hostile stance to American business that the radicals propose." He smiled indulgently. "If you are displeased with my position, señora, you should hear our young friend Prudencio Nadal."

"That's because he's more of a realist than you are," Annie retorted, not one whit abashed. "Your independence is some kind of pie in the sky. Full sovereignty, but all sorts of special relationships. Who is going to pay for an army and navy? Who is going to encourage investment and allow a hostile foreign policy? You're kidding yourself if you think American industry is here for any reason other than getting tax benefits and staying on American soil. This Nadal kid is green, but he knows that two and two are four. And that's why he can make inroads into your supporters."

She had hit a sore point.

"You should moderate your enthusiasm for Prudencio Nadal, señora. He has as little use for American labor leaders as for American businessmen. And the last two weeks have shown that he has a violent way of expressing his dislikes."

Annie's brusque gesture bordered on the indecent. "That for Nadal! I listened to him for a week. He's another elitist, just like you. If the workers don't agree with him, then they have to be educated. If the voters aren't ready to jettison the commonwealth, it's because they've been hypnotized by the father figure of Muñoz. Bah!" She leaned forward, peering intently at her companion. "Take a good look at me. Do you see anything approaching charisma?"

It was an awkward question for a man with courtly manners, even in the midst of a heated argument. Complete honesty would have compelled Ramírez to admit that he had rarely seen so unprepossessing a woman.

"No," he said.

"Yet I can swing over ten thousand voters any day. Not because I've hypnotized anybody, but because over the long haul I've been right more often than I've been wrong. And people notice little things like that. You and Nadal should stop talking about education and mesmerism and consider another possibility. Maybe Puerto Ricans are right and you're wrong!"

Happily this was something Ramírez could deal with.

"No stateman," he said, figuratively wrapping himself in his mantle of greatness, "has ever been led by the people. By the very nature of things, he must lead them."

Annie cast her mind back over recent history. "I wouldn't be too sure of that. From where I sit, it looks an awful lot as if somebody has been leading you and Nadal and the Governor right where he wants to."

20. Notions

Volumes have been written explaining how to attain success in business as well as in life. They all append simple infallible rules. Build a better mousetrap, give the public what it wants, tighten the chain of command, watch the overhead, prune the deadwood, THINK—the list of precepts is endless. Both life and business have become too complex for anything so primitive as the Ten Commandments.

John Thatcher was skeptical of most rules of thumb. The supporting evidence was always so scanty. Doctors told him that eating wheat germ improved executive decision-making; business schools told him that charting break-evens guaranteed profits. Everything, of course, is possible but Thatcher had doubts about wheat germ, let alone those charts.

Nevertheless, the years had given him considerable experience with success, and he had some thoughts of his own on the subject. Success in life and business, as in football, came more often than not to those who kept their eye on the ball. A specific goal, distinctly defined and unwaveringly pursued, went far toward solving all intervening problems.

Annie Galiano was an illustration. She had blown into Puerto Rico ready to take on all comers. After laying about her mightily, did she pause to take breath? She did not. She had charged off to remind Puerto Rico of her political clout and, from what Thatcher heard, to level Francisco Ramírez Rivera in passing. Diverse as these activities might seem, however, they were not detours: all of Annie Galiano's will and energy at every moment was focused on one unmistakable cause—the health and vigor of the ILGWU.

The Sloan Guaranty Trust, Thatcher was happy to find, inspired in its servants the same single-mindedness—although on a less flamboyant scale. Neither Dudley Humble nor Pete Olmsted was letting outside events distract him. Each was working wholeheartedly for the well-being of the Sloan Guaranty Trust. Even the continuing schism between Commercial Credit and International was not being allowed to rock the boat.

Of course by now, Thatcher could see, Olmsted was not troubling himself with policy implications; Olmsted was concentrating on the Sloan's three-million-dollar loan to Slax Unlimited.

He was growing seriously worried about it.

"It's a goddam mess!" he said. "David's running off to New York has really put the lid on things! Oh, hi, Dud!"

"John and I are just off to attend that symposium about the free port," said Dudley Humble, consulting his watch. "We don't want to be late." Humble was trying hard to keep Slax and its manifold problems from monopolizing Thatcher during this fortuitous return to Hato Rey. "We're due at the Caribe Hilton any minute, Pete. This is a steering committee to get the move for the free port organized."

"Nobody's making any decisions," said Olmsted, still absorbed in his own concerns. "What about next fall's line? What about reorders? Norma's just sitting on everything. But she still insists they're not going to sell."

"It's really inevitable, is it?" Thatcher commented. "That Slax is going to have to sell off the Bayamón plant?"

Olmsted scowled. "Let me put it this way, John," he said. "If they don't sell soon, things are going to stop being bad and start being lousy. The Sloan may find itself owning a pants shop yet!"

Thatcher recognized hyperbole, but Humble took foreclosures seriously. "Good God, Pete," he said, "haven't you explained the situation to Mrs. Lippert?"

Olmsted took a deep breath. "I've explained until I'm blue in the face. So have Marten and Aguilera. So did David—before he beat it. But there's a limit to what anyone can say, you know. You can't tell a woman that the real reason she should sell is that her husband is a dummy."

Thatcher recalled another view of Norma and David Lippert. "What about Annie Galiano's remark? She said Norma wanted to get David out of town."

"Oh, there's no doubt about that," Olmsted replied. "You heard Cesar and Eric. Norma's gone crazy. She's shipped David off to New York. She won't sell. She won't listen to reason. She's stirring up bad feeling wherever she can."

Thatcher contemplated this catalogue, then asked, "Has she got any justification for being insane with worry? Do you think she can be genuinely alarmed about David?"

"She's genuinely alarmed about something, all right," Olmsted replied. "It may be just that she's afraid David will be the logical scapegoat if Nadal is cleared. On the other hand, everybody knows that the last time he saw them Harry had a fight with the Lipperts—even though they both keep trying to play it down."

Humble had a contribution. "Maybe Mrs. Lippert remembers something about that Monday morning that makes her suspicious of her husband."

Thatcher could see another possibility. "Either that or she's afraid David will remember something that will make him suspicious." He noticed Humble's expression, then added, "Don't underestimate women. You remember what they say about the female of the species?"

"You know, you may be right, John." Olmsted was ready to go one step further. "Norma's a pretty tough cooky underneath. She doesn't let much faze her. I've always wondered if she really fainted the day we found Domínguez' body."

By now, Humble was horrified. He looked significantly at his watch and started to say something, but Olmsted continued.

"When I think of how enthusiastic Harry was about opening up in Puerto Rico," he said, looking sadly into the past. "God, if I had known then what I know now."

This innocuous self-indulgence flicked Humble on the raw. He still was not happy at any mention of Harry Zimmerman's name. It was too apt to remind him of the body he had found.

Then, too, there was the home-town spirit.

"Now, just a minute, Pete," he said. "God knows I sympathize with . . . with you. Slax has been one disaster after another. But Puerto Rico was—and is—a damned smart place to open a garment plant. You know Slax better than I do, and if you say they can't make a go of it, you're right. But somebody else will. So don't blame this on Puerto Rico. Harry Zimmerman could have been run over by a car in New Jersey, you know."

The fight had gone out of Olmsted. "Yeah," he said dispiritedly. "Of course, a lot of trouble started before Harry got it. They had that goddam murder, then the fire and all the sabotage. You don't claim that would have happened in New Jersey, too, do you, Dud?"

"I understand from what I read," said Humble, "that doing business in New Jersey is not always a bed of roses."

Dudley may have been in Puerto Rico too long, thought Thatcher with some amusement.

"You can't believe everything you read, Humble," he advised kindly. "Even about New Jersey."

"Certainly not," said Humble. "I just wanted to point out that student radicals and violence are not peculiar to Puerto Rico."

"No one is claiming they are."

Unexpectedly Olmsted said, "You're right about one thing."

"The radicals?" Humble asked, again looking at his watch.

"Radicals? Oh, them," said Olmsted, in effect waving them away. "No, you're right about the real trouble. It started when Harry got killed. After all, before that happened Slax wasn't in real commercial difficulties. There was no talk about selling."

Thatcher prepared to accompany Humble. He had one more question. "What are they doing at Slax now?" he asked.

"What can they do?" Olmsted asked rhetorically. "On the face of things, everything looks great. All the shifts are running. Cesar's got everything humming. They're sending a shipment up to New York next week. Eric's got that all lined up. Fine and dandy. This way it will take months for David to boot things. He'll louse up orders, lose customers, decide on the wrong models!"

"Well, we'd better be going . . ."

"And how long Cesar and Marten are going to hang around is anybody's guess. They're no fools. They can see the handwriting on the wall. Just let either of them walk out and Norma's really going to find herself in the soup."

Thatcher thought back, while Humble fidgeted meaning-
Lippert sooner than Olmsted expected. Still, since there was
no apparent end to Slax troubles, he said, "Well, I'll look
fully near the door. Things might come to a head for Norma
forward to seeing what happens. Pete. I'm flying back this
evening."

Feelingly, Olmsted told them both that he wished he were, too.

Dudley refrained from comment until they were in the taxi. "I know Pete's under a strain," he said, "but I don't think he's got a balanced picture of Puerto Rico. After all, everything's just about back to normal now."

Idly Thatcher viewed the scenes they were inching past. San Juan presented a crowded, colorful picture. Buses debarked students, shoppers, workers; the honking of automobiles and taxis and trucks filled the air with a cheerful din. On the sidewalks, women sauntered past shop windows. In school yards, children played merrily; vendors peddled fresh fruit at every corner. One of the enduring truths about every great city of the world, thought Thatcher, is that it is strong and resilient—like San Juan. Riots, police, armed Guardsmen, blockades had come; now they were gone. It was as if they never had been.

Thatcher leaned back and asked Humble if the plebiscite was likely to interrupt this peace.

"I keep forgetting that you've gotten a distorted impression of Puerto Rico, too—thanks to Slax," said Humble. "The plebiscite will cause about as much excitement as any election at home. Speeches, advertising—that's it. Puerto Rico doesn't go in for revolutions. As a matter of fact, all of this excitement has nothing to do with the real Puerto Rico. You're going to see that now."

The gathering at the Caribe Hilton was certainly real. Prosperous businessmen, newspaper editors, government officials—they were supporting the drive to have Vieques declared a free port. They were substantial men, and predominantly middle-aged. It was a far cry from the world of Prudencio Nadal.

In fact, Thatcher mused, accepting a name tag for his lapel, he could define the distance more exactly: it was precisely the same as that between Wall Street and the world of SDS.

This distance, of course, was not infinite. For here was the establishment of Puerto Rico. And, of course, only establishments can produce Prudencio Nadals and SDS's. They are, after all, somebody's children. And who else can afford them?

But the real Puerto Rico? Thatcher would only go so far as to say that these well-tailored, hardheaded men were probably a closer and more accurate reflection than was Nadal. Establishments are not all imposed; many are homegrown, with roots that run deep.

He followed Humble into the conference room. Fortunately, their timing was perfect. They arrived too late for introductions, in time for the formalities. First came a deputy director from Fomento. He produced reams of statistics about projected costs, benefits and employment to be realized by Puerto Rico if a free port were established.

". . . additional construction, with housing starts, utilities and other outlays by the private sector. Not only would this produce revenue, it would stimulate further investment. . . ."

Fomento was succeeded by the Chamber of Commerce, with several unwieldy cardboard diagrams.

". . . Now, here, this red line shows the projected rate of profits. Then . . . this dotted line is our projection of the retail space that would be required. If we plan on four thousand persons per thousand dollars . . ."

Finally, there was a representative from the Banco Popular. He was a tall, handsome man, who opened his remarks with a graceful reference to his brethren of the American banking community. He then unfurled a building program suggesting that the Banco Popular intended to keep any new gravy to itself.

Humble leaned forward and listened intently.

Thatcher did not. Instead, he casually inspected the rest of the audience. The American presence was strong. Besides Humble, there were the other bankers, there were delegates from the airlines, from shipping lines, from government offices. But the Puerto Rican element was not dwarfed. Row on row was filled with local businessmen. There were Puerto Rican banks in Hato Rey as well as New York banks; there were locally owned department stores, restaurants and hotels. There were builders, architects, surveyors who had been born on the island. Like businessmen everywhere in the world, these men were here because of a simple, uncomplicated interest in profits. Enormous sums would be made when— and if—Puerto Rico were granted the right to maintain a free port. A golden stream of tourists could be diverted from the Virgin Islands, bringing a boom of major proportions.

Plenty of Puerto Ricans, Thatcher could see, were ready to fight for their fair share.

The Banco Popular yielded to the Governor, who was greeted with a standing ovation.

Thatcher resettled himself and again withdrew his attention. While Prudencio Nadal and his followers spouted half-digested slogans, while Francisco Ramírez Rivera mouthed fuzzy romantic nonsense about *hispanidad,* the presumably firm supporters of the status quo sitting here today were the only ones really willing to fight the Americanization of Puerto Rico. Their armories did not include propaganda, let alone bombs and bullets. They were going to risk dollars and cents. But they were on the front line.

For these men knew that change is inevitable. It cannot be staved off by wishful thinking. Accepting this, they were ready to venture into the arena of economic competition. Others, including the Governor, might settle the questions of form. Substance rested with Puerto Rico's merchants, bankers and businessmen.

"How good are the chances that a free port will be established?" Thatcher asked after the meeting broke up with a stirring peroration from the Governor.

"Dim," said Humble. "In fact, I'd guess that it's very unlikely. We have to attend, of course, to show we're on the side of the angels. But between you and me, I wouldn't bet they'll push it through. And I've read literally dozens of reports about it. Everybody's projecting really tremendous possibilities—but from where I sit, I still think it's pretty visionary."

Thatcher was happy to see that Humble's boosterism was

tempered by realism. This boded well for the Sloan in Hato Rey.

"That's one of life's little problems down here," Humble confided. "Everybody churns out statistics. They're all growth-minded. So you have to take everything with a grain of salt."

This was a fundamental of the banker's creed. Glowing balance sheets emanate from companies whose every asset has been looted; impressively large sums are inscribed on checks for which there have never been sufficient funds. Paper camouflages embezzlement, fraud and even worse crimes.

He should have thought of that before, Thatcher suddenly realized. It was so obvious, in view of some of the things he had been reading. A banker should have seen through one of the anomalies at Slax immediately.

No doubt the police had—as witness Captain Vallejo's return to Bayamón.

But, just as suddenly, two other bankers' comments returned to him. And he was by no means sure that the police *could* have anticipated them.

One had been made by Pete Olmsted, only this morning.

The other, oddly enough, had been enunciated by Bradford Withers.

"Out of the mouths of babes," he murmured incautiously. "No, no, Dudley. I was just thinking aloud."

Two bankers had stated two simple undeniable truths.

This was not much to build on. But perhaps, in the wild tangle of senseless violence and unmotivated evil, it might be the beginning—the loose thread that unravels the knot.

He frowned in thought. There were facts that could substantiate the argument he was postulating.

He looked back over the conversations he had held and the people he had met.

Oddly enough, in each case it was a woman who could answer his question.

21. Threading the Needle

John Thatcher spent a busy and productive evening. Every query was answered except one, and that soon would be.

When he arrived at Hato Rey the following morning, he found Mrs. Schroeder tidying the office. She seemed determined to wipe out every trace of his presence. This fanciful impression was reinforced when she looked up and caught sight of him.

"Mr. Thatcher!" she cried. "I thought you left yesterday."

Although he had more serious matters on his mind, Thatcher noted the true secretary. Here was Mrs. Schroeder—Patsy—a cheerful, bouncy woman. Yet, let her temporary employer take any step of which she was not forewarned, and the air grew heavy with reproach.

"Something important has come up," he replied. "Humble's office has prepared some information for me. Will you see if it's ready, please?"

Within minutes he was scanning a two-page report. The last query was now answered. He thought for a moment, then came to a decision.

"See if you can get hold of Captain Vallejo," he said. "Here is his card. I want to talk to him as soon as possible."

He elicited a reaction worthy of Miss Corsa. Mrs. Schroeder, he could see, did not approve of associating the Sloan with police investigations. On the whole, he did not, either. But it became unavoidable when the Sloan had been made part of a murderer's calculus.

His telephone calls to Señora Aguilera and Annie Galiano —together with Humble's material—left no room for doubt.

Captain Vallejo was cooperative. "Not at all, Mr. Thatcher," he said. "As I told you, I welcome any help you can provide. Perhaps some coffee . . ."

Thatcher agreed, not solely out of deference to Mrs. Schroeder. The coffee shop, with its neutral ambiance, would let his case stand, or fall, on its own merits.

On his way out, Thatcher asked Mrs. Schroeder to tell Miss Corsa that he was staying over.

"I will," she promised.

Briefly, Thatcher debated suggesting that she confine herself to the facts. Then he decided against it. Who was he to deprive people of pleasure? It would give Mrs. Schroeder satisfaction to report that Miss Corsa's Mr. Thatcher was dallying with the police. Presumably Miss Corsa would report that this never happened when Mr. Thatcher was safe in New York. There is too little simple enjoyment in this world.

In the coffee shop, Captain Vallejo's inexpressive countenance did not reveal eagerness. Nonetheless it was there.

"You said you had run across something," he said when the waitress had served them. "About Domínguez?"

It was natural for him to think so, Thatcher realized. He chose his words carefully. "In a way. Yesterday I came across a suggestive connection. I think it may interest you. I have checked it out through a series of, er, personal inquiries. As well as double-checking through some Sloan sources."

Vallejo remained attentive, so Thatcher added, "I believe it does bear on the murder of Benito Domínguez. As well as Harry Zimmerman's. In fact, I don't believe it's too much to say that it explains almost everything that has happened. This is what occurred to me . . ."

Vallejo leaned forward fractionally. He did not interrupt.

Thatcher was concise and well organized. Even so, it took him several minutes to present his thesis. He did not editorialize, except in his conclusion: ". . . from this warped point of view, everything—including two murders—must have seemed eminently reasonable. More than reasonable, inevitable. If at first you don't succeed . . ."

"Ah!" Vallejo expelled a long sigh. Then he too contemplated the train of events started—and finished—with murder. "Yes, I can see that. Each crime occurred because a previous crime failed. Until Harry Zimmerman himself had to be murdered. So now the murderer is successful, is he not?"

Thatcher thought back over some recent conversations.

"That remains to be seen," he said.

Vallejo was following his own train of thought. "Except, of course, now we know who he is. Oh, yes, Mr. Thatcher, I have no doubts. All along, we have concentrated on those who had opportunity to commit these crimes. But we have also searched for a motive. Why? Why do this? We asked questions about families and money."

"Not a bad line to explore," Thatcher said, handing him Humble's report. "As this proves." He did not add that the Sloan Guaranty Trust had more access to the relevant information about *some* families and *some* money than any police force in the world.

"Of course!" said Vallejo, slamming the report on the table with a violence that rattled the cups. "But you remember what I told David Lippert—before his wife sent him beyond our reach?"

"You mean evidence," Thatcher said.

Vallejo nodded. He did not have to labor the point as he had done that night in Cataño. Motive and opportunity were not enough. Where was the proof?

No one had seen murder done.

No one had seen a fire set.

This was what had been worrying Thatcher since he had hung up for the last time yesterday.

"But somebody does know he lied," he pointed out. "In fact, many people do—if they only realized it. He lied again and again."

Vallejo looked disappointed. "You mean, for example, Prudencio Nadal? But he is still at large."

"I was thinking of someone less dramatic," said Thatcher. "Someone reliable, someone who is completely credible."

Like, for example, Annie Galiano.

But it was the big lie that was critical. And Thatcher thought he knew how to pinpoint it.

"I don't know his name," he said. "But I've been reviewing everything that's happened since the Domínguez murder. And I believe there is one man who can help us—the man who sent the last shipment from the warehouse the day of the fire."

"Wilfredo Moreno," said Captain Vallejo promptly. "The freight forwarder. We talked to him."

"You were asking him the wrong questions," Thatcher

commented. "The right questions should give you something very different."

Captain Vallejo was already halfway out of his chair.

Wilfredo Moreno, a telephone call established, was not at his office. He had taken the day off. His son's family was visiting from Fajardo.

So Thatcher found himself accompanying Vallejo to a large house tucked around the corner from the downtown shopping area. Shuttered against the midmorning sun, it looked forbidding. But inside there was life abundant. While Vallejo and Thatcher waited in the small square sitting room, a rather flustered matron went off to find the master of the house. Voices, laughter, music drifted back to them. Wilfredo Moreno's family was large and high-spirited.

"Gentlemen?" he said, bustling in to greet them with no sign of irritation at this interruption.

Captain Vallejo apologized and explained that a matter of high importance forced them to intrude.

"Sit down, sit down," said Moreno, who was a small, genial man. "I confess I am curious, but you will explain. Any way I can assist you, I will. Although I can assure you, Captain, that I tried scrupulously to tell you everything I know."

"It was I who neglected to ask the correct questions." Vallejo apologized again.

Thatcher was beginning to wonder how long these courtesies could go on, when Captain Vallejo introduced him and asked him to explain their interest in freight forwarding.

Rarely had Thatcher had a more enthralled audience. Moreno punctuated his dry recital with little cries. Finally, when Thatcher finished, he burst out: "But yes! What you suggest is exactly true! But what consummate villainy! To use me as a cat's-paw!"

Both Vallejo and Thatcher were taken aback.

"And this explains much that puzzled me about Señor Zimmerman!" Moreno was gathering steam when another idea came to him. "So my son was right, after all! The radicals did not create this trouble! Words fail me."

But he was ready to continue, so Vallejo cut in. "And yet the murderer may escape unpunished!"

"Unthinkable!"

"Unless you, Señor Moreno, will consent to assist us."

Moreno swelled. "Any way I can help see justice done. I am but a humble businessman. But I will not be used! In the cause of honor, no one shall say that Wilfredo Moreno held back. My esteem and respect for Señor Zimmerman—"

Vallejo was forced to break in again, to explain what they wanted.

"It will not take you from your family long," he concluded. "But it is essential."

Moreno rose. "First I shall inform my wife."

He left on a Napoleonic note.

"We are lucky," said Vallejo softly. "First, that he has no doubt about his acting ability. And second that he is willing to help the police trap a murderer."

He did not have to tell Thatcher that not everybody is.

"Señores," said Moreno, back once again and dressed formally for the occasion, "I place myself at your disposal!"

". . . and so, of course, you see why I have been disturbed," Moreno was telling the phone not long afterward. "I explained this very carefully to Señor Zimmerman—excuse me if I raise a subject that I know must be painful for you. He understood that there must have been some confusion. But now that Señor Zimmerman is gone, I wish Slax to understand my position."

Like the good actor that he was, he did not glance at the reel of tape recording every word he said, every response he evoked. Nor did he glance at the men around him. Moreno might have been at his desk, making a business call. He was in fact at police headquarters in San Juan.

"Yes," he continued. "I value my association with Slax and do not wish to see it imperiled. . . . Ah, you can assure me that my position is understood? Good. . . . And no one is under any misapprehension? Excellent. You will understand what relief that brings me. I very much appreciate your words. Accept again . . ."

When he finished, he looked around with pride. "There!" he said. "I believe that is what you requested. My only regret is that we do not hang people like this. Ah, well, it does not do to dwell on the darker side of life. You must excuse me. I return to my house. My grandsons expect me to show them El Morro. Youth must be served. . . ."

He was still talking when Vallejo escorted him to the car that would speed him home.

"One of God's happy ones," Vallejo commented when he returned. He flicked on the recorder.

This time they could hear both sides of the conversation. The murderer too was businesslike.

"Although it must have been a blow," Thatcher said, rising, "to realize that Moreno could blow the story sky-high."

Vallejo revealed a certain gallows humor. "Not so much of a blow as it will be when I arrive," he said with an echo of Moreno's magniloquence, "with a warrant!"

With Vallejo proceeding to Bayamón and an arrest, Thatcher returned to Hato Rey. He had no particular desire to be in Puerto Rico when someone he had known was branded a cold-blooded murderer, but one more task awaited him before he could turn northward to the tranquillity of Wall Street. Someone had to prepare Pete Olmsted for this latest blow.

By now, Mrs. Schroeder was projecting heavy resignation.

"I spoke to Miss Corsa," she said when he arrived. "She wants to remind you that you have an important appointment tomorrow afternoon."

Only years of practice kept Thatcher from sounding defensive. "I hope I'll be catching the evening plane," he said crisply. "Will you please see if you can locate Olmsted for me? He may be out in Bayamón. Wherever he is, I want to see him."

She took note. Then: "Mrs. Lippert called, too. I had to tell her that I didn't know when to expect you."

"If she calls again, repeat it," he said. Today he did not want to talk to Norma Zimmerman Lippert.

"Shall I call Miss Corsa?"

"Just get Olmsted," he ordered, striding past. It was a good thing this whole Puerto Rican episode was winding up. He scented an alliance between Miss Corsa and Mrs. Schroeder in the offing.

Fortunately, Olmsted had just come into the building. "Still here?" he asked incuriously.

"Have you been out at Slax this morning?" Thatcher asked abruptly.

Olmsted dropped into a chair. "Where else? I keep going

through the motions. But what good does it do? Now they're not even turning up at the office. Norma's running around telling every crazy story that pops into her head. Cesar's out somewhere. Probably still trying to find another job. Eric is chasing around looking for a warehouse—"

"What?" Thatcher said sharply. "Are you saying that there was nobody out in Bayamón?"

Olmsted nodded. "Nobody but the foremen. The plant is running okay. But what kind of way is that to run— John?"

Thatcher was obviously not listening. An hour ago, the murderer had been at Slax, taking a business call from Wilfredo Moreno. Now the murderer was somewhere else . . .

A chilling thought assailed him.

"John, what's the matter?" Olmsted demanded.

Thatcher was already at the door.

"Mrs. Schroeder," he barked, "I want you to call Wilfredo Moreno's home. He lives somewhere in the Santurce district. I don't believe he's there—but find out. And if not, make them tell you where he is. And—" he broke off for a moment —"make sure they don't give the information to anybody else."

"But, Mr. Thatcher!" she protested, scandalized.

This was no time for protocol.

"Say you're from the police, if necessary," he said. "And hurry."

Could he be wrong? Perhaps the killer had not been alarmed by Moreno. But two murders already made it too great a risk to take.

In minutes, his premonition was amply confirmed. Señora Moreno was as voluble as her husband. No, Wilfredo was not at home. He had taken Armando and Felipe to El Morro. She would have him call back—unless this was the party who had called earlier . . .

"Too late," Thatcher muttered. "Now, Mrs. Schroeder, you call the police right now and repeat this to them. Tell them to get in touch with Captain Vallejo."

He grasped Olmsted's arm and was steering him toward the door when she called after them. "Where will you be, Mr. Thatcher?"

"Yes," Olmsted began, "where—?"

"El Morro," said John Putnam Thatcher ferociously.

22. Gather at the Neck

Meanwhile, Captain Vallejo was striding out of Slax in a bad temper, mocking the refrain he had just heard.

"No, no one is here. No, I do not know . . ."

"Stupid girls," he grumbled to himself. Vallejo had been balked too long to be patient now. He was reviewing a list of places where he might run his quarry to ground when his driver waved to get his attention.

The radio was stuttering out a message.

Vallejo barely had time to assimilate Thatcher's information when another operator broke in. His voice was choked with excitement.

"All cars . . . all cars . . ."

Prudencio Nadal had been sighted in Old San Juan.

Wilfredo Moreno was just parking his car beneath the imposing walls of El Morro. Beside him, two little boys sat wide-eyed.

"Ah hah!" he said. "It is something to see, is it not? Now, what can you tell me about El Morro?"

Armando and Felipe were struck dumb.

"Shameful," said their grandfather severely, taking each by the hand and starting up the path. "I shall have to tell you."

El Morro is the mighty fortress commanding the heights over the narrow channel that leads into San Juan harbor. Bestriding the headland, El Morro is the very embodiment of history. Once the guns of English and Dutch men-of-war challenged its batteries. Once Sir Francis Drake ran the gauntlet of its artillery.

Today, El Morro is a monument. The ships passing below are tankers and freighters; the sparkling Atlantic is dotted with dazzling sailboats, scudding before the wind. Imperial Spain is a memory.

Yet El Morro is still a cause for wonder, even to visitors older than Armando and Felipe. Towering above the sea, with walls ten and sometimes twenty feet thick, it is almost a world of its own, from dark dungeons far below to the lighthouse that rears above the whole sprawling complex. Soldiers of Spain lived and worked here, in barracks and storerooms. They prayed here in the chapel; they stood guard on the parapets. There are towers and turrets, stairways and ramps. And there are cannons—silent, rusting, yet still menacing.

"Now, you must promise to be good," said Moreno, leading his charges under the great arch that is El Morro's entrance. "Bad boys could be lost if they wander away. Or if they run up and down the stairs, they could get hurt."

Armando and Felipe promised fervently to be good.

"Excellent," said their grandfather.

El Morro was too majestically isolated on its promontory for them to hear the wail of the sirens that were beginning to snake through the narrow streets of the city behind them.

Captain Vallejo was swearing to himself as his driver cut in front of other traffic on the expressway.

The radio was rapping out a barrage of calls.

". . . Car Thirty-three . . . to the corner of Calle Luna . . ."

"Car Fourteen now proceeding through Santurce . . ."

Calls were bursting forth every second. The operators sounded electric. And why not? Every policeman in San Juan had been waiting for this moment.

Angrily Vallejo reached for the hand microphone.

"Vallejo here," he snapped. "Get somebody to El Morro . . ."

But did it get through the babble of voices?

"Riot patrols ordered to the Plaza de Armas . . ."

". . . at the bridge . . ."

Vallejo rapped out an obscenity, then turned savagely to his driver. "Switch on that siren!"

"At this rate, we're never going to get there," said Thatcher when Olmsted jammed to a halt. Traffic was at a standstill. Somewhere up ahead, out of sight, there was an obstruction.

Olmsted was sweating. Thatcher did not think it was because of the heat.

"I can't believe it," he repeated.

Thatcher's synopsis had floored him.

"You've said that before," Thatcher reminded him. "Does that mean you think we're on a fool's errand?"

Olmsted replied by jerking the car into motion, forcing a truck onto the curb as he swung wide.

It was a grim prospect. A decent, innocent man stalked by someone who did not hesitate to kill.

Thatcher preferred not to think of the two grandsons.

Olmsted cocked his head to the window. "Do you hear what I hear?" he said.

Somewhere behind them, a police siren was howling.

"I hope that means that Mrs. Schroeder got through to Vallejo," Thatcher said.

"If she did," Olmsted commented, "this sets a record for efficiency in Puerto Rico."

Thatcher checked his watch. Olmsted was quite right. Behind them another siren sounded.

The murderer was just entering Old San Juan when his rear-view mirror reflected the flashing light of a squad car. His hands tightened briefly on the steering wheel. Then the police sped past. He relaxed. There was no sign of anxiety on his face.

He drove on. By now he was almost drained of human emotion. He had become an automaton, doing what had to be done—no matter what it was.

Just now, he had to remove one man who could reveal a lie.

It had been a mistake, he thought. Almost everything had been a mistake.

Nothing had gone according to plan, he thought with the rage that gripped him more and more compulsively. They had made him continue—by their obstinate stupidity.

Norma . . .

He shook his head slightly. He would take care of Norma too, when the time came. Now he had to concentrate on Wilfredo Moreno. It should not be difficult. It could be made to look like an accident.

Things could always be disguised.

Another squad car sped past. Something must be going on,

the murderer thought. He considered this; then, without haste, he turned toward the parking lot near the post office. Old San Juan was crowded. Americans forsaking their hotels, Brazilian sailors on shore leave, schoolchildren, messenger boys, loiterers. The narrow streets were thronged.

It would be safer to continue on foot.

He parked the car. As he did so, a motorcycle trooper sped up to a bored patrolman, leaned forward and spoke urgently.

The murderer saw them, then started walking. Toward El Morro.

Hundreds of policemen were pouring into Old San Juan, in squad cars, in trucks, in patrol wagons. Up and down the streets, policemen were hammering on doors, walking through bars and restaurants, examining the pedestrians.

"If Prudencio Nadal is indeed nearby," said one sergeant, directing his men to spread out, "he can spend his life here. It would take an army— yes, Captain?"

Vallejo's car had finally gotten through. "Get some men up to El Morro," he snapped.

The sergeant was embarrassed. "My orders—" he began.

"Damn your orders!" Vallejo roared. "Get some men up there or else!"

"But, Captain . . ."

The murderer had reached the top of the hill. He paused, looking behind him with a frown. Police were everywhere, more and more of them. Resolutely he pushed on.

The guard at the sentry box waved him through.

The murderer began walking up the long tree-lined roadway. He did not see the small boys flying kites over the ocean. He did not see the tourist buses parking.

He saw only El Morro rising ahead of him.

"If this is what your pal Vallejo produced," Olmsted said disgustedly, "I think he may be overdoing."

They were backed up behind squad cars, motorcycle police and units of the riot squad.

"I'm beginning to wonder," said Thatcher. "Why are so many police milling around here? Unless they're trying to cut him off."

Olmsted inched ahead. "The place to cut him off is up there," he said.

"You're right," said Thatcher.

The murderer paused, dwarfed by the ramparts above him. As he stood there, a group of schoolchildren swept past him into the fortress.

Four Americans were taking pictures of each other, first posed before the walls, then silhouetted against the sea.

They smiled at him.

He smiled back, and went inside.

"Finally!" said Thatcher a minute later. They had managed to push through the clogged city to the windswept approaches of El Morro. But his satisfaction was short-lived. As Olmsted raced up to the walls and parked, there were no signs of police activity here.

The Americans were still taking pictures. They looked up and smiled at the two men hurtling past.

Thatcher and Olmsted did not smile back.

For a moment they hesitated. The office was filled to overflowing with schoolchildren, organizing for a tour. The guides were fully occupied.

"You go that way," said Thatcher, leading Olmsted to the courtyard. He pointed to stairs on their left as he himself set off toward the right.

Nuns. Some American teenagers. A Puerto Rican family with a small baby.

He did not see Wilfredo Moreno—or the murderer.

He looked up. There were figures on the parapets, figures up by the lighthouse.

". . . and here," Moreno was saying authoritatively after surreptitiously memorizing the plaque, "this lighthouse. It is not the original. Do you know what that means, Armando?"

He was not a baby, Armando said.

"Fine. This was built by the Americans. Their guns destroyed the original. So you see . . ."

Suddenly a shadow fell across his path. Moreno turned, then stiffened.

The murderer stood there, ten feet away.

Nothing was said.

"Boys," said Moreno, his voice suddenly lifeless. "Go down to the courtyard." He saw the murderer shift. "Go look at the cannonballs."

Armando and Felipe scampered off.

Moreno remained where he was. He knew quite well he was looking at death. The murderer took a step forward.

Moreno backed away.

Thatcher rounded a corner, struggling for breath. Climbing to the heights of El Morro had been more strenuous than he expected. If Wilfredo Moreno was not here . . .

Thatcher froze.

The tableau before him was nightmarish—brilliant sunshine, the ramparts overlooking the sea and, in the distance, groups of tourists looking, gasping, chattering.

But in the foreground were two men tied to each other by silence and fear.

The murderer took another step.

Thatcher shouted a name against the wind and started forward.

No one heard him.

From the ramp leading to the far side of the lighthouse platform, there was an authoritative clatter. Captain Vallejo and three of his men pounded up into view.

The murderer's spell was broken. Moreno, with an inarticulate cry, clawed at the wall. The murderer's head whipped around. Then he pivoted and ran.

"Stop him!"

"Halt!"

"Bring him down!"

They were too late. He was already clambering to the top of the battlement. Another instant and he had pushed himself into space.

Far, far below lay the rocky pits from which El Morro's stone had been quarried.

23. Stitch, Stitch, Stitch

It was nearly a month since Eric Marten's suicide.

"I suppose I should have realized earlier that Eric was behind everything," Cesar Aguilera said thoughtfully.

"That's why he laid down such a heavy political smoke screen," Thatcher replied. "Like a conjuror, he had to rely on misdirection. Most of us were looking the wrong way for too long."

He looked around the table affably and decided that the overriding character of Seventh Avenue, where they were lunching, had been set for all time. He and Olmsted, Aguilera and Annie Galiano, were all eating cheese blintzes.

Pete Olmsted was bearing out the official Sloan assessment of his abilities. Slow but sure, they said affectionately down in Commercial Credit, that's our Pete. He may take a while getting there, but he covers all the ground.

"I don't see how you can say that," he protested. "I would have gone on looking that way forever. The one thing that seemed clear about the troubles at Slax was that the Radical Independents were involved."

Thatcher shook his head. "No. When you stopped to think—and of course Marten tried to keep the pace of events so rapid that you didn't—what evidence was there linking the radicals to Slax? There was the membership card found in Benito Domínguez' pocket, there was a sheet of paper pinned to the watchman's shirt at the warehouse, there was a kidnap note sent to the editor of a newspaper."

"That is not entirely a fair summary." Cesar Aguilera was looking at scenes from the past. "It is easy to see that you were not in Bayamón when several hundred students descended, calling for a strike."

Automatically, Annie snorted.

"I know the students emerged then, after Slax had made

headlines with the Domínguez murder. But let me leave that for a moment and finish this point." Thatcher turned to Olmsted. "The evidence was all paper evidence, Pete. More important, it was a series of unconfirmed statements by the writer. That's the kind of evidence you never accept in business dealings. If a corporation tells you that it has fourteen million dollars in assets, you ask for corroboration by an independent auditor. If somebody offers to pay you with a check for ten thousand dollars, you don't accept it until his bank says that he has funds to cover it."

Olmsted thought he had spotted a flaw in this reasoning. "Those are self-serving statements. If somebody admits he's just been fired for incompetence or he's just come out of jail, he's not likely to be lying."

"Has it occurred to you, Pete, that there are different views of self-serving statements? Just as there are different views of laudable actions. Eric Marten was clever enough to realize that the students would not publicly disassociate themselves from the harassment of an American company until too late. In fact, they played into his hands until the roar of protest at the kidnapping."

· Olmsted munched his way to a solemn conclusion. "Good God! I never thought of it, but there are probably lots of students in Cambridge and Berkeley boasting to their parents about taking part in riots they watched from the sidelines."

"Exactly. The documents linking the radicals to Slax might be valid, but there was nothing on their face to make them so. And one thing we know is that anyone could pick up a good deal of radical material. Membership cards are casually issued at meetings, flyers are handed out on street corners, material is sent through the mail."

Annie Galiano was enthusiastically scraping sour cream from a small bowl. She paused, spoon in hand, to intervene. "But you can look at something besides the paperwork. Cesar says the kids turned out in force for the strike agitation. But that proves your point, in a way. There was nothing to show they ever heard of Slax until the newspapers carried the story of Domínguez' murder. There was nothing to show they knew of the fire in Cataño or Harry's disappearance until after these things were public."

Thatcher beamed at her. He was in a good mood. That

morning the Sloan had severed its ties with Slax Unlimited. For good, he hoped.

"Once you approached the subject with an open mind, there were many questions you could ask."

Cesar Aguilera was inclined to take that as personal criticism.

"You mean that I should have asked these questions?" His handsome face clouded. "I think perhaps you are right."

The others immediately applied themselves to the task of lifting his spirits.

"Christ, Cesar, you had enough on your plate keeping the plant running," Olmsted said stoutly. "And you did a damn good job."

Annie took a more belligerent line. "Handling the Lipperts is a full-time job by itself."

Thatcher thought the best thing he could do was hurry on. "If you had been sitting miles away with nothing else to do, you would have come to the same conclusion I did several weeks later. You would have looked at the character of the sabotage itself."

"Like all sabotage, it was designed to do as much damage as possible." Olmsted was so anxious to support the diversion from Aguilera that he spoke too quickly.

"That's not true. After all, what are we celebrating today?"

Pete looked puzzled. "We've just signed all the papers on the sale of the Bayamón plant by Slax Unlimited," he said warily.

"Put it another way," Thatcher advised. "A perfectly standard garment factory, in good working condition, has been sold."

He might have known that this would awaken partisan instincts.

"We've saved the jobs of three hundred and fifty garment workers without a single hour's layoff," said Annie Galiano piously. This had been her chief, but not her only, concern during the negotiations.

"Puerto Rico now has a modern garment factory which is fifty percent American-owned and fifty percent Puerto Rican-owned." Aguilera's white teeth glinted briefly as he relaxed into the vernacular: "And I'm in charge of the whole shebang."

Olmsted happily flipped a blintz onto its side. "And the Sloan has recovered its three million from the purchase price."

"Yes, yes!" Thatcher might have been waving away a swarm of gnats. "My point, however, was that there is a garment factory to sell, and one without substantial damage. Which is rather surprising, if you accept the theory that it has been the target of sustained attacks by Nadal and his followers. They don't specialize in subtle methods. Puerto Rican students have thrown bombs before. And with an inside man like Domínguez to help them, they could have leveled the plant. Instead, what do we find? A good deal of harm to finished goods, to supplies, to a warehouse. It was almost as if the factory itself were being carefully preserved."

"All right, I'll grant you that," Annie conceded. "But there had to be an inside man. That business of changing the thread on the bobbins was done by someone who knew his business. Are you telling me Domínguez didn't do that?"

It was Aguilera who answered. "I doubt it. I have doubted it since acid was used at the warehouse. What bothered me about the saboteur was his mobility. Domínguez was a foreman. He didn't have anything to do with the warehouse."

"Already we have established a good deal about the saboteur," Thatcher summarized. "He was someone in the garment business, someone who moved freely between Slax's various sites and someone who did not wish to destroy the basic value of the plant. He does not sound like a promising recruit to Prudencio Nadal's organization. You could add that Slax was never a reasonable choice for a radical assault. What do students all over the world attack? They concentrate on the big, visible symbols of the establishment they oppose—universities, the military, defense contractors, the government. On balance, I was inclined to decide that this saboteur had nothing to do with the Radical Independents. What, then, was his motive? That brought me to two interesting statements made by Brad Withers."

Olmsted goggled.

"Withers?" he repeated unbelievingly.

Before the outside world, Thatcher thought it best to ignore this incredulity.

"Brad," he said firmly, "in reviewing everything that happened up to the kidnapping, said that the only change, after everything settled down, would be the sale of one garment factory at distress prices. Then you, later on, said that Slax could weather sabotage. It was Zimmerman's murder that forced the sale of Bayamón. Naturally, that made me think. If there was to be only one significant result, maybe that was what the murderer had in mind all along. Furthermore, it explained the death of Benito Domínguez. As we have all agreed, the radicals didn't even know anything was going on until his murder. But when they learned of it, they reacted precisely as Eric Marten planned. He had taken Prudencio Nadal's measure very accurately."

Annie shoved aside an empty plate. "That," she pointed out, "isn't very hard to do. Nadal thought the Domínguez murder was a gift from heaven."

"I doubt if he'd phrase it that way. And I suppose it was irresistible to him. A Puerto Rican, who has been described by the press as a Radical Independent, has been murdered in an American plant. The implication is plain that management fired the gun. Prudencio Nadal doesn't stop to think. He swallows the story whole and organizes demonstrations at Bayamón, embracing Domínguez as a martyr to the cause for independence. So far, everything has gone according to Marten's plan. At this point, he hits two snags."

"Two?" asked Annie, who did not suffer from false modesty.

Thatcher was gracious. "You, of course, were the big one. But I think Nadal himself was a disappointment to Marten. Oh, I don't mean in losing his rounds with you. I mean in his generally peaceful approach to the situation. Marten, I am afraid, was overimpressed by Prudencio Nadal's publicity. He expected some kind of revolutionary ferment—trucks overturned, buildings occupied, all work effectively halted. He did not allow for the fact that Nadal was out of place in a garment factory. Nadal instinctively recognized that tactics appropriate in a university would be wrong at Slax. I know you don't have a high opinion of the boy, but he recognized from the start that he had to win the sympathy of the workers. He could not count on the carefree indulgence he would get from students. When you close a university, you are not taking bread from the mouths of the students. He knew that the only way he could usefully close Slax was by having the workers do it themselves. And you took care of that, very neatly. All Nadal could do was retreat. And he did. Give him that much credit."

"Sure," said Annie generously.

Cesar Aguilera emerged from his coffee cup. "I confess I discounted Nadal myself. But I was not so ready to dismiss politics entirely. For a while, I found myself suspicious of Dr. Ramírez. It was clear that Prudencio Nadal was being lured beyond his depth. And I asked myself who would profit from this. One answer was that Ramírez was smearing a potential opponent. When we all left the Convento to watch the fire, all of us except Ramírez, I wondered if he had no need to follow us. Most *independistas* in Puerto Rico are opposed to violence, indeed they are afraid of it. The fire would have disgusted many people with Nadal."

"What did you think when the kidnap note came?" Thatcher asked curiously.

"Then I knew Ramírez was out of the picture entirely. He was bound to suffer from the consequences. The whole independence movement had been discredited."

The plebiscite returns, which had been announced the day before, made further discussion unnecessary. The independence vote had been minuscule.

"I came to the same conclusion about Ramírez," Thatcher said. "Quite clearly, he is not a man to undertake violence. Moving behind the scenes, making alliances, exerting pressure—those are the tactics he would employ."

"He sees himself as an ambassador to the United Nations," Annie said with vast contempt.

There was so much sinister meaning in her voice that Thatcher would have liked to pursue the topic, but Pete Olmsted had no intention of leaving the tale unfinished.

"All right," he allowed, "so politics was out. Somebody was going to buy Bayamón at rock-bottom prices. But who? I can see Marten doing it. But then I could make out a reason for David Lippert doing it, particularly with Harry's murder. Excuse me, Cesar, but you could have done it. And for a while I almost convinced myself that Norma had wiped Domínguez out as the easiest way of getting Slax back to normal."

Thatcher became meditative. "I think you'll find that some of your suspicions cancel each other out, Pete. Norma had no motive for the sabotage, and no one has denied that she was genuinely attached to her brother. If she murdered Domínguez, then nothing else was explained. David had a motive for murdering Harry Zimmerman, but not for the sabotage. It was the sabotage that was the thread linking everything together. If you refused to be distracted from the sabotage, then there were only two reasonable suspects." He smiled apologetically at Aguilera. "You and Marten. And with Zimmerman's murder, there was no longer any choice at all."

"I follow you down to the two," Olmsted said doggedly, "but there you lose me. Harry must have found something out, so Harry was murdered. That's the way it looks to me, but it doesn't eliminate anybody."

Cesar took up the case against himself with some gusto. "That is correct. Harry was upset all that day, we have any amount of evidence to that effect. But he had started the morning by quarreling with David. That may have accounted for it. We cannot assume he discovered anything."

"Come, now. The David argument won't wash. Zimmerman was always finding some mistake by his brother-in-law. We know how he reacted." Thatcher ticked off the possibilities. "Either he decided to ignore David's sensitivities and solve the problem, in which case everyone at Slax heard about it, or he decided peace in the family was more important. His intention to leave Puerto Rico right away suggested that David's feelings had won this time. We have every right to assume Zimmerman discovered something, because something very unusual happened that Monday."

"The fire," Annie supplied.

It was rare enough that Annie Galiano made an error. Thatcher rather enjoyed putting her right.

"No," he said genially. "Zimmerman was dead before the fire. You have forgotten that fifty thousand dollars' worth of finished goods moved unexpectedly out of the Cataño warehouse. And Harry Zimmerman was at the docks that morning. It was afterward that he launched into his abnormal activity. We now know what happened. He went to the freight forwarder's office to complain. There he learned that no effort at all had been made to move the stalled goods. Zimmerman did not need a diagram. He knew immediately that Eric Marten was doing the unforgivable. He was holding back shipments, destroying good will, losing customers. At best. I expect that Zimmerman could have predicted a fire at that moment. He went into action on the spot. First he ordered the freight forwarder to take immediate action. Then he headed for San Juan and a showdown with Marten. He should have been more careful in tangling with a murderer."

"But," Olmsted protested, "Harry said he was going to the ILGWU."

"Where he expected to find Marten," Thatcher retorted. "If you think back to Zimmerman's schedule, it all makes sense. Sunday evening, before anything had happened and when he still thought he had plenty of time in Puerto Rico, he promised Annie that Marten would look over some details in the union agreement. Right?"

Mutely Pete Olmsted nodded.

"Monday morning Zimmerman's schedule changes," Thatcher rolled on remorselessly. "He fights with the Lipperts and decides on an early departure. His next stop is Bayamón, where he sees Eric Marten. Marten, remember, is going to San Juan only a few blocks from the ILGWU office. Zimmerman, who wants everything ironed out before he leaves, tells Marten to check over the agreement. He admits to a fight with David. Then, probably because he is still irritated and wants to take it out on somebody, he goes to the freight forwarder. At that point, all his thinking changes."

Aguilera had been following the recital intently. Now he nodded suddenly. "That explains something that has always puzzled me. When he called me from the docks, Harry said nothing about leaving that day. He did ask me about the snarl at the freight forwarder, but I thought he was simply annoyed that David had left all that to Marten."

"He had abandoned all thought of leaving Puerto Rico. That's why he didn't mention it to you or to Pete when he stopped at the Sloan. He intended to corner Marten at the ILGWU and have things out with him. Of course, as soon as he saw Annie's empty office and heard she wasn't there, he knew Eric wasn't there, either."

"It's a shame I wasn't there," Annie reflected. "I would have gotten the whole story out of Harry in five minutes."

"And settled Eric Marten's hash in another five, I'm sure," Thatcher rejoined gallantly.

"Well, then, what did happen?" Olmsted impatiently rose above this exchange.

"I imagine he met Marten on the street. Remember, Marten was just leaving an appointment two blocks away, and Marten drove himself into San Juan. They probably got into Marten's car and within a very few minutes Marten knew that his only salvation lay in murdering Zimmerman and tying it in with an atrocity by radical students."

"You mean Harry just got into a car with a murderer?" Olmsted protested.

"I doubt if he was thinking of Marten as a murderer. He was thinking of him as a sabotage expert. Zimmerman wasn't in Puerto Rico when Domínguez was murdered, and he was always more concerned with the attack on Slax. Nor had he given up the idea that Nadal was the prime mover. He may well have thought of Marten as a paid tool of the radicals."

"It makes sense," Annie said almost grudgingly. "And it left Marten wide open on the freight-forwarder story."

"Yes, that's why he went berserk at the end. Nothing could explain away the anomalies there. Freight forwarders who are being pushed for action don't suddenly make a major shipment without telling anyone. Marten was stunned, after the fire, when he found out what Harry had done. He knew that, if anyone started looking in his direction, there were too many clues for comfort."

"Such as?" Annie demanded.

"Whom would Zimmerman be looking for at the ILGWU, other than you? Aguilera was always at the plant. That was his job. His very immobility made it unlikely that he was the saboteur, or that he had any meeting with Harry anywhere except in Bayamón. The Lipperts were not having anything to do with the ILGWU settlement, or with you. And, in spite of the fantasy about an invitation from Prudencio Nadal, Zimmerman was in no mood for meetings under the second oak tree from the left. If he had consented to see the boy at all, it would have been at the office. Then we come to the fiesta. Eric Marten was the one wandering around alone. He said he was escaping from his wife's cultural activities, but he was late to dinner, too. He had ample time to set the fire. And it was there, at the fiesta, that he tried to dodge Annie's question about coming up to the ILGWU offices."

Annie was getting into the spirit of things. "Then there was the talk about looking for a job. Everybody kept saying that Cesar was looking for a job. Why wasn't Eric?"

"I never thought of that," Pete Olmsted admitted. "He had his job already planned, hadn't he?"

"I think so," Thatcher said. "I had a few words with Señora Aguilera and she gave me a good deal of information about Marten's in-laws."

Cesar grinned. "Elena told me about that. You couldn't have gone to a better source. Of course, Marten's in-laws were all eager for a good investment. He would have had no trouble forming a company, taking over Bayamón and continuing as manager, if not part owner. As a matter of fact, I did understand that part of his behavior. He was quite wild when Norma decided not to sell. It was not difficult to guess that he was planning to make a rock-bottom offer. But I thought he was simply exploiting a situation someone else had brought about."

"Eric Marten was not the man to wait for chance to provide exploitable situations. He created his own." Thatcher paused. "The mystery to me is that he took so long to develop into a murderer."

"Elena has a theory about that." Aguilera searched for words with which to express his wife's swooping flights into speculation. "She says that until recently he was content to drift. You know he had spent his whole life in the islands, wandering from one to another. Then, a year ago, he married and became part of a clan. Elena thinks his vision of himself changed. He was ready to become a man of substance, a patriarch. And that role did not include being an employee. I know he began to resent having to recognize David as his superior."

"And about that time, there were riots at the university," Thatcher mused. "That may have been the beginning of his idea to use the student radicals as a smoke screen for his own activities."

Olmsted disliked this entire line of conversation. The decision by the Sloan Guaranty Trust to hand Puerto Rico over to International still rankled. Innes' offer to let Commercial Credit stay in the picture long enough to wind up the transfer of Slax's Bayamón plant had added insult to injury. Now Thatcher was telling him that murder had been brewing for months.

"Speaking of student radicals," he said firmly, "what did they ever do with Prudencio Nadal? They caught him down in the Old City when we were up at El Morro. When is he coming up for trial?"

"What trial?" Aguilera was surprised. "What could they charge him with? He did not do anything—except keep quiet and take the credit for various deeds of sabotage."

"You mean he didn't do anything at all?"

"Not a thing." Aguilera looked into the future. "That may be the course of his whole professional career. And you do not arrive in a jail cell that way."

"Oh, he'll get there yet," Annie prophesied, "unless he learns to start looking a gift horse in the mouth."

"So Ramírez ends up the winner on that duel," Olmsted concluded. "I suppose he'll pick up some of Nadal's support."

"Ramírez has other interests as well." Cesar Aguilera was obscurely amused. "I suspect that one of the new owners of the Bayamón plant is a straw man for Ramírez."

"You can be very sure of it. We looked into that." Thatcher never let straw men stop him when he was interested in principals.

"All things considered, they came up with a pretty good price," said Olmsted, once again a functioning banker. "It didn't take Norma long to straighten out and make up her mind to sell, once the murder was solved."

Cesar Aguilera still responded to his old loyalties. "Norma was never in any confusion about the correct business decision. She did not consider business important if David was in danger."

"She must have been damned sure that he was the murderer then."

Aguilera shook his head. "I do not think it was that simple. Norma had two men who were important to her. She had just lost one. She was not taking any chance at all on losing the second. Originally I think she may have suspected David of killing Domínguez. She could have understood the motive there. Then, when it seemed as if Harry had been kidnapped in revenge for Domínguez, she turned against David in her grief and guilt. But that was momentary hysteria. Certainly they are very happy now."

"Have you seen them?" Thatcher asked curiously.

"Oh, yes. I had dinner with them last night in Scarsdale. David is in charge of the New York office now." For a moment Cesar Aguilera shed his years and became mischievous. "I understand Norma drops in to help occasionally."

Unexpectedly Annie commented, "I expect them to make a

go of it. The Slax plant in Georgia is going great guns. We've renegotiated our contract there. I'll be able to get along with them fine."

Pete Olmsted could not believe his ears. "You mean to say you and David are getting along without any trouble?"

"David?" Annie blinked. "Don't be silly. As soon as Norma has those kids in school, she'll take over. She's just getting on with the business of life right now. And it'll be a good day for Slax when she's not tied up any more. She may be stubborn as a mule, but she's not beyond listening to reason —eventually."

Cesar Aguilera and Pete Olmsted were lost in bemused silence. It was left to Thatcher to say weakly, "Oh, yes?"

Annie expanded her encomium. "Why, it didn't take me more than six or seven sessions to persuade her about that day-care center in Georgia. It's going to be called the Harry Zimmerman Center. I knew Norma would want some kind of memorial for Harry," she concluded solemnly.

"Now, wait a minute, Annie." Olmsted was incensed. "You've just held up the sale of Bayamón for over a week because of their damned nursery school. You said the new management had to go ahead with it."

Organized labor on the other side of the table drew itself up stiffly. "Of course they had to go ahead with it. The work line had received a promise."

Olmsted was proving he could add one and one. "But that means you've come out of this with two day-care centers," he said in tones of outrage.

Annie produced a battered look of innocence.

"Well, now," she marveled, "what do you know about that?"